PRAISE FOR *CHERIS*

T0046841

"*Cherish Farrah* got me shivering in [a] ... telligent, insightful, and absolutely cre[epy] ... mystery and intensity with such powerful intent. Bethany C. Morrow knows how to make a reader squirm, and thank goodness for that."

—Victor LaValle, author of *The Changeling* and *The Ballad of Black Tom*

"*Cherish Farrah* is a delicious page-turner [with a] strong intellectual foundation, set in a world that on the surface feels disturbingly glossy with its champagne and perfect dresses and two Black girls who are clinging to each other."

—Megan Giddings, author of *Lakewood*

"[*Cherish Farrah*] spirals into the dysphoric and surreal, ultimately turning into the kind of unnerving social horror Jordan Peele popularized in the 2017 film *Get Out*. . . . It's shot-through with its narrator's destabilizing visions and occasional hallucinations, which make its world feel queasily, feverishly strange. . . . [It's] not a book for the faint of heart. . . . At once restrained and ferocious; like Farrah, it maintains control until it can't anymore, and then it erupts. Morrow uses her heroine's warped perspective to examine painful truths about race and class in America, but this isn't a book intended to teach anyone a lesson, except maybe: Be careful. You never know who's really in control."

—*Los Angeles Times*

"A spine-tingling thriller."

—*PopSugar*

"One of those slow-burn thrillers with an electrifying end; this is a highly buzzed-about title this spring."

—*Amazon Book Review*

"I don't believe the word 'mind-blowing' is an adequate description of Bethany C. Morrow's *Cherish Farrah*, but it's the closest that language has to offer. Although I've always been drawn to horror in both literature and film, Morrow's book is a different breed: It grips the senses and left me wanting more and feeling desperate for an abrupt end to its viciousness, all at the same time . . . Bodies of work focusing on social horror, like Morrow's, show how complicated existence is for Blacks while stripping away the privilege of illusion for white people. There's nowhere to hide. No way to deflect. All of us are left facing down the naked truth. Ensnared by the light of a horror that society can't turn off."
　　　　　　　　　　　　　　　　　　　　　　　　—*The Rumpus*

"*Cherish Farrah* is a stunning one-two punch of social horror and psychological thriller."
　　　　　　　　　　　　　　　　　　　　　　—*CrimeReads*

"Bethany C. Morrow has created a masterpiece. . . . It is a slow burn and well worth the wait. . . . Morrow is skilled with her words as we can feel the tension slowly building between each character, which brings us to a conclusion that is both jaw-dropping and also a little weird. . . . I certainly won't forget *Cherish Farrah* for a long time." —*Mystery & Suspense Magazine*

"Bethany C. Morrow's latest cinematic social-horror novel, *Cherish Farrah*, is right at home among . . . uneasy, atmospheric narratives. . . . Farrah's chillingly claustrophobic perspective infuses *Cherish Farrah* with a deep and creepy dread." —*Alta*

"Ever since we read Bethany C. Morrow's dystopian novel *Mem*, we've been eager to see how she'd follow it up. She's gone in unexpected directions since then, covering a lot of stylistic ground, and we are—as the saying goes—here for it. *Cherish Farrah* is about the fraught friendship between two teenage girls and the unsettling secrets hidden within one of their families, making for a haunting denouement." —*Vol. 1 Brooklyn*

"Bethany C. Morrow's second novel for adults addresses class-ism and racism, as well as families and friendships. It's a slow burn from page one and ends in discomfort for all. Like *Mem*, Morrow's first novel, *Cherish Farrah* is beautifully written, with poetic language and passages full of vivid, intricate imagery. Unlike *Mem*, her newest novel puts race in the forefront."

—*The Massachusetts Review*

"Bestselling author Bethany C. Morrow gives us a new adult social horror novel that I did not want to stop reading. . . . This is the kind of book that is supposed to disturb readers and make us think, and Morrow achieved both of these goals. This was my first novel by Bethany C. Morrow but will not be my last."

—Black Girl Nerds

"If you like unsettling books about manipulative people worm-ing their way into someone else's life, then get ready for this great novel!"   —Book Riot

"Morrow returns to adult fiction with a chilling thriller about race, class, and female friendship. . . . The shocking ending to this suspenseful novel with a masterfully drawn narrative voice will leave readers breathless."   —*Booklist*

"[A] slow-burning tale of power and manipulation." —*BookPage*

CHERISH FARRAH

A NOVEL

BETHANY C. MORROW

DUTTON

DUTTON

An imprint of Penguin Random House LLC
penguinrandomhouse.com

Previously published as a Dutton hardcover in February 2022
First Dutton trade paperback printing: February 2023
Copyright © 2022 by Bethany C. Morrow
Penguin Random House supports copyright. Copyright fuels creativity, encourages diverse voices, promotes free speech, and creates a vibrant culture. Thank you for buying an authorized edition of this book and for complying with copyright laws by not reproducing, scanning, or distributing any part of it in any form without permission. You are supporting writers and allowing Penguin Random House to continue to publish books for every reader.

DUTTON and the D colophon are registered trademarks
of Penguin Random House LLC.

LIBRARY OF CONGRESS CATALOGING-IN-PUBLICATION DATA
Names: Morrow, Bethany C., author.
Title: Cherish Farrah: a novel / Bethany C. Morrow.
Description: 1. | New York, New York: Dutton, Penguin Random House, [2022]
Identifiers: LCCN 2021029396 (print) | LCCN 2021029397 (ebook) |
ISBN 9780593185384 (hardcover) | ISBN 9780593185407 (ebook) |
ISBN 9780593471685 (export edition)
Classification: LCC PS3613.O7783 C54 2022 (print) |
LCC PS3613.O7783 (ebook) | DDC 813/.6—dc23
LC record available at https://lccn.loc.gov/2021029396
LC ebook record available at https://lccn.loc.gov/202102939

Dutton trade paperback ISBN (9780593185391)

Printed in the United States of America
1st Printing

Hand-lettered type by Vi-An Nguyen
Title page art © Shutterstock / Tymonko Galyna
Book design by Ashley Tucker

Beware the day they change their minds . . .

CHERISH
FARRAH

I'm sitting in a bedroom with the kind of vaulted ceiling I wanted in my own, in a house much larger and more extravagant than the one I can't go back to, and the fact that I can't enjoy it upsets me.

I feel fickle. Angsty. Defensive. Like an ordinary teenage girl, when all I'm ever doing is pretending to be one.

The house where I used to live is only a few blocks away, and being told it's no longer mine is destroying me on the inside. It's making it hard to eat, to maintain a train of thought about anything else. To decide what needs to happen next.

And something has to be done.

I cannot become accustomed to someone else being in control. Not just of what happens on the outside, but worse, of what's happening on the inside of me.

I won't allow it.

I would burn it all first.

When Cherish Whitman was ten years old, her parents orchestrated twelve days of Christmas for her. It doesn't matter how spoiled you think you are; a reindeer playdate tops everything. Making angels in the snow when it's unseasonably warm and the powder's been brought in special is an experience that sets a standard, and Brianne and Jerry Whitman did not shy away from it. They didn't worry about what expectations or extravagance would have to come next. They taught Cherish that she deserved it.

They taught us both, and I am a quick study.

Last year, I was part of the planning committee for Cherish's sweet sixteen. My own had involved a dance hall, and a theme, and all the white kids we've gone to the academy with all these years. It wasn't sensational and it wasn't embarrassingly modest; it was perfectly forgettable, even if my parents' budgetary reminders weren't. When it came time for Cherish's, my mother joked with the Whitmans that maybe I could do them a favor and suggest something equally modest for their daughter's celebration, having been so reasonable about mine. I smiled along with them and then suggested a "quick" plane ride to the city for dinner and party-dress shopping—and Brianne Whitman was elated. The "recovery" mud baths and Swedish massages were entirely her idea.

Cherish is easy to love, but I'm almost equally enamored of the Whitmans. It's the way they love her. It's the unapologetic extravagance they dole out to their daughter, the way they never temper their coddling of her, that makes them remarkable. It shouldn't, and I'm sure it doesn't sound out of the ordinary until you know what makes their family unique. It becomes clear very quickly. It's difficult to miss, even if you've known them as long as I have.

Color blindness requires the kind of delusional naïveté that I have only ever believed in Cherish. For one thing, you can't be the intended beneficiary of color's power and refuse to see it; that's just refusing accountability. Only someone susceptible to its harm, who honestly and impressively never develops an awareness of that fact, could claim it. Cherish is just such a masterpiece, and the Whitmans are why.

"The guests are arriving, ladies," Mr. Whitman informs us from the doorway of Cherish's bedroom. Our bedroom, for the past couple of weeks. He's got his hand over his eyes like one of us is a blushing bride and it's bad luck to see us before the ceremony.

"Dad." Cherish laughs, and it covers the groan I don't mean to make out loud. "You can look!"

"Jerry!" Mrs. Whitman stops cornrowing Cherish's hair and sends one of her trademark twinkling laughs toward the high ceiling. They're always like the final stage of an exorcism, as though her joy will come billowing from her open mouth like a swarm of locusts. I almost see it, a cloud of gold above her head.

Both Cherish and her mother look at me with smiles or gaping amusement, asking with their expressions whether or not I can believe this wholesome, adorable scene, but I can't muster a grin. I raise one corner of my mouth, and Cherish is satisfied, going back to her reflection in the vanity too quickly to notice anything's off. Mrs. Whitman's brow creases a little, but when I drop her gaze, she doesn't let on.

She's a consummate professional, Mrs. Brianne LePage Whitman. Her day job involves an ornate showroom, a pencil skirt and modest button-down, a classic chignon, and any of a thousand silk scarves tossed across one or both of her shoulders like she meant to do something with it but just casually ran out of time. She somehow conversationally explains one antiquity or another in the most intriguing detail, but as though it's just something she knows, and then someone bids their entire net worth to take it home. When I was younger, I literally did not know she was paid for this; I thought it was just something wealthy white women do.

Today Brianne's hair is down, and she's wearing something she calls a garden dress, paired with her plain wedding band and an arrangement of light accessories Cherish would tell me are "tasteful" for the occasion. It's little details like having jewelry for every occasion and knowing precisely how many there will be that taught me the difference between my family's money and theirs. The Whitmans' property backs up to the twelfth hole of the golf course, and I used to live a very short drive away, but there's a difference between working to afford this community and choosing this community so you can still travel four times a year.

Cherish is their saving grace, or rather I'm close enough to their daughter to know that if the Whitmans stole the whole world, it would only end up at her feet. It makes it difficult to hold their privileged position against them, but I still feel so sick to my stomach right now that I could throw up all over what I'm sure is an irreplaceable antique rug. It's Turkish mohair from the beginning of last century—*that* I specifically recall from the first time I tiptoed across it and Brianne set a sea of golden laughter free above her head.

"RahRah, you want Mom to braid your hair like mine?" Cherish is asking, two tight cornrows framing her face as though to keep her voluminous twist out contained.

"I'm happy to." Brianne smiles at me, a trace of concern visible in her soft smile, her hands delicately clasped in front of her the way they sometimes are while exhibits are being positioned at the auction house.

This is what I'm talking about. Of course Brianne Whitman, blond, and svelte, and demure, knows how to cornrow. I mean, of course, because that's the kind of mother she is. She's not cunning like my mother and me, but she's conscientious— and since she's only Cherish's mom, that's enough. When Brianne found out she was going to have a Black daughter, of course she was mindful enough to take a class. Not just in Black

American studies, either. On hair care, on skin and makeup, too. She wasn't going to bring home a baby who looked nothing like her and act like her love was enough. That's not who the Whitmans are.

Cherish is still occasionally checking me out in the mirror, and Mrs. Whitman hasn't stopped looking at me like she wants to open her arms and swallow me inside, even as she wipes the rest of the gel from the back of her hand and applies it to Cherish's edges.

"I've got a small headache," I lie, and lightly crease my brow like I'm resisting a full grimace.

"Okay, definitely pass on the braids, then," my friend says with a laugh. "You know my mom braids like she's trying to cinch your scalp."

Mrs. Whitman waves us off, jovially, because she knows how to graciously escape a compliment.

"Five minutes, okay, girls?" she chirps on her way out of the bedroom, but Cherish hops up from her mirror immediately after.

"I'm ready," she says, joining me on the huge bed we share. "You wanna go snatch wigs and whatnot?"

"Snatch wigs?" I repeat back to her with all the intended judgment. "Is that what the white kids at the academy say these days?"

"You know they do. But seriously, there'll definitely be a few toupees and hairpieces at this thing, and I will absolutely use my birthday pass on embarrassing blue bloods."

"There's no such thing as a birthday pass," I reply, falling back into the crook of her arm.

"There for sure is. Everyone knows that."

"Maybe for the *actual* wigs."

"WGS? Really? Has that come back around already?"

"It never left."

"You know you can be white girl spoiled even if your parents are Black, right?"

"Mmm," I hum, so she hears the skepticism. There's no use explaining what she couldn't possibly understand. I've learned to coddle Cherish over the years, too.

"Okay, my hair's gonna get flat," Cherish says, forcing me back up when she rises. "Let's get into it."

"Would you be upset if I didn't come down today?"

Her head falls to the side. "Would I be upset if you didn't come to my birthday party because you wanted to stay upstairs and sulk?"

"Che. You don't get to have three birthday functions in one weekend and then act salty when somebody gets tired. And—" Then my voice breaks.

I hate it because it's not something I planned.

The break isn't intentional. It's not the execution of a subtle strategy, timed to elicit a specific response.

When the tears almost come, they're because I'm not used to slipping.

"I'm not sulking. Thanks for being so supportive."

However I look when I can't choose between anger and sadness, the snarky expression slips from Cherish's face, and it'd be satisfying if I'd done it on purpose. When she grabs me by the shoulders, pulling me in, I have to fight the urge to pinch her the way I used to pinch myself under the dining table, or beneath my desk the first few months at the academy, when I needed to bring the pain to the surface for release. I perfected the kind of pinch that breaks capillaries and really burns, and then leaves a bruise that's like a tiny drop of purple ink that slowly spreads.

Most people grab a hunk of arm, but I've always had self-control. Because the key—after choosing just the right spot, like the place just above the elbow, on the inside—is to trap what almost seems like too small an amount of skin between finger and thumb, so that at first you don't expect the pain. Then, as you tighten, you twist.

It'd be easy enough to reach that spot on Cherish when we draw back from the embrace, if I let my hands slide down her arms, but I won't. I'm just sick of feeling unlike myself, of feeling physically ill, and Cherish is just being Cherish. Sometimes obtuse, often insufferably spoiled . . . but always mine.

Even now, even without pinching her, I feel slightly better when I'm wrapped up in her arms.

"BB! I'm so sorry, RahRah, don't cry," she says into my hair, and like I'm any other teenage girl, her reaction ensures that I must. I want to be sick right this minute, just to purge the unfamiliar ache and frailty. I am exhausted at feeling like I could break.

"I'm sorry, Che." I can't wipe my eyes because she's trapped my arms between us and she's hugging me too tight. For a moment, I consider that this was *her* strategy. That she meant to bring me to tears. I wonder what it's like to be this fragile all the time, and whether she's decided I have to find out.

"*I'm* sorry. I wasn't thinking, I was trying to make light of it, but I shouldn't have." She moans into me the way Mrs. Whitman does when she's heartsore for someone.

I believe her—until she speaks again.

"I'll never act white girl spoiled again. Promise."

She only says it to make me laugh. Which I do, my shoulders relaxing when my suspicion fades.

"Yeah, right. You are not capable of that kind of self-control."

"Okay, you're probably right. Also, it's just really fun." This time we both laugh. "Being a spoiled white girl when you're Black is literally my favorite thing ever. It confuses very literally everyone."

"That's the only reason I put up with it."

"Whatever. You love me."

"Ugh. Don't remind me." We both try to check our reflections in the vanity at the same time and end up shoving each other, playfully. "Fiiine," I say through a sigh. "Let's get the finale over with."

Cherish hoots, grabbing my hand and pulling me down the long staircase, through the house, and out into the backyard.

The Whitmans' sprawling, triple-tiered backyard is nothing short of a private park. The front has no yard at all, instead boasting an ocean of stone pavers in varying shades of gray and the perfect sprinkling of cloudy blue all the way up to the door. The back more than makes up for it, and today the park is decked out with garden lighting, waitstaff circulating hors d'oeuvres so small you'd have to sneak a tiny army of them off the platter to make them count, and half the city's rich and/or local famous. There are way more adults than teenagers, which makes sense because we've finally arrived at the event geared toward applauding Cherish's parents for raising an amazing daughter. There's always one.

As soon as we make our appearance, Cherish and I are wrangled back up toward the house, up the rolling lawn to the patio and pool, and Mr. Whitman holds the mic up to his wife's glass, which she clinks with a knife to get the crowd's attention.

"Oh, you can stay in the pool, gang. This'll only take a moment," she says, leaning closer to the microphone than necessary, like she doesn't know exactly how the contraption works. It isn't age; Mrs. Whitman is barely older than my mom, and her twinkling laugh and bouncy blond hair almost make up for the fact that she doesn't have her daughter's built-in font of youth, melanin. She's just used to a discreet headset during auctions.

"Che, can you come here, honey?" Mr. Whitman beckons her from my side, and a few of their guests clap like she's receiving an award.

"As you all know, this is our baby girl, our universe, our shared heartbeat, Cherish." Mrs. Whitman is already dabbing at her eyes, but she'll keep it together. Brianne LePage Whitman has never flubbed a speech or an auction yet.

"You surprise me, every year," Brianne's saying directly to Cherish now, and when I see them standing together, they just look like a family.

Mr. Whitman's the kind of fit dad whose abs you can make out through his polo, and he doesn't even have the decency to be graying or thinning yet, which my dad says is like hitting the white-guy lottery because it's hard for them to look corporate professional with a shaved head. What's worse, Jerry doesn't seem obsessively conscious of his full head of hair, rarely reaching up to flaunt or confirm its thickness. He never looks like he has a worry in the world, especially not right this minute, while he smiles down at his daughter and lovingly tugs on one of her braids.

"I know people hate us," Brianne jests to gentle resistance from her audience, while Cherish's attention volleys between her parents. "But we say it because it's true. You have never given us a day's worry or trouble."

This is where someone could've quipped that Cherish never gave her a contraction or stretch mark, either. It'd be shocking, but only because the Whitmans do not keep tasteless company. As adoptions go, transracial ones leave pretty few doubts, on sight. But the Whitmans don't casually talk adoption, which I've come to appreciate. Cherish is their daughter; they've made sure of that.

"You're brilliant, and beautiful." And then Brianne looks at me for longer than her trademark engaging-the-audience glance. "And an amazing judge of character. Farrah, honey, you come over here, too!"

"Crap," I mutter through a smile when, as expected, all eyes descend on me. If I were more myself, I would've seen this coming. I would have decided ahead of time which way I wanted to play it, and why. Without forethought, I'm forced to settle for the most remedial and cliché response.

I gingerly make my way across the expanse of lush green, not letting my eyes land on any particular partygoer for too long. The key is letting my smile fluctuate as though I'm trying to convince myself I shouldn't be self-conscious. I do know a few of them. My hair stylist and my pediatrician are here, the former because I referred her to Cherish, and the latter because Mr. and Mrs. Whitman convinced my parents it was a big deal for me to have a Black doctor, given what Black girls and women face with the healthcare industry. Cherish's pediatrician became mine, too; same with her orthodontist in eighth grade. Brianne said raising a well-adjusted and protected Black girl takes intentionality, and she and my mom were pretty close friends after that.

When the walk to the Whitmans genuinely begins to feel longer than it should, I realize I do actually feel exposed. It isn't part of the act. I'm not myself. I'm not in control, which was proved upstairs with Cherish, even if it was only a small break. And even though it's my parents' fault, it's made worse by the fact that they aren't even here. Out of a queasy stomach, a hot bolt of anger flashes up my spine because I really wanted them to be.

They were supposed to be here for this. They were supposed to be here so that, at the very least, I wouldn't look orphaned. They were supposed to be here so that I would not be facing the side glances and too-gentle smiles on my own.

Polite society is a misnomer.

In this community, there'll be no rounding a corner to find someone heatedly exchanging details of the Turner family's foreclosure—but that's because everyone already knows.

My parents are supposed to be here so it doesn't look like they're trying to save face. Especially when I don't get to. But they aren't here, and I get no reassuring squeeze from my mother, no forehead kiss from my dad. I ball my hands into tight fists at my sides, but it's not for comfort. It's for control.

It's because I am tired of feeling betrayed, and it's getting harder to keep my mask in place.

Finally, I reach Brianne Whitman, and when I tuck into her extended arm, she pulls me into her side the way she clearly wanted to upstairs. And I do feel better.

"For those of you who don't know, this is Farrah Turner, and she and Cherish have been best girlfriends—sisters!—basically since the day they met. What was that, fourth grade?"

"Third," Jerry corrects her without even consulting us, but he's right, and Cherish and I both laugh. "But fourth grade is when it happened."

"Oh my gosh," I say, and put my face in my hands, to everyone's amusement.

"Dad," Cherish whines.

"Oh, you have to tell it. Is it okay if he tells it, girls? It's so precious!" Brianne gives the microphone to her husband, putting her other arm around me and lacing her fingers together at my hip before she starts the unconscious mom-sway. I let my head drop against her shoulder, face still in my hands, but fingers splayed so I can see Mr. Whitman getting ready to tell the family's favorite story of Cherish and me.

"Hi, all, I'm Jerry Whitman," he begins, and his friends laugh. "Better known as Cherish Whitman's dad, you know how it is." He's a natural, just like his wife, but he makes you feel like he hadn't planned to tell you anything, and now he's just charmingly rambling in a way that makes perfect sense. "That started at church when Cherish was about four years old.

People stopped greeting me and just spoke to the adorable little girl in my arms, which, I mean, I couldn't blame them. She had these huge eyes." He stops, like he just realized his daughter's right there and he can look into the eyes he's describing. "She still does."

Cherish does what she always does under the warmth of her parents' adoration; she glows. Her dimple is at maximum deepness, and her hair moves like a cloud over her shoulder when she dips her head.

"Anyway." The mic rests against his chin and he scratches his forehead. "So, Farrah and Cherish met in third grade, and it was obvious that they adored each other, but when they were in fourth grade," he emphasizes, as though to remind us that he had it right, "that's when Brianne and I really fell in love with Farrah. I was still flipping houses back then."

A murmur carries through the yard, and Jerry waves it off without looking.

"I know, I know, everybody did it. We all did. HGTV destroyed a generation. So, I was going to check on a property in renovation, and I took the girls with me—they probably had some rehearsal or something." He glances between us. "Dance? Were you still doing ballet? Anyway, I had them both with me, and we go to the property, and of course, I get totally sidetracked with the workers and putting out a half million fires. And there was a bunch of base moldings that had been torn out and stored on the side of the house, because the dumpster also hadn't been delivered yet. I know, flipping is a nightmare from start to finish," he says, as though he can actually make out the playfully annoyed murmurs of friends who've apparently gone through house-flipping phases of their own. "So, as kids do, Cherish and Farrah found said base moldings, complete with probably an inch and a half of nail shooting up from them every so often. And before you report me, this was the first and last time I ever brought either of them to a renovation site. Because, of course, the girls decided to make a game of stomping the nails to the side. Not their brightest moment, but they really are smart girls, I promise."

I can feel my face getting hot, and eventually Brianne notices how hard I'm cringing. She laughs, the way I knew she would, and jostles me between her arms.

"And so finally, Cherish stomps her little foot down to really give it to a nail, and because the universe will not be mocked, the nail decides instead to really give it to her. Goes straight into her foot."

There are gasps and moans from the partygoers, which Jerry accepts with sage nodding, his free hand kneading his daughter's shoulder.

Cherish lets her head fall before swiveling it in my direction, her bottom lip caught between her teeth when her eyes meet mine. She's trying not to smile so wide, and now I can't help it. Because no one knows what we're thinking right now; it's just ours. When my best friend rolls her eyes skyward and then closes them, only I know why, and instead of wearing a blushing expression, I swell. My chest rises until Brianne Whitman's hold of me is taut, and then I let the breath out, slow and satisfied.

No one knows why but Cherish and me.

"That's not when I found them," Jerry Whitman is saying.

"Because I think Cherish was so shocked, she didn't even scream, and Farrah didn't come racing into the house to find me and say that Cherish was hurt. No. Farrah—seeing her best friend hurt, and not knowing how to help her or spare her or make it stop hurting—slams her foot down on one of the nails. I kid you not. She impaled her little foot to share in her best friend's pain."

What began as gasps and gapes of probable disapproval become sighs and coos. They're being told of an absolutely ridiculous act of comradery that only a child would be silly enough to think rational, and it suddenly makes sense with the benefit of hindsight, the proper framing of a generously catered birthday party, and a charming storyteller.

"And I told Cherish that day, at the doctor's office, where the girls were getting tetanus shots . . . I'm glad you found Farrah."

All the Whitmans turn to me, and despite the dozens and dozens of eyes trained on us, and despite my parents' inexcusable absence, the warmth I feel isn't embarrassment or anger. It's quiet like the hush that's fallen across the many tiers of the yard, and peaceful, like I haven't felt often enough lately.

Mere moments ago, I didn't want to be here. I didn't want to be with my parents, either, in the unbearably small house they're renting on the other side of town. Ever since this nightmare began, I've only wanted to be in a house they no longer own. I've made myself sick wanting it—when all along the Whitmans have wanted me. They're taking a toast to the birthday girl and turning it into a celebration of us both. Of me.

"Thank you for loving our daughter the way we do, Farrah," Jerry Whitman tells me.

When our audience claps politely, Brianne motions for the microphone and her husband hands it over.

"I just want to say one more thing, and then you girls are free." One arm still holding on to me, Cherish's mom looks directly into my eyes.

It always puts me on edge, being looked at that directly. Not by Cherish, but by anyone else. Not just since my world started falling apart; since forever. It feels threatening. Like the person is looking for something. Trying to work something out, the way I do. Trying to know what I decide is secret or told.

Just as quickly as the warmth flowed, it ebbs. Whatever Brianne Whitman intends to say, I steel myself for it.

"I just want you to know, Farrah, that we love you," she says, "and we're so glad you're here with us now. You complete our family."

She kisses my forehead but somehow doesn't feel how clammy my skin immediately becomes.

I can't decide what to say. I try to thank her—to end the exchange—but my breath hitches somewhere at the start, and there isn't enough force to carry the words. When I nod, my eyes fall, and I feel my brow creasing.

None of these are choices. I am not exerting any measure of control.

This sea of faces is impossible to decipher. If their attention is laced with pity, I can't tell. If instead of feeling I'm deserving of this public invitation of adoption, they'll spend the next few hours quietly discussing the Turner family failures that made it necessary, I want to know. For now, they're all too quiet, as though they refuse to drown out the hiccupping, inconsistent heartbeat I can hear in my ears.

Enamored of the Whitmans or not, I must consider that this is an attack. It's a statement on my parents' absence, on my need of a home. In front of all their friends and guests, would Brianne Whitman have said something like that otherwise?

I refuse to cry. Not only because it's out of character—or would have been just one month ago. I refuse to cry at my best friend's party in the arms of her mother, who sounds convincingly like she's just trying to tell me I'm welcome here. I'm wearing a dress I bought yesterday with the prepaid credit card the Whitmans gave me to match the one they gave Cherish, and if I don't get back inside, I'm going to be sick down the front.

Slowly, I back away. While friends of her parents come to surround and toast and congratulate Cherish on aging a year, occasionally slipping folded bills into her hand like they're eccentric uncles or defiant grandparents—or like money must be flashed whenever my eyes look, and the gift giving is choreographed so that I never miss it—I take small steps until I'm back at the door, and then I duck inside.

I barely make it to the bathroom in time.

III

*M*y mother sometimes pretends she doesn't know her daughter. She pretends that I am the only one wearing a mask. That just because we both hide it well, I don't know who she is. Who we are.

I'd packed up for another weeklong stay with my best friend's family. Despite their well-established stance on slumber parties, my parents had become uncharacteristically permissive. Sleepovers were meant to last one night, I'd been taught all my life, not the entire weekend. That's the way it'd always been, but things were changing. My parents had been having hushed conversations, or meeting up outside the house—as though they didn't suspect the app I'd downloaded to their phones let me know exactly where. Something was happening, and they should've known that I could tell.

My mother should have known. She must have.

"Since when do you not want to stay with Cherish?"

Nichole Turner knew she would offend me with what was clearly a rhetorical question. It was delivered convincingly enough—if I were anyone else. If I were like Cherish, or at least some common manner of adolescent, I'd be trapped. Confused. Misdirected so that my response would be to defend my love of my best friend's company.

"I'm smarter than that," I reminded my mother instead.

We were sitting in the car, and outside our soundproof bubble, Brianne waited at her front door. She smiled down the driveway, one hand on her narrow hip and the other shielding her eyes from the sun. She was impatient for me, and I couldn't enjoy it. Not when there was a warning to issue.

"I want my life back," I said.

We were alone, if visible, and my mask was not altogether in place yet. It didn't have to be. When it's only me and my mother, I can uncoil the part of myself that only someone with a matching part would understand. Anyone else would consider my age and be completely incapable of interpreting my conversation as anything more potent than teenage disrespect. The fact that my mother never stoops to chastising, that she never bests me with allusions to an established familial hierarchy, is the confirmation Nichole Turner refuses to verbalize.

The day I made my desires clear, Brianne was doing the polite work of intentionally avoiding looking directly into the car, lest she infringe on our privacy. This was a difficult time for the Turner family, she understood; otherwise there would have been no need and no permission for my long visits. This one would become an extended stay, but I couldn't know that yet.

Nichole Turner said nothing while I delivered what turned out to be a futile demand.

"I want *my* house, with *my* pool, where *I* live. I won't adjust to anything else. Not even this."

When I looked at her, my mother's oval face was turned toward me. She was ignoring her dear friend, and I thought it meant she understood.

"Farrah," she said through a sigh.

"I can't make it any easier," I said before she could speak again. "I'm telling you exactly what I want."

We have the same jewel-brown eyes. No one would understand, but that's part of how I know we're alike. Her eyes can glint the same way mine do. They can carry a message, or a warning, that leaves the rest of her face untouched. Brianne could fix her gaze directly on my mother or me and she still wouldn't see. She wouldn't notice the facets of my mother's eyes, that there are fragments of Nichole Turner's real self hidden across them. No amount of study would reveal what Nichole—what we—artfully conceal.

But my mother has a flaw. A hint of a dimple in her left cheek. She wasn't born with it; she says she fell when she was a child, that it's damaged tissue, not an adorable feature like Cherish's—but that's the way it looks. It softens her when she needs to look assertive. It tells on the slightest twitch of her lips and makes her look uncertain. Vulnerable.

Maybe that's why she lost everything. Maybe it's the only way someone like us could.

I'm glad she fell. It means the dimple was never going to be hereditary.

"Whatever you have to do," I told her, lowering my chin and relaxing the muscles in my face as though preparing a canvas. I was going to get out of the car soon and go bounding over to my best friend's mom in a show of girlish exuberance that was doomed to collapse. "Get it back."

She didn't.

I don't live at the Whitmans' now because I decided it's what I would prefer when my parents moved into a rental. I did not plant the idea in my parents' minds. I'm here because they decided it would be easier for me, and they settled it with Brianne and Jerry before they ever broached the subject with me.

That's what makes it unbearable. That's why I've been sick. Cherish thinks it's the stress of having my world upended that's disrupting my body, but I know better. I know what's curdling deep in my guts, jostling my thoughts, and depleting any energy I try to cull to plot my own course.

Control, I think as I stare at my reflection. Water still clings to my face, and a harsh, acidic taste persists in dotting my tongue no matter how many times I rinse my mouth. I've gone to Cherish's en suite, where no party guest will stumble onto me, but I know it's only a matter of time before my best friend comes looking.

There is no excuse for my weakness, betrayed or not. Especially when betrayed. I am teaching my parents and anyone paying attention that—like everyone else—I am weakened by defeat.

I refuse to be when there's an alternative they do not expect.

So, control. Of what—and when—I let them see.

Where are you? I text my mother. *I want to go home.*

I stare at the words, but I don't send them.

This is Nichole Turner I'm talking to. I will not beg. I can't afford to make her doubt who we both are.

I expect you to be here soon, I send instead, and my mother texts right back.

I'm sorry, baby, I thought I'd be out of here by now! I know you're uncomfortable, Fair, and I meant to be there.

She's speaking through the mask, like we have an audience again. Like she's standing next to my dad and she wants me to know.

Can't afford to turn down contracts, no matter how far out of the way the clients are. Coming straight from here, I promise. But it might be a bit.

And Dad? I type, curious how she'll explain his absence without admitting he's there with her, but before I can send it, she starts to type something else. And before the bubbles stop dancing and the text appears, I already know what she's going to say.

It means the world that Brianne and Jerry want you there. They've been adamant that you stay with Cherish, and I know it's where you'd rather be.

She says it like it's the rented house's fault that it's embarrassingly cramped, and not hers for choosing it. Like anything should've been more important than what I told her I could not accept.

I am not demanding because—like my mother—I cannot live with someone else in control.

This tug-of-war we're in is only natural, because we're mother and child. She's got the advantage right now, but it's my own fault. I taste the acid on my tongue. I've been too indulgent with my devastation, so my mother's texts go on and on.

I know this is difficult, and I really wish it weren't. I didn't think it would be.

But it's so important we are gracious with them. No one wanted your life uprooted over all this, least of all your dad and I.

This is a good thing, Farrah . . . even if you can't say you decided it.

She signs off with a kiss, and I'm left swallowing the hard lump in my throat because Nichole Turner has managed to have her say before tidily closing the conversation. Texting back would look weak. Confrontational.

I'm standing in my best friend's bathroom, clutching my phone while I try to regulate my breathing. I run my eyes over the glass basin beneath the elegant faucet, look at the oversized mirror and the extravagant assortment of organic skin conditioners, pre-poo treatments, scalp serums, tangle teasers, and the kinds of unprocessed concoctions that come with minimalist labels and impressive price tags.

It shouldn't be a luxury to find products designed specifically for you, Brianne says, and no matter how long I've known the things she says, I never stop being impressed that she knows them, too. Even if I sometimes wonder why she says them to *me*.

Gracious.

"RahRah?" Cherish's voice comes gently through the door. "You okay?"

I take a look in the mirror and pat the moisture on my face. My eyes aren't red or puffy, thank God. The whites of my eyes are bright. I'm alert.

Gracious, Nichole Turner instructed, but I tug back.

Control.

I slide the door open before I answer Cherish.

"Thought I got my period while we were talking down there," I say, and roll my eyes as if in relief.

"I'm not due for a week," she says, thrusting a finger at me. "If you sync me up and I get it early, I will fight you."

"C'mere," I say, and I grab her and push my abdomen against hers.

"Farrah!"

"Yeeeeah," I say, both of us laughing as I smoosh us together and wriggle. "Join forces, O mighty uteruses! Together we shall rule them all!"

"You're such a freak," she says, shoving me at last. "C'mon, the boys are waiting."

Ugh.

"Don't. I know you wanna see Tariq." She drops her lids low, all sultry and suggestive, even though she knows Tariq and I don't get down like that. Not yet anyway. Neither of us is the impulsive type.

"At a party surrounded by old folks, including the Honorable Judge Campbell? Not really."

"They're not waiting downstairs, dummy—they're waiting in the *car*." Cherish applies gloss to her lips and smacks them.

"It's your birthday party. You can't *leave*."

"Farrah. This is the third event in three days. It's really not that serious."

But earlier I *had* to come down.

Cherish bounces out of the bedroom, her heels high with each excited step like any moment she'll twirl on her toes.

I could trip her, easily. Send her careening down the stairs even more quickly than we do as we check over our shoulders and hustle out the front door. We pass the hired valets, who say a respectful "happy birthday" without specifying which of us they're talking to. They know one thing in particular about the Whitmans' daughter, despite never having met her, but Cherish and I both fit that bill.

"Thank you," I answer, before Cherish squeals at the sight of Tariq's silver Ferrari Spider gliding up the long brick driveway.

"Come on," she says, grabbing my hand and pulling me down the paver path currently flanked on both sides by luxury vehicles. For the most part they're much more understated than the sleek head turner with the custom plates.

CMPBLCRT. As in Campbell court. As in this Black boy driving this outlandishly expensive vehicle is the son of Judge Leslie Campbell. Pull him over at your own risk.

"I don't know why we couldn't wait at valet," I'm saying, but the approaching car is vibrating with bass, and it's reverberating up the drive. "Cherish, it's a two-seater."

She isn't listening. Tariq isn't the one driving his car, and he's also not the reason we're ditching Cherish's last birthday event early.

"Ay, birthday girl!" Kelly yells over the music, and just as he's put the car in park, he hops up and leaps over the door, slipping an arm around her back. He doesn't pull her all the way in. He doesn't have to and he knows it. Her dimple's on full display while she bites her lower lip and pushes against his chest like she wants to keep her distance.

Ugh.

"Happy Birthday, Cherish. Hey, Farrah," Tariq says, after

turning down the music and opening the passenger-side door like a regular person.

"Hey," I say back, and then awkwardly step in like I'm planning to hug him, only we accidentally make eye contact first, and his gorgeous brown eyes are peeking between the thin dreads that populate only as much headspace as his flat top used to. They're entwined, twisted together and forward like bangs, and when he flicks his chin to the side to clear them from his view, the longest sweeps across his nose. For a moment, we both look like we're trying to decide whether to hug or to shake hands.

"Oh my God, will you kiss already?" Kelly calls, lobbing the Ferrari keys to the polo-wearing valet who's jogged down the drive to meet us. "The other Campbell car, bruh, thanks."

When the young man's driven off, and before he returns with the keys to the group-accommodating car Judge Campbell drove to the party, Kelly crosses the space and grabs the back of Tariq's head like he might push our heads together.

"Man, stop." Tariq breaks free, while Cherish giggles, wrapping both of her arms around one of Kelly's tatted biceps. Tariq glances back at me and smooths the bottom half of his scalp, checking that his recent fade is undisturbed and tossing the dreads from his eyes again with a second flick of his neck.

I'm certain I ovulate in reply.

I might not be impulsive, but I could stand for our somewhat Victorian courtship to pick up the pace, so I finally step into Tariq's arms and hug him, intentionally holding my breath like if I don't, I'll breathe in too deep and give myself away. I lay one palm flat, high in the middle of his back, and I let it linger a moment longer than the rest of me so I know he'll feel it, then slide it down a little before disengaging.

"I'll take those," Kelly says when Tariq's eyes are still on mine, and I'm only watching him with my peripherals. I watch his friend snag the keys to Judge Campbell's SUV from the returned valet.

"Shotgun," Cherish chirps up at Kelly, to his satisfaction.

"Maybe you should let Tariq drive his dad's car," I suggest, and then immediately regret it.

Kelly trains his gaze on me and curls his lip. His honey-brown skin is glowing in the sunlight, which also glints off the grill covering his bottom teeth.

"Maybe you should find your own place to live," he snaps.

"Hey," Tariq says.

"Kelly." Cherish hits him in the belly with the back of her hand. "Mind your business."

It's too late, though. Something curdles in the bottom of my stomach like bad milk, and I look down so neither my best friend nor the boy I'm crushing on can catch my eye.

It's not embarrassment. I'm shocked at myself. I'm seething that I spoke without meaning to because it means I am not in control. It doesn't matter that it was harmless, that no one would guess from that outburst what is really behind the mask I wear in front of Kelly. I know that it wasn't what I meant to say. I know that I didn't mean to say anything.

What Kelly said back is of no consequence at all. How could it be? It makes no sense. Kelly isn't a Campbell. He may be as good as adopted, but he's not *adopted* adopted like Tariq is. Judge Campbell's his guardian, and he's Tariq's best friend—though that's sometimes hard to tell—but they're not *actually* brothers. They have matching chains and they match in height, but that's by choice and lucky coincidence. Kelly has lived with the Campbells, off and on, for literal years, but he still always finds some way to imply I'm materially benefiting from my friendship with Cherish. Materially, because his remedial thinking could only ever factor in the tangible. Still, he flaunts every privilege he gets for being a child in the Campbell court, flagrantly without gratitude or self-control, but it's supposed to matter that *he* has a problem with *me*.

If their silence is any indication, no one seems to notice the hypocrisy. Worse, Cherish has fallen for him despite his behavior. When I confessed I wanted Tariq, she immediately matched it with a confession about his best friend. It must satisfy some basic teenage drama for her, the coupling off and the copycat declarations—but Kelly and I do not get along.

Or we wouldn't, if I didn't go along. If I didn't drop my eyes and let my silence suggest that Kelly's bullying actually hurt my feelings, my meticulously crafted mask would slip free. Because if I responded to Kelly, I could easily find another outlet for my recent lapse in control. I could transmute this frustratingly foreign stress sickness into something useful, like immutable rage. I could let it rush out of me and over him.

It would be so easy. As simple as starting with the truth. I could tell him how disposable he is in a world like the Campbell court—in any world, really. I'd catalog his flaws and estimate his fears, and do it without embellishment or exaggeration, in the way most people don't or can't. It would eat his flesh down to the bone like a shoal of piranha.

Not projection. It wouldn't be more about me than him, and it wouldn't be an emotional outburst, tapering off as regret seeped in. There would be none.

I never regret. I don't have to, because unlike Kelly, I think ahead. I mentally play through the scenario, all the way, not just up to the moment of satisfaction, but beyond. I make sure it's worth it—or that I can make it.

That's what I did the day a young Farrah and Cherish disobeyed her dad. Because whether Jerry Whitman remembers it or not, we'd been warned about playing with the materials on the side of the house he was renovating. We'd been cautioned about the nails, which of course is how we knew they were there in the first place, and when he took exponentially longer than he said he would, we went to find them.

It's like a little ritual when you're impatient, I told Cherish, when she was hesitant at first: do something you've been told not to do, and the parent who's kept you waiting for what feels like an eternity will magically appear. And Cherish and I wanted to go for ice cream after ballet, as we'd been promised. So we laid out the molding, nails pointed skyward, and decided to try our balance and skill by standing nearly en pointe between them. We weren't that far in ballet, of course, so it was inevitable that our little exercise would result in someone's foot falling backward onto a nail. I just assumed Cherish knew that, too.

The first time that happened, the nail was crushed to the side without incident. That became the new game, laying the nails down, one by one, by stepping on them just right. Knowing that one false step would end in pain.

"You just have to step down really hard," I instructed

Cherish, and showed her as though I hadn't just learned by accident the moment before.

"That's easy," she replied, and broke one of the nail's necks with merciless force.

It *was* easy for a while. The nails were crippled one by one, and the threat of pain seemed more and more distant. Maybe they weren't made of metal at all. They seemed so much more malleable, and the warning we'd been given was easily chalked up to parental paranoia. Until Cherish brought her foot down hard and went still and rigid.

"Che?" I said, tipping my head to the side to try to catch her gaze, but she was staring off at nothing, and her eyes were welling with tears. I knew the cries were coming, and when her mouth gaped, I leapt.

I grabbed her, one hand on the back of her head and the other clamped over her mouth.

"Shh!" I shook my head, my eyes as wide as hers then, or wider. "Don't cry!"

It's been years, but I still remember what I thought. That we were nine years old and she was the only friend I had. She was the reason I'd begun to understand what children were supposed to be like. What I wasn't—only she didn't seem to notice. She was teaching me what I was expected to be without even trying. Clarifying the kinds of things other children didn't see—like her mother's golden halo when she laughed. When I'd described it to her, Cherish thought I meant it was a feeling; she didn't know that it was real, there, in the air, and that I could see it. So little by little, I stopped.

Control.

Cherish is how I knew what I should pretend not to know or see. She was useful to me.

The Whitmans were already lovely to me, but there were other things Cherish didn't seem to understand. Like what it meant that her parents didn't look like mine. That they could change their minds about me without even knowing what was beneath the mask I was fashioning after Cherish. I couldn't be myself, but that was with anyone besides my mother. How exceptional did I have to be to stay in the Whitmans' favor? I wasn't sure. What I knew for certain was that I could not be responsible for hurting their child.

But I *was* hurting Cherish, I could tell. She was trying to claw my hand off her face because I'd covered the bottom of her nose, too, but she was afraid to move too much and jostle her impaled foot, so she whimpered and cried beneath my hand.

I didn't let go. I looked down and found an uncurved nail.

"Look," I whispered to her, but she didn't. I had to grip her tighter, shake her hard, and command her again. When she finally glanced down, her tears running into the tight seal my hand was making, and her snot wetting the palm of my hand, I did it.

I slammed my foot down on the upright nail, and I barely winced.

"See? It's okay."

At first, Cherish's brows ribboned above her eyes.

"See?" I loosened my grip on her just enough to show that if she was quiet, I could let go. "See, Che? Just like you."

I had to make it easy, but after a moment she understood, and she only sniffled calmly when I released her.

"Just like at the academy," I told her, because by then I'd already overheard her parents' relief. "It's me and you. Okay?"

Cherish just nodded. She can't help it that I have to explain everything, feeding her only as much information as she can process, in the simplest of terms. It's part of being white girl spoiled, so even when it makes my life more difficult, I don't hold it against her. I remember that it's why she means so much to me.

"I'm gonna hold the wood down," I told her, kneeling like it didn't tear my foot even more, "and you yank your foot up, okay?"

"RahRah," she whimpered, and shook her head. "Let's just call Daddy."

"After we're free. And we'll tell him how it happened to both of us."

"But you only did it to make me feel better," she said, and I stopped. Because of course she thought that—and if she did, so could they. It was brilliant, the way she could accidentally be.

"We'll tell him that," I said, nodding reassuringly. "But only after we're free. So all he sees is that we're hurt. Not that we disobeyed."

The lie would never have worked on my parents, but Cherish's parents were white. It was the first time I remember thinking she might be lucky.

It was harder than I'd told her it would be, and by the time it was my turn, the nail had wiggled around inside my foot so many times I was crying real tears, too. But one of the workers saw us limping and called for Jerry Whitman, and when he came, he came in a hurry. He knelt down and put one arm around each of us, even though it would've been totally fair to be more concerned with his own daughter. He carried us both to the car, and he never asked whose idea the game had been. He never assumed it was mine, and that I was a corrupting influence on his daughter. He never said she should find someone else to play with, even though there were several girls at the academy who lived on their street and whose families looked more like his.

But you only get so many of those moments, where chaos can be invited and you know it's still safe. When the other party is as docile and benign as Cherish or Jerry Whitman, I learned, control doesn't have to be as tightly maintained.

Kelly is another story. Or rather, Kelly while he has Cherish's and Tariq's favor is another story. I could unravel him without hesitation, but then I'd see their faces. The looks I saw on other children, before Cherish, when I said too much and scared them. Those looks had let me know—not just that they weren't ready to see all of me, but that they didn't see the teacher melt when she upset them. That they couldn't visualize terrible things as vividly as they could see daylight. If I punished Kelly even verbally, I knew how Tariq's expression would change, and I'd know I should've feigned weakness, not let an amateur bully like Kelly unmask me.

I have to let Kelly's behavior steamroll me and be grateful that it lacks impact, because when Cherish does speak up, it's never any more chastising than a gentle tsk-tsk, and she's always careful to simultaneously communicate that he's not canceled over it. But I don't expect Cherish to know better. I don't expect that one day she's going to actually grow, when I know why she can't.

It'd be unfair to expect more from Kelly's best friend than I do from mine, so I don't bother wondering why Tariq never steps in. He's not exactly the confrontational type, anyway, and that's part of his appeal. Tariq Campbell is the first person in a long time I didn't immediately suspect. I never thought he was nice for a reason, never thought he might be calculating something. He's too much like Cherish, simple and sweet, though his void—if he has one—isn't so glaring. I don't want any of that to change, so it doesn't. Even when he gestures toward the car.

"You can drive, Kel," Tariq tells him.

"I know," the boy replies, and then looks back at me before biting the air. It's a feral show of aggression, and it should make everyone in his presence recoil—but it doesn't.

"Hey," Cherish "chastises" him again. And then she swats his butt when they've turned away, because the point was getting to put her hands on him, and nothing more.

There should be a penalty for being that weak, if there isn't one for disloyalty. There should be a nail in front of her, and it should drive itself deep into her foot, embed itself in the tender meat directly in its center, so that she'd have to beg me to pull her free again.

"You okay?" Tariq asks me when the other two are out of earshot.

I cinch my shoulders involuntarily under the scrutiny of his concerned gaze. What does it matter if Kelly really humiliated me or not, if Tariq thinks he did and is worrying over my wounds? And then, like the sweet, intrinsically good person he always is, Tariq says just the right thing to calm my nerves.

"Not about Kelly. I know you could level him if you wanted to. I meant, are you settling in okay?"

"Yeah. Okay," I say, my lips spreading into a smile that is far too genuine for how dishonest I'm being.

It's been almost two weeks and I am *not* settling in okay.

I knew my parents were hurriedly packing our lives into boxes, that the word *foreclosure* kept being discussed in suddenly discontinued conversations when they weren't sure whether or not I was eavesdropping, and that everyone apparently thought not seeing any of it would keep it from upsetting me.

Instead it felt like someone made me look away, while just out of sight, but still close enough to hear, my whole world was being demoed. I told my mother that not seeing it, being infantilized, was much, much worse. That it should never have happened in the first place.

When Kelly pulls the Campbell SUV from its place between the other cars and makes an unnecessarily sharp turn before speeding down the drive, I fall to the side, narrowly avoiding Tariq's lap with my stabilizing hand. If it were anyone else driving, I'd ask them to take it easy, but I only speak to Kelly if I'm intentionally looking to garner sympathy—and right now the thought of that makes my skin hot.

"So where are you taking me for my birthday?" Cherish asks, while recording us all with the front-facing camera on her phone. When I know I'm in view, I filter through the appropriate number of smiles and poses while Tariq does the same. As soon as she's done, we go back to silently sitting side by side, occasionally bracing against Kelly's reckless driving.

"Anywhere you wanna go," Kelly charms her, grabbing her chin in his hand for a minute, which is easy enough since he only drives with one hand, and sometimes not even that.

"Meaning you didn't plan anything," I say, and without the blaring music they were playing in the Ferrari, everyone hears me.

He catches my eye in the rearview, but before Kelly can say anything, Tariq throws himself on the grenade.

"Yeah, way to go, Kel. Who rides in to sweep someone off their feet with no idea what to do next? You can do better, Cherish."

"Hey," Kelly says directly to her, like there's not a road in front of him that requires his attention. His tongue is tracing his grill for a moment, so whatever he's about to say, it's certain to be upsetting. "Nobody's disputing that. I'm just saying you can do me, too."

"All right," I say under my breath.

I don't have to worry about anyone hearing me this time, because in reply, Cherish pounces. She's got her arms around Kelly's neck, her body strewn across the center console, and her lips muffling Kelly's laughter.

"Um." Tariq looks from the spectacle to me, but I look away.

It's their first kiss, if what Cherish tells me is true, and we all got to be there for it. I'm sure that makes this little dalliance official, to my great disappointment.

When she pulls back, Cherish is playing coy, dropping her eyes and pretending to stifle a smile.

"That doesn't count as my birthday gift, either," she tells him like there aren't two other people in the car, forced to experience this with them. "*I* gave it to *you*."

"I got you," Kelly says through a low, suggestive breath.

If I could reach the steering wheel, I'd drive us off the road.

"Please find someplace to go and let us out," Tariq says, for both of us.

Cherish is insufferable, but only to a point, so she responds with playful laughter and goes back to her side of the car, before twisting in the passenger's seat and smiling at me.

"RahRah's choice," she says, grasping the leather like if she doesn't, fireworks might start shooting out through her fingertips. Her eyes are sparkling like there's a light show in them, too, and I want to shake it out of her.

I don't.

With a teenage girl as typical as Cherish, there's a good chance that my disapproval of Kelly would drive her farther into his arms, and farther from me. I'd like to think she's better than that, but it isn't a hypothesis I'm willing to test.

Besides that, without Kelly to pine over, Cherish might've fallen for Tariq. It is admittedly a much less devastating concern, but it isn't ideal.

"So?" Cherish grins at me. "Where are we going?"

"I wouldn't mind some popcorn," I say, shrugging one shoulder. "Wanna see a movie?"

If I'm lucky, two hours will fly by, and we'll have to hurry back to the party when it's done.

"Movie sounds good," Tariq agrees, turning to look at me with a small, adorable smile.

"As you wish," Cherish says, and lowers her head in reverence, or something, and then, to Kelly, in an overly loud British accent, "To the theater, my good man!"

CHERISH KNEW I wasn't going to have a good time no matter where we went; letting me choose was a way to make that fact my own fault.

When we got to the theater, not only did the boys want to see a plotless collection of fight scenes, they insisted we watch it in the simulation seats. The only upside to being jostled in perfect sync with nonsensical action sequences for ninety minutes was that I was visibly queasy and miserable by the end. Despite clearly wanting to make it a long night with Kelly, Cherish insisted that she'd better take me home. Part of me hoped he'd resist, that he'd at least suggest they dump me on the Whitman porch and go on as a trio. I was disappointed he was able to muster the bare minimum decency required to acquiesce—even though he whispered instructions for her to text him later.

"Did you guys at least kiss?" Cherish asks when Tariq and Kelly are peeling back out of her driveway. A number of the guests have already headed home, including Judge Campbell in Tariq's Ferrari.

"Who, me and Tariq?" I almost blush. "Of course not. We were watching the movie."

Cherish lets me go into the house ahead of her.

"Okay, and? I watched the movie, too."

I toss her a very unconvinced expression. I would love to erase the image of Kelly's hand stealing toward Cherish halfway into the movie. I thought I couldn't feel sicker, and then I saw reflected light bouncing off Kelly's watch in the darkened theater.

"I did! It was about a singing pig or something. Who went on a journey, probably. To save a kingdom and his . . . friends. Who were elves."

"Stupid."

"Hey!" Mr. Whitman catches sight of us in the entryway and smiles, extending his arm like he's either inviting us over or pointing us out to the guests he's talking to at the foot of the stairs. "There are my girls." And then to us: "I've been looking for you two."

"Then how long were we gone?" Cherish asks with an abundance of nonguilt.

"An astute question. And one I would absolutely answer," he says, nodding, "because I noticed your absence immediately, and boy are you in trouble—"

"Uh-huh," she says through a laugh. Charisma is definitely a nurture, not a nature trait, and Cherish Whitman gets hers from her dad. The friends he was talking to when we entered are smiling between the two of them, clearly on the verge of audibly cooing.

There was a time I thought it was a performance, the way Cherish's parents are with her. It's playful and familiar in a way that's different from my family. When Cherish and I were young, I wasn't sure which differences to attribute to her parents being a different race, and to be honest, I'm still not always sure.

Now Jerry Whitman is feigning sternness.

"I'm gonna let you both off the hook this one time because I think Farrah's mom would like to see her."

"She's finally here?" I clip, and then offer a tittering laugh that isn't too belated.

"She's around here somewhere, and I think she has something to tell you," he says, looking around like she wouldn't be easily spotted if she were anywhere in the open space near the stairs. Finally, he waves me off. "Go on, get out of here, go find her."

I'm trying not to race around the downstairs like a giddy kid, and only barely succeeding. It's silly, and I know it; it's only been a couple of days since I've seen her, and if she had news, she's had plenty of chances to tell me. If she was going to tell me my house belongs to me again, she could have said so earlier, in her multitude of texts—unless she wanted to see the look on my face when I heard it. Because they *have* had plenty of time and space to set this right. Two weeks without having to take care of me— not to mention all the times they dropped me off here before.

Now my mom is back, and Jerry Whitman says she has news.

My chest is warm at the thought; I cannot calm down.

"I'm gonna check out back," I tell Cherish, and she nods.

"I'll keep looking in here."

"Thanks," I say before she squeezes my hand and we part ways to search.

You'd think there was going to be a rescue, the way my heart is galloping, and the way my best friend has adopted my anticipation. There's no reason for her to be as excitable as me at my mother's arrival, except that Cherish thinks I miss her.

I pause a moment to watch my best friend dash and dip between people. She politely smiles at a party guest wishing her a happy birthday, and then slips away before they can launch a full-on conversation, and I smile.

I wish I'd chosen this. My mother was right—this is where I'd prefer to be, given a choice between a rental home and staying near Cherish. If I'd chosen it, it would've made all the difference. I wouldn't have been sick to my stomach, fixated on what it feels like when someone else decides. I wouldn't have had to reject it, and make myself miserable. Because Cherish *is* the most important thing to me. Even when I'm imagining tiny tortures to inflict upon her, I never go through with them, not the ones that couldn't be explained away—and being near her is how I learned which are which.

Cherish is why I'm not burning everything down.

We go together. We still will when my parents have set everything right and I choose to stay here anyway.

I've zigzagged through the tiers of the Whitmans' backyard, among the guests still milling around even though the catering staff has obviously begun deconstruction and the property is being restored to its former, unstaged glory. I still haven't found my mother, so I give up and pull out my phone.

Where are you? I text, and then take a deep, painful breath.

I'm finished with the heart palpitations, the insistent acid reflux, and the way it feels like my blood is lava sometimes. I'm finished with the symptoms of a Farrah who is completely at someone else's mercy. Who doesn't know what's coming next.

Enough.

I force myself to take another breath, this one just as deep.

When it still pinches, I take a third. Because this will not continue, and I will not wait to hear my mother say the words to know that this nightmare state of being is over. I will not allow her voice to relieve the pressure.

My parents have done what I asked.

I am getting my home back.

I am in control and I am keeping Cherish. I will bask in the Whitmans' adoration without distraction.

I take a fourth breath, and it's full and easy.

I'm already heading back up to the house when my phone buzzes.

It isn't Nichole Turner.

Found her. Come to my room—QUIETLY.

I bunch my eyebrows, but when I get inside, I *don't* bound up the stairs like a reverse Christmas morning scene. I see Cherish standing outside her slightly open double doors, holding a finger in front of her lips, and I widen my eyes to let her know I get it. This isn't my first time eavesdropping.

She both motions and mouths that my mom is inside, and I nod before quietly taking my place opposite her to listen to whatever's happening on the other side of the bedroom doors.

Immediately I wish I hadn't. Or I wish I were at least hearing this alone.

"I don't know how I'm going to tell her." It's supposed to be my mother, but she's speaking in a voice I'm not used to. Nichole Turner is sure of every word that escapes her lips. Whoever is speaking right now sounds wounded, and it doesn't make sense.

This can't be my mother—unless this is a mask I've never seen.

"I've been racking my brain the entire drive, but I—" She gives up then, and I recoil like I've been hit. "Brianne."

Something about the way she says her friend's name draws my guts into a knot. The Whitman house is a comfortable temperature, as always, even with the constant in and out of the guests today, but I feel sweat pricking my upper lip. Because she seems . . . genuine. Which makes me pay attention to what she's saying.

I don't know how I'm going to tell her.

Because apparently what's happened so far hasn't been the worst thing. Someone else deciding what I lose and what I keep is somehow going to be outdone.

Maybe I haven't been giving myself enough credit. Maybe the sick anxiety that's plagued me hasn't been a kind of self-flagellation; maybe it's been knowing. An internal alarm system, warning me that this is not rock bottom. Because now my mother has something new to tell me and it can't just be losing the same house twice. It's making her sound like someone else.

"Farrah won't understand."

"What do you mean?" Brianne Whitman asks. "Of course she will. She'll be upset, Nicki, but—"

"Brianne," she says, and something in her tone alters again. There's one thing she's afraid to tell me, but there's something else she's considering telling her friend. Something she hasn't even tried to tell my dad.

I won't burst into the room. I'm not going to stop her, even though I can already hear her in my head. I can replay the times Nichole Turner has tried to ease into the subject with me, even though I never acknowledged it. Because part of maintaining her own mask has always entailed criticizing mine, and I've never understood why.

"Farrah's," she begins, and then she stops. She falters immediately—or else she wants Brianne Whitman to pry it out of her. She knows it isn't the kind of thing that can be believed without evidence. And I haven't given the Whitmans any, despite my funk.

In the hallway, I smile.

Control.

"Farrah can be demanding. Difficult."

"I don't think I know a teenager who isn't," Brianne answers easily.

"I know. Of course." There's a heavy sigh.

"Nichole. What's the matter?"

There it is. The invitation my mother was hoping would make this easier to say. Brianne is curious. Now I wait to see how far she'll go.

Even if she says it in plain English, Cherish won't understand. At least there's that. I can tend to the dark smoke curling out of Cherish's open door, pouring out of my mother's mouth and crawling along the floor as though it will spill all the way down the stairs and soil the whole house. I can stop the murky cloud before it passes our feet and I can cover Cherish with it. Just for now. While Cherish doesn't matter, while nothing I learned from her is of any use because it's the real me my mother is trying to describe. I can blot Cherish out because she isn't even the one my mother is telling, not on purpose.

Brianne is the one sitting across from my mother on my best friend's bed; Brianne, who recently told me in front of a garden full of people that I complete her family. That I am welcome here. That's who my mother is trying to poison—but she's hesitating.

"I don't know," and then Nichole Turner whispers it again. "I don't know. I wish I were seeing things sometimes. I tell myself I am. But I know my daughter. I know there's a look she gets in her eyes . . . and I know it scares me sometimes."

Control.

Even though that surprised me. Even though that wasn't enough, it was too much. That was more than tug-of-war.

There's silence between her and Brianne Whitman, but my mother can't wait it out.

"You don't believe me," she says, and it doesn't sound like she's surprised.

"I," Brianne starts to answer, and then takes a thoughtful moment. As though to demonstrate to my mother what she should have done. "I haven't raised any white daughters. But, Nichole, something tells me, if I had, and I could say the same about them? No one would raise any alarms."

The curling cloud stops flowing out of the bedroom. It pauses abruptly and then it rewinds; it pulls back the other way and goes back inside Cherish's room.

"I'm not saying you aren't worried about your daughter," Brianne continues. "I'm not even saying you don't have cause; look at everything you three are going through right now." I'm not in the room, but I know that Cherish's mom has laid her hand over my mother's. "All I'm saying is, Black girls don't get to be difficult without people accusing them of something far worse.

I'm not preaching at you, Nicki, I know you already know this. But even if she is. So what? I say . . . let her be."

It takes everything in me not to laugh out loud.

This family is exquisite. Every imperfection more perfect than the last.

I want to show myself now. I want to press the doors open and let both women know I've heard them, to see whether there's the appropriate amount of shame on my mother's face. Whether her dimple infantilizes her attempt at an unrepentant expression and makes it clear that Brianne Whitman has just eviscerated her attempt to slander me. Brianne, who has made her identity protecting and mothering a little Black girl, so that she cannot fathom what my mother is describing or that it does not have something to do with Brianne Whitman's hard-won expertise.

I don't walk inside the bedroom, and I don't walk away.

I am two of me. I'm shivering with the euphoria of knowing that Brianne Whitman cannot see me, and I am still because I know. Nothing will mitigate my mother's betrayal.

There's silence, but it's too complete. There should be the dull echo of footsteps elsewhere in the house, the dim and distant sound of quiet conversation and instructions between the staff. I should be able to hear Brianne and my mother adjusting on the bed, or Cherish's breathing. The fact that I hear nothing means I haven't just disappeared Cherish; I've muted the world. I am alone with my mother's failed confession, and I'm deciding what must be done.

The answer never changes.

Control.

Cherish's breath returns first. Even across the expanse of the open doors, I hear the air flow in and out of her, as I have so many times before. She is visible again, and when my gaze slides to her throat, I fix it there until I am so attentive to the soft brown skin at her neck that I can faintly make out the beating of her heart. I believe that I can see her pulse beneath her skin. It ticks, like the trembling hand of an alarm clock. It is skittish, not steady. Uncertain instead of strong.

Cherish draws my eyes to hers, and instead of confusion, or perception, or inquisitiveness over the way I've been studying her, her gaze offers me a familiar vacancy. The void that only I have identified. I have given it a name, and still she doesn't understand. I've told her in so many words—in three, to be exact—that she is adored to the point of coddling to the point of infantilization to the point of arrested development. The Whitmans set out to change the world for her, but they have loved her to the point of transformation instead. She couldn't see or understand the world no matter how close it stands.

It is remarkable. A feat, on a child that looks like her. A triumph, though they don't even know it.

Because Cherish is still who she is. She's white girl spoiled, but she isn't white—which is why I can fill that void. It's why she doesn't just let me—she wants me to. She wants me close, and no failed confession will change that.

She is perfect, and she is mine.

I've forgotten there was anything else my mother came to say until Brianne Whitman speaks again. "You don't have to be the one to tell her," she says, and though her voice is gentle, it's also slightly charged. Maybe she's implying that my mother disparaged me as an excuse to avoid whatever news she doesn't want to deliver, but that is far too merciful.

"I can't make Ben do it," my mother answers, and I'm pleased to hear her so deflated. Her voice sounds weak, like one of her lungs has collapsed. "He's just doing what he thinks is best. It has to come from me; otherwise . . ."

I'm sure my mother shakes her head, pretends to be careful or discreet, though the damage has already been attempted.

"Farrah won't accept it unless it comes from me," she says conclusively.

"What makes you say that?" Brianne asks, because she has not heard a word.

I wish I could see my mother's face, to see what expression conveys that she has resigned herself to being the only one who knows the truth.

"I don't want this getting framed as something he's doing *to* us," she says, but I know it isn't in reply. She's pivoting to a conversation Brianne can understand. "No one could have foreseen these past eighteen months, least of all him."

"And it isn't your fault, Nichole."

My mother lets out a heavy breath. "I don't know. I'm the one who got laid off."

That part, I knew.

"I was the one who spent six months trying to replace that position rather than take a pay cut."

That part, I didn't.

"Which was totally understandable," Brianne insists. "You and I have talked about it. Nobody wants to go backward, Nichole."

"Yes, but, Bri. Our situation isn't like yours."

For a moment, I think she's going to mention the Whitman trust. For a moment, I think the woman who just tried to unmask me is going to show her dear friend that like mother, like daughter.

I want her mask to slip. I want her to unhesitatingly tell Brianne Whitman a simple truth, and see if she doesn't sound as difficult as she accused me of being.

Because my parents didn't inherit a family home, which they then sold to Mr. Whitman's younger brother before buying the one they *really* wanted. That is Jerry and Brianne's story.

I genuinely want her to show herself, even though Cherish is listening, too. My lip is sweating again, and so are the palms of my hands, and abruptly the clenching returns so that any minute I might have to run to the toilet. I stay where I am because my mother is more than a boardroom beast; she can be merciless. I know that, even if I've only ever seen it glint in her eye. I know that even though she's refused to let it show. I always thought she was holding it back to teach me how, but that was before she started criticizing the glint in mine.

Brianne didn't understand her disparaging me, so maybe my mother will show herself now. Maybe all it took was Mrs. Whitman speaking on a subject that she couldn't possibly know from experience. She's raising a Black daughter, but she's never been a Black woman. There's no class for that. She's echoing my mother's very personally experienced concerns, but when

Brianne Whitman talks about unequal pay, she means between herself and white men; I doubt she's ever seen the salary disparities that favor her. She has no idea what it costs for women like my mother to lean in.

Control.

If my mother unmasks right now, I will trust her again.

I will forgive without reservation.

All my mother has to do is tell Brianne LePage Whitman a truth. That her family's stability is not the result of good financial planning and choices. That one catastrophe can cost some people everything, while others have more safety nets than they could've possibly earned.

It's something I hadn't known until my parents' finances flatlined, so why should Brianne be assumed any wiser?

I want my mother to uncoil herself. But she doesn't say any of that.

"Neither of us can afford our life without the other," she says instead, and whatever I was looking at, I look away. "I knew that. I knew the strain I was putting on Ben, to take that risk."

"But you were right when you said Black women are overqualified and underpaid, Nichole. Of *course* you didn't want to lose ground."

And the queasy churning immediately calms. Because my mother is always smarter than I give her credit for.

Of course she chose those exact words to elicit that exact response.

Of course the point was getting Brianne Whitman to remind her*self* that my mother lives with a double bind.

If only she'd paired it with honest contrition for her attack on me.

"No, I didn't want to lose ground," Mom repeats through a sigh. "But the gamble didn't pay off. Which I'd stupidly convinced myself wasn't an option. And now we're here."

"So, what? He's going to force you to change everything? Move out of state, pull Farrah out of the academy, separate the girls, and—"

"No one wants that."

Cherish and I lock eyes, and then we take turns closing them in relief.

"But," my mom goes on, "if that's what it takes to get on our feet again, how can I refuse?"

It's quiet inside the bedroom for a minute. Cherish is gaping at me, wanting me to give her some sign that I heard it, too, but I can't.

It isn't just that my parents think I'll accept being separated from Cherish. It isn't just that they're telling someone else before they told me.

They lied.

On top of everything, my parents have been lying to me.

My father isn't working overtime in a last-ditch effort to get our house back. He's looking for work somewhere else. No, he's found it. Which means he's already given up on the life they promised me they were going to save; they both have.

"Nicki, I know it's cliché, but *you're* the strong one," Brianne begins.

"I know," my mother snaps, too familiar with that particular brand of encouragement to accept it with good humor. "Which is why it's important that I side with him. Farrah has to know we're united on this."

The heels of my hands suddenly hurt and I unclench my fists to find deep red imprints where my fingernails were digging in. A little more pressure and I could have broken the skin. Because my mother has always chosen my father over me.

Control, I tell myself and force my fingers straight.

"You don't have to decide today, right this minute," Cherish's mom is saying, because Brianne Whitman doesn't know when she's lost. "There's no reason you have to tell Farrah until he gets an official job-offer letter—"

"He did," Mom says, and it's quiet again for a moment.

Outside the door, Cherish's eyes snap back to mine, but I'm unmoved. She's surprised because she doesn't always know how to put the pieces together. Cherish doubts the proven, even when I try to warn her. She says things like, "Not everyone is out to get you, Farrah," because her parents lovingly debilitated her.

She really is a masterpiece.

"I'm not supposed to tell anyone until he gets back," my mother says, "and we have a chance to sit Farrah down together . . . but it's already done."

"I didn't realize," is all Brianne Whitman replies.

"I should find Farrah," Mom says, and then there's a shuffling sound. "Have you seen my phone?"

"Oh. I think I was sitting on it, I'm sorry."

Amid more sounds of movement and rearranging, I hustle back down the stairs with Cherish right behind me, just in case my mother's about to respond to my text.

When my phone vibrates, I've just pulled the front door closed behind Cherish and me, and my mother's calling.

"RahRah? Are you gonna answer it?"

I look down at my phone, and the picture of my mom glancing back at me over her shoulder. I took this picture while she was standing in what used to be our massive kitchen watching my dad cook, her nightly glass of rosé in hand.

"RahRah?"

I reject the call.

I pull Cherish away from the house and toward the perpendicular three-car garage, all of whose doors are open, as though for display. "Pick a car, any car."

ess than a five-minute drive from the Whitmans' sprawl-ing Greek Renaissance homestead is the cul-de-sac where I learned to ride a bike.

I don't know why that's the first memory that comes to mind. It's something a parent would say. If Jerry Whitman were telling a heartwarming story about the house at the end of the street, nestled in the curve, it's something he would include. It's a brief detail that would convey exactly what this place means to me.

But I don't need to say it to Cherish. I don't need to give a defense. When I say I want her to take me home, she doesn't ask why. She just looks me in the eye after fastening her seat belt and nods like she would've gone anywhere I asked.

In a moment or two, we'll be there, and everything will feel right again.

Whether the house is nothing but a house, whatever hap-pens next will be my choice. Whether I choose to make it an emblem or I relinquish it, everything after tonight will be control.

I can't see the house as we come down the street, not really. There's an island roundabout in the bowl of the street, directly in front of my house, and a smattering of white-bark birch trees that match the ones on my property serve as a kind of privacy barrier.

The Turner family home isn't as stately as the ones closer to the golf course, but it does have the same lovely trees that speckle the grounds. My dad loves the white bark; he said it felt like proof that we were still a part of the community—despite the fact that our garage could only accommodate two cars. Ours is only a mid-length drive, setting the house back from the street and making room for more trees on either side; there isn't room for a valet to line up a dozen or so cars for party guests.

You used to catalog every flaw, my mother's voice accuses me.

She's right. I had a list of ways my home didn't measure up to places like the Whitmans' back when I didn't know houses could be lost. Now, when Cherish stops the car half in the driveway and half in the street, like at the last minute she remembered we no longer have a right to be here, I do not match her hesitation.

This house is perfect, and it's still mine.

"What is that?" I ask, but I don't wait for Cherish to reply. I get out of the car and stand in the headlights to investigate a strange addition to the lawn. Just beyond the curb, staked in the soft ground outside the staggered line of our personal birches, a long white post holds up a transparent box.

Inside there are packets.

"A Charming Country Home with Country Club Ameni-ties," I read, and then there's a lurch in my stomach because of the photo bannering the top. It's my house, but it's impersonal. My mother's deep barrels don't flank the front door with fra-grant and colorful bouquets. There's no welcome mat that reads *The Turners*. It's been stripped of us—of me—in hopes of entic-ing someone new.

"This four-bedroom, five-bath—hey, I didn't know you had the same number of bathrooms as us."

"We don't," I answer Cherish, but neither of us looks away from the page. "Your house has five full baths and two half."

"Does it?"

"Pitched rooflines and a hidden two-car garage add to the curb appeal of this thirty-one-hundred-square-foot jewel"—I continue reading so she knows I'm not going to answer her—"whose gourmet kitchen, elegant master suite, and outdoor liv-ing spaces must be seen to be believed."

I don't like the way that's written.

"Like you'd never believe how amazing the inside is?" Cher-ish echoes my irritation in that way she's always had. It says that even though she's not as discerning as I am, because I've filled the void, she can still sometimes read my mind. "I don't think you reel in buyers by saying you don't think the house has enough curb appeal."

"Maybe people aren't interested," I say, and I don't mean to sound so quiet and hopeful that the house I sometimes thought wasn't good enough won't be good enough for someone else. That maybe if no one else wants it, I can still take it back.

It's already done.

It's been less than fifteen minutes and I'd already forgotten.

My parents lied.

They don't want it back. They don't want to keep what's mine. They're ready to leave for good—and if that weren't enough, my mother hoped to poison the Whitmans against me so I couldn't possibly stay.

Gracious, she said, as though I have to be for them to let me stay.

I know it's where you'd rather be, she told me—only she tried to take their home from me, too. Because Nichole Turner doesn't care where I am, so long as she decides it. She has no preference but control, because my mother and I are alike.

The house doesn't matter. Not the layout or the square footage. What matters—what my mother understood would matter most—is that it's mine.

I kick the white stake, and the transparent box reverberates.

"Whoa!" Cherish jumps back, her hands flying up in surrender. "Are you okay?"

This time she watches me kick the stake. She's ready for the suddenness of the violent sound, even when the second strike causes splintering and pieces like dozens of toothpicks rain down onto the lawn.

"Why are you asking if I'm okay?" I ask, before kicking the stake again. I made the first two look easy, but the third attempt doesn't connect as precisely, and the sole of my shoe slides off without causing any more damage.

When I snort in amusement, Cherish's hands slowly come down, and she smiles like she's relieved.

"Go ahead, if you can do better," I tell her, gesturing at the lopsided stake and smiling back.

"If I can do better than the first two, or that weak last one?"

She leans back to wind up, and when she releases her foot and it connects with a thunderous crack, we squeal in celebration.

Whatever it looked like before—however my mother might have presented it as an evidentiary exhibit when it was only me—now it's a teen prank. It's harmless, a pointless bit of destructive fun, but not one that speaks to a troubling pattern. It can't be thought upsetting unless I do something sinister later. Unless we both do.

Cherish and I alternate now, each taking turns like it's a piñata, until finally the stake snaps, and the top half comes down like a felled tree. The transparent box crash-lands and sprays informational packets across the lawn.

"Grab them," I tell Cherish through huffs, and we collect them all, Cherish picking up the box, while I retrieve the top half of what used to be a white stake. Now its paint is strewn throughout the grass around the sad, beaten base that remains. "Come on!"

Giggling, and dropping packets along the way so that we keep having to double back and start again, Cherish and I run across the street to the forest island in front of my house.

"Hide it," I tell her, but we're laughing too hard to whisper, and while we haphazardly bury the half stake and box and packets, we have to fight to keep from collapsing against each other.

"Shh, it's done," Cherish says, patting handfuls of fallen birch leaves over our victims. "No one will ever know."

"This house belongs to me," I pant, and we stand upright. Our laughter dissipates for a moment while we tower over the burial site. Cherish lays her head on my shoulder and sighs, and it sounds so satisfied that I can't help but smile.

Behind us, the car's still parked halfway in the drive, its headlights still illuminating the bottom of the stake. We walk past it up the driveway, without dimming them.

"How do you even get hired by someone in a different state?" I ask.

"I don't know."

"That probably means they've been lying to me this whole time," I say, as though the thought is new. I temper the strength of my conviction so that Cherish doesn't think I'm being paranoid—or demanding.

"Doesn't it?" I ask, nudging her with my words as we futilely peek through the panels on either side of the door and into the darkened entryway. "If he's got a job offer, doesn't it mean he's known for longer than the two weeks I've been at your place? Probably, right? It seems like he had to know we were never moving back home."

"I don't know how any of this works . . ."

I feel my face go slack as I pretend I'm still looking through the narrow window on my side of the door. Because maybe she doesn't mean for it to sound the way it does.

It sounds like I may be accustomed to unfortunate situations now, but they are still entirely foreign to her. But she wouldn't act WGS right now, this very minute, unless she wanted to humiliate me.

There's a prickle at the back of my neck, but there's no breeze tonight. The air is completely still, but it feels like something is teasing my skin for a response. I shrug and then make a circle with my shoulders.

Gracious, I hear in my mom's voice, before my chin ticks in a discreet refusal.

Control.

Because there's a chance Cherish is just being honest. She should be smarter. She should think of how her words will sound to someone in my position, but she's probably never known anyone who lost a house. I haven't.

The night I moved in with Cherish, when we stayed up all night just holding each other and staring at the ceiling, she'd said she didn't even know banks were involved in homeownership. I almost pinched the tender skin above her elbow then, too—but I hadn't known it, either.

"Come on," I say, and I take her hand before I steal around the side of my house. There's a simple gate there, enclosing our impressive "outdoor living spaces," but all I have to do is reach over and unlatch it to gain entry because nothing has changed.

This house is still mine, and neither the bank nor my parents nor anyone else has anything to say about it. I'll give it up if and when I decide to. Not before.

I pull Cherish inside the gate behind me, and now there's a little bit of electricity in the air. We're both smiling wide, only barely holding back the resurgence of giggling and then letting some out on purpose. There's an accelerating current inside me, like I'm somewhere I'm not supposed to be—or like I know something no one else does.

This is still my backyard.

The covered back porch is wide, as always, but it doesn't have any lights spiraling down the posts, and the patio outside my parents' back door is missing its charming bistro table and chairs. The brick fireplace is empty, has clearly benefited from a deeper clean than we ever gave it, and although the waterfall isn't running, the pool lights are.

It's like it knew I'd be coming.

The stone mosaics inside the pool and the spa are illuminated in a warm and calming glow, the way they were every night I can remember. The light dances across the small stones, waves of it undulating beneath mostly still water, making it easy to believe that everything's still just as it was.

"How many times did we sneak out here to swim in the middle of the night after my parents went to bed?" I ask.

Cherish laughs and glances back at their door, like any minute they might wake up and catch us, even though they never did.

"So ridiculously unsafe," I say, shaking my head as though at young Che and RahRah.

I want to see how Cherish responds. She heard what my mother said. I need to know whether she understood it. More than that, I need to know that she still belongs to me.

"Pfft," she says with a roll of her eyes. "We knew how to swim."

"Accidents happen," I tell her, and then my eyes drift from

the stones that only look soft because they're under peaceful water. Because there's brick bordering the pool, and stones that might constitute boulders separating the pool from the spa— and because skin breaks so easily. "What if we'd slipped on the way in or out of the water and cracked our skulls out here? One of us could easily have drowned before anyone knew we were out of bed."

"O . . . kay. That wasn't *not* creepy." But she still laughs. She's still holding my hand.

She isn't staring or startled by all the sharp edges I mentioned. She isn't imagining how blood might plume beautifully in the illuminated water, like I am. All she's thinking of is the memory I've recalled, and the idea it's implanted.

"Are we doing this or what?" Cherish asks, like the thought is hers.

"Are we doing what?"

When I look at her, Cherish untangles our fingers and pulls her shirt over her head. She pulls her voluminous twist out up and off her neck, binding it in a high bun and leaving her two long cornrows to frame her face.

"Che."

She glances at me, unzipping her Bermuda shorts and sliding them down over her narrow hips.

"We can't." I resist again so she'll prove her resolve.

She continues looking at me, prying one shoe off with the toe of the other. It's a silent challenge—or so she thinks—and she does a good job maintaining the expressionless calm. She almost looks like she's not doing anything out of the ordinary, while telling me with her eyes that I have to do the same.

I'm chewing my bottom lip again, but it's only to fight the wide grin threatening to spread my lips and expose my teeth.

I stare back at my best friend and start undoing the three buttons on my shirtdress so that Cherish finally breaks into a smile. In a moment, we're laughing again, and I'm so warm inside that the paler brown skin on my chest might be flushed.

Once undressed, I part my hair and start a French braid with one half, before Cherish takes the other half and does the same, binding her fingers in my hair and then freeing them to do the next crisscross. When both my braids are done, she ties their ends in a knot at the back of my head and then pulls me backward into her by the shoulders.

"Ready?"

I nod before I answer. "Ready."

She pushes and I leap, and between the force of both of us, I go careening into the water, howling. It breaks to let me in, and I descend into the bright light, the sound of Cherish's whoop abruptly muffled because I've been swallowed up.

It's cool—much chillier than I'm used to, because we always regulated the temperature—and it feels so good seeping into my scalp, through my underwear, soaking into my skin. It's so refreshing that I stay under until Cherish is there, too, and then I open my eyes to greet her. When she and I rejoin hands and turn over at the same time to float on our backs, the fronts of our bodies are exposed not just to the night sky, but also to the occasional breeze we couldn't feel before we came in. It sets goose bumps on our skin and makes our teeth chatter, but we stay in the pool.

We're not whooping or hollering now; we aren't laughing, either. The only sound is the water lapping against the edge of the pool and the popping sound our feet make when they slowly slip beneath the surface and then crest again.

After a while I can't feel Cherish's hand in mine anymore, but I know it's there, under the water.

That's what happens when you hold anything long enough; you stop feeling it, no matter how much you want to. No matter how much you try to treasure it, you can't—and maybe that's as far as most people ever know. That if you hold on, you lose the feeling. But I know there's always a way to get the feeling back.

You have to disrupt the calm. You have to tighten your grip, crush it a little, to remember you've got a hold on something.

"RahRah?" Cherish's voice is somehow both booming and muffled. It comes to me through the water and through the air, like it won't take any chances of not finding my ear.

"Yeah?"

"What do you love most about me?"

Water sloshes against the side of my face, refilling one of my ears so that if I wanted to, I could tell Cherish I didn't hear her question. It'd be half-true, except that I know what she said. It isn't the first time she's interrogated me this way.

Maybe it's perfectly natural, something anyone would do. Maybe people often wear their neediness on their sleeves and it isn't unique to Cherish. Maybe it's not her void that makes her want an itemized recollection of the lovable things about her—but it's the void I love most, and I will never tell her that.

"That's too easy," I say, as though to the night sky, and then I turn my head in the water and look at her. She bobs, or I do, both our bodies swaying with the water. "What do you love about you?"

Cherish smiles and looks back toward the stars. A lifetime as Brianne Whitman's daughter, subject to incessant encouragement about self-love and validation, has prepared her to field my redirection.

"I'm kind," she says, calm, as though she's done the corresponding breathing exercises, too. "And I have a dimple."

"Oh my God."

Her laughter peels out of her and she has to press her head farther back into the water to keep from capsizing. I smile.

"RahRah?" she asks when she's recovered. Her voice is smaller somehow and I know what she's going to say this time, too.

"Yeah, Che."

"I don't want you to move away."

I watch the stars, and what must be a satellite slowly crossing between them.

"I know, Che."

"You can't let them separate us," she says. "I need you."

Tears that probably look very much like pool water returning to its source slip down the sides of my face. It's not because I didn't know; it's just because I love that, too.

I know it's where you'd rather be . . .

. . . even if you can't say you decided it.

So, I decide.

I choose the Whitmans' house. I choose Cherish for my home, the way I should've done from the start. She's the only person I still love when I hate her.

I pull my feet deeper into the pool and stand upright.

"I'll stay," I promise her, and water rushes from the crown of my head and splits into a million streams and rivers as it escapes my thick hair and runs down my chest and back.

Cherish is still on her back beside me, and when I turn to look down at her floating body, she closes her eyes against the pellets raining down from mine, but she doesn't stand up to escape. I raise my hand above her so that thick droplets rush down the length of my fingers and fall across her torso. Eventually the water begins to run low, accumulating at the tips of my fingers torturously slow, like it doesn't want to part with me. There are several beats between the pearls of water I send crashing onto her forehead, and Cherish squeezes her eyes shut until there's nothing left.

After that, I trace my damp finger down her face slowly, from hairline to the space between her brows, and then again, horizontally, to cross it.

In response, she closes her arms over her chest, and when I can tell she's holding her breath, I lay my hands on my best friend's chest and stomach, then I press all the way down.

There's something so peaceful about the way she sinks below the surface. She's calm, only tensing when her body tries to turn or rotate from beneath my grasp. She forces herself to stay under my hands, and I wait.

I need to witness her resolve.

Underwater, glowing in the pool's light, her eyes bat open after a moment and she watches me, but Cherish doesn't fight.

Staring back at her, I start to smile as I take deep, antagonizing breaths, because she can't.

Because the truth is, if we were going to get hurt when we were younger—sneaking into the pool under cover of darkness, after my parents were long asleep—there wouldn't have been any blood. It wouldn't have been the brick or the boulders or a freak accident.

It would've been one of our baptisms gone wrong. It would've been that one of us trusted the other too long, that we didn't know we'd held our breaths past the point of good sense. That we'd cared too much about proving ourselves to each other in the secret way we somehow devised without ever putting it into words.

Tonight, I'm satisfied.

I'm ready to relent.

I'm about to take Cherish by the bra straps and heave her out of the water toward me, when a light bounces across my face, and a man's voice booms through my backyard.

"Who's there?!"

I can't see him with the flashlight beaming directly into my face, but I know he's one of the community security guards, called no doubt by a concerned neighbor.

"What are you doing? Is someone in the water?"

He's blaring the light into the pool now, and it must have nearly blinded Cherish before she closed her eyes—but she still doesn't come up.

"Get out of the pool!" he bellows. "Ma'am! Both of you need to come out of the pool, or I'll call the police!"

I don't move. I'm standing in waist-deep water, in a soaking-wet bra, and he's near hysterics, but I wait. This is all still up to me.

"Ma'am!"

I wait. Just as he bends down to untie his shoes, a first

gesture of many meant to indicate he's coming in the water after us, I hoist Cherish out.

The security guard looks at us, Cherish fresh from baptism, water pouring down her face and chest, both of us calm and silent. Cherish is recovering quietly and his chest is rising and falling quickly by comparison. The look on his face blends confusion and discomfort beautifully.

"What are you doing?" he asks, but any authority has drained from his voice. The color in his face follows, the longer Cherish and I stand before him, silent.

Instead of yelling any further commands, he merely gestures with his flashlight for us to come out of the water, and looks away from us when we finally do.

MY MOTHER MUST have been gone by the time the Whitmans were called, because when they arrive to pick us up from the security office, there's only Jerry and Brianne.

When the still disturbed guard explains that we were trespassing on private property and tells them the address, he's clearly not expecting the way their concern melts into compassionate sighs.

"That's where she used to live," Jerry informs him, suggesting with a lift of his chin that the man should at least pretend to understand. "I'm sure there's no harm done. But it won't happen again."

He turns to a still wet Cherish and me, and we echo him in unison.

"It won't happen again."

"I'm sure next time you girls can swim in our pool, at home," he says, with a lighthearted shake of his head.

"They weren't swimming," the guard interjects, and then he turns his head slightly away from the two of us, like we won't hear what he says next. Or else like he still doesn't want to look directly at Cherish and me. "They were holding each other underwater."

Jerry scrunches his brow and glances at us. I assume Cherish gives the same blank and innocent expression I do.

"It's just a game," Brianne assures him, as though she's ever seen it done—but the guard won't let it go.

"It wasn't a game," he insists, and his eyes stray over to me before leaping away. "She wouldn't let her up. I told her to multiple times, but she kept holding her down."

There's no expression or response I can give. It has to be Cherish.

All I can do is wait.

A giggle peels out of her, and the stiffness that might have collected in her parents' posture never solidifies.

"What are you talking about?" she asks through the kind of laugh that cuts through certainty and self-esteem.

Immediately, the guard's mouth gapes, and when I join Cherish in laughter, I make sure to keep mine restrained. I can't be the one cutting into his credibility; my attempts to curb my amusement have to seem pitying.

"Somebody's a hypochondriac," she says, rolling her eyes and letting her tongue peek between her teeth when she snorts back a laugh. "Are you afraid of the water? Is that why you didn't come in and rescue me?"

"Cherish, be nice," Jerry chides her halfheartedly. "I'm sorry about these two. It's the end of a very long, very eventful birthday weekend. Thank you for calling us; it won't happen again."

And when he flashes Cherish and me a glance, we echo him again.

"It won't happen again."

WHEN WE'RE HOME, no one tells us to wait in the foyer while they go retrieve a towel. No one asks what we were thinking, going swimming in our underwear, without a towel or a change of clothes. The Whitmans are permissive in the way parents can be when they don't clean their own houses or vehicles and the cost isn't a concern.

It's nice not to have to tiptoe. It's nice when every single instance of freedom isn't followed by a consequence, even one as trivial as taking extra care before collapsing into bed.

It's nice that the permission applies to me now, too.

Jerry wishes Cherish a happy birthday one last time, and both parents kiss us each on the forehead or the cheek.

"Good night, sweet hoodlums," Mr. Whitman calls after us as we mount the stairs. "Please don't ever make me speak to that security guard again."

"No promises," Cherish calls back.

Upstairs, we rock-paper-scissors to decide who gets the bathroom first, and I make sure she wins. She loves to throw scissors, so I slide out paper and then shrug like a gracious loser when she bounces off to take what I know will be one of her ridiculously long, scalding-hot showers. Alone in our room, I wrap my terry-cloth turban around my wet French braids and relax on my side of the bed to stare up into our vaulted ceiling by myself.

There's a simple package on the nightstand beside me. It's wrapped, but the weight and size can't obscure the fact that it's clearly a book. When I lift a corner of it, it's just enough to verify that there's no accompanying card for the gift.

"It's for you." Mrs. Whitman's voice carries from the hall. She's standing almost where I was when she sat on the bed with my mother, except the top half of her body is curling around the slightly open door and she wants me to know she's there.

"For me?" I ask to see what else she'll say.

"May I come in?"

I nod, and she slips inside, closing the door behind her.

"Jerry and I . . . we knew this weekend would probably be a little much to take. Birthday celebrations are fun, but. Maybe this year less so?" She makes it to the bed and sits on Cherish's side, twisting to place her hand close to me without touching.

She's being careful, tiptoeing around something. If she'd decided what to say before I got home, it was easier in theory. Now she's afraid to upset me.

"I heard you talking to my mom," I say as though in confession, choosing the apologetic tone in case she already knows, and so that she thinks it was an accident. But I wonder if that's why there's a present for me on the night of my best friend's final birthday party.

"Oh, honey," she says through a sigh. "I thought you might have, when your mom couldn't reach you."

Whenever I've been swimming, it takes hours before my body realizes I'm no longer in the pool, and inside my head it feels like I'm swaying like a buoy. I focus on the feeling when I let my eyes slip, and seem to absentmindedly rub one arm with the opposite hand.

"I'm sorry you're going through all of this," Brianne says, and lays her hand over mine at last. "And I'm also really glad you're here. We all are. We want you to know you're welcome as long as you like. Which is why we wanted to get you a little something, too."

I don't mention the shopping spree they gave me yesterday, because in their minds that was probably part of Cherish's gift. Instead, I lift the bundle again and turn it over and over, looking for the seams. Brianne Whitman is a marvel with all things décor and craft, and I can't find anyplace to start delicately unwrapping the gift, so I just tear. Maybe that makes me seem anxious to see it, and she smiles like she's happy at the sight of me making one long, continuous spiral of the paper.

Inside, it's exactly what the shape implied. A book. I'm not exactly thrilled, but I don't have to perform excitement for Mrs. Whitman; a much more measured thoughtfulness will please her, so I inspect it.

The book is old. If the clear sleeve protecting it wasn't evidence enough, the condition makes it pretty clear. There's no dust jacket, the title and border and illustration are printed directly on the hardcover, and there are flecks of color missing from all three. The background is blue and tan, with an old-fashioned scene depicted in red and white. It's colonial or European, involving a horse, and a soldier and two boys in old-fashioned clothes. I have absolutely no idea what's going on in the picture, and I've never heard the title before.

"*The Whipping Boy*," I read aloud.

I play enamored now, the way I trace my finger across the front like I want to feel the cover's texture through the protective layer. Because this is not a spur-of-the-moment gift, found and given because of an exhausting weekend. This book would have taken some searching, if they just wanted something old and obscure; if the Whitmans wanted this exact title, who knows how much longer.

This gift is specific, and intentional, and chosen with me in mind. Why else would Brianne be hovering so close as I take it in?

I have absolutely no use for this book I've never heard of— but that's beside the point.

The waves I still feel inside me after tonight's swim swell. The content of the package doesn't matter. It's the fact that, once again, Cherish's parents have gone out of their way to make me feel special. To make me feel a part. The way Brianne was clearly trying to when she said I complete the family, even though, at first, I suspected it was an attack.

What could be more Whitman than a gift that is both extravagant and completely pointless? What could be more satisfying than a present that doesn't fill a need? Whose only purpose is to make the recipient feel exceptional for owning it?

If I were Cherish, I would take the book out of the sleeve, turn the no-doubt delicate pages, searching for some reason why. Why *this* particular present? If a book, why *this* book?

The Whipping Boy sounds terribly old and boring, hardly intriguing for a teenager with almost limitless entertainment options at her fingertips. Cherish would ruin the moment trying desperately to find some reason to appreciate it. That her mother is some sort of fine art and antiquities specialist would factor into her assessment, but only enough to reduce the present to some sort of selfish projection of Brianne's interests onto the recipient.

I know that the gift is reason enough, regardless of what it is. If it's more an extension of Brianne Whitman's expertise, even better. It means she is giving me herself.

The book is an emblem, the way my house has been. A tangible representation of Brianne's affection for me; it doesn't have to be anything else.

"It's marvelous," I say, because I've heard Brianne describe antiques that way. I let my eyes continue searching the unspectacular illustration because she never spends fewer than two full minutes studying a single detail on a new find.

"I'm so glad," she tells me, and I can hear the exhilaration in her voice. She scoots closer to me. "It's not for reading, of course, it's far too delicate for that. Everyone should have something very old, just to cherish. Although . . ." And she reaches for the book, which I give her so that she can carefully open the sleeve and take a deep breath. She offers me the open end, and I do the same. "There's no harm in enjoying the aroma."

I smile at the way it smells warm and almost roasted, and the way Mrs. Whitman keeps leaning closer and closer so that now our shoulders and our legs are touching.

She beams.

"It's entrancing, isn't it? If I never read a book again, I'd still fill my house with them, just for that smell."

She's still smiling at me, and for a moment her gaze is

unwavering. There's a kind of insistence in the way she's look-ing at me, and even though I can't completely translate it, I'm careful to match it. I want her to know I'm not thrown off, the way I was after her party toast.

"It's so lovely. Thank you, Mrs. Whitman."

"Of course, honey." She puts one arm around me and lets our heads rest together so that when a shiver courses through her, I feel it. Her shudder leaks from her body into mine, and even if I'll never look at the book again, I'm intoxicated.

Maybe she can be home, too. Cherish is the one I've cho-sen, but there's no reason I couldn't have Brianne as well. Par-ents who already love one child they didn't bear, and who always see her in the best possible light. A mother who refuses to hear the child she adores disparaged. Never asking for evi-dence or example because she never meaningfully considered my mother's complaint.

I will choose the Whitmans, too.

When Cherish's shower quiets, Brianne sits up with a start, breaking our contact.

I didn't expect that.

Maybe Brianne is worried about how Cherish will respond— but there's also the chance that this moment has been dear to her. Enough to keep it secret.

"This is just for you, remember," she tells me, and, to my delight, she takes the book out of my hands and closes it in the drawer of the nightstand beside me. Then, as though to down-play the act, she waves and makes a frivolous gesture. "Cherish has gotten more than her share of presents this year, that's all."

But she pauses for one last steady gaze before she says, "It's only fair to keep something for yourself. All right?"

Once Brianne Whitman looks away to collect the spiral of wrapping paper, and while she stands up and smooths her dress, I smile. A deep breath escapes, like the ones I intentionally took while Cherish was underwater.

"Thank you," I say. "Really. I'll treasure this."

"I know you will, Farrah, and you're more than welcome. Now you girls get some sleep."

And after blowing me a kiss, Che's mom slips back out of the bedroom before her daughter reenters. Of course, I know she was never in any danger of being caught, because unlike Brianne Whitman, I know how long Cherish preens before coming out, even once her shower's done. I know her habits and routines as well as I know my own because we're close in a way Cherish isn't with anyone else.

I know something about both Cherish and Brianne Whitman that neither knows about the other, even if it's as simple as the length of a shower.

Before Cherish comes to bed, I open my phone.

Love you, Mommy, I text.

She'll hear the sickly sweetness in the written words, if only because of what I have never called her aloud.

My mother is clever, and this is as good as a confession. That I know what she attempted today, and that I'm not only feeling well again.

I'm better.

I am winning.

V

There's only a week left of school, and it's not even a full one, Monday to Thursday—and only for those whose parents haven't already whisked them off on a first summer vacation.

Yes, academy families tend to vacation in flights. Typically, there's what I call the Primer, then the Party, and finally the Pièce de Résistance. The Primer involves jet-setting, but usually just to one location, and only for something like a week. It's perfect for the family who knows their child will need summer tutoring or some manner of coaching, and will have to forgo one or both of the other flights. After the Primer comes the Party circuit, during which people are back in town long enough to gush about where they've been and where they're being *dragged* to in August. Partiers will appear as though out of a Primer livestream to pop up at a few choice events, and maybe hop over to a music festival with a small group of friends.

After which, there's the Pièce de Résistance. The vacation that'll dominate all social media accounts, that'll be something like competitive, obscure-destination hopping.

Two summers ago—when life was as it should be—Cherish and I won.

Yacht selfies off the coast of Ibiza weren't exactly a strong start with three academy families Primering together in Morocco for eight days, but from Spain, our parents took us to Lamu Island in Kenya, and since no one we know has visited any part of Africa between the northernmost coastline and Johannesburg—no contest. Aside from the stray fake-incredulous comments—"I didn't know people vacationed in Africa!"—our schoolmates had a pretty difficult time hiding their envy and awe.

There won't be any Lamu Island this summer, not for my family anyway. No Primer, either, and no use for a Party circuit when there's nothing bookending it. Which makes the last few days of school an exercise in avoiding holiday talk. For a reigning champion, that's impossible. Several times just today, I've ducked into the restroom or pulled out my phone under the guise of a vibrating notification, because staying quiet isn't an option. It culls attention. Inspires questions. They might pretend the questions are benign, that they're only asking where I'm heading over summer break, but I hear what they really mean.

"How are you guys gonna top Kenya?" means *Hope you enjoyed it while it lasted.*

It means *The life you thought you had is pretty much over, and we knew it wouldn't last.*

You and Cherish might be sister-friends, but she's still a Whitman.

In the silence, when someone miraculously doesn't ask me anything vacation-related, I know that they're thinking the worst: *Living with Cherish won't make you like her.*

In the Humanities Wing break room, the blinds cast a patterned shadow across the round tabletop and my forearms. I've tucked myself away in the corner to nurse a glass orb of apple juice during my free period, and I'm happy to be completely alone.

I'm subjecting myself to dinner at my parents' rented house to confirm what I already know—that they've been quietly preparing for a completely new life—and will leverage it to secure an indefinite stay at the Whitmans. I need to run through the scenarios.

In the break room, I've been content to sit with the lights off, scrolling through my phone as I open one app and then immediately close it before choosing another. It's a rigorous and pointless finger exercise, but it leaves my mind free to work out the puzzles without suspicion.

"Hey." Cherish's voice infiltrates my cocoon. "There you are."

"Hey."

"Having fun in the dark?"

She weaves around the tables as she makes her way to me, her academy blue plaid jumpsuit rolled up to show sheeny brown shins above braided thong sandals. Her sleeves are rolled, too, and her waist is cinched with a thin brown belt, because only Cherish and I have figured out how to make the chimney sweep onesies look good, and with the year basically over, no one will bother dress-coding her for it. It's the kind of stylish alteration I'd usually be making to one of our uniforms, too.

Today I prefer strict adherence to uniformity: knee-length pleated skirt, *not* rolled up at the waist to shorten it, and instead of my own accessories, I'm sticking to the academy-crest studs and nothing else. Onlookers will likely assume either that I'm striving for near invisibility or else that I'm too somber for creative alterations.

"Looking all good," Cherish purrs at me, unsurprisingly oblivious.

"Shush," I say, closing my phone. "How'd you find me?"

"We are one, RahRah. Our hearts beat in tandem."

I blink.

"Or I've been checking all the break rooms, whatever. I need you to hear me out. You *have* to come with me after school today," she says, and I start to shake my head because we've already been over this. "I knooow, you're supposed to go see your folks. I'm just saying, Kelly and Tariq—"

"Aren't going anywhere."

Cherish winces, almost imperceptibly, before I go on.

"We've got all summer; that's all I meant. Or we hope we do anyway, so I have to see my parents, Che."

"I know, I just thought maybe an hour. One. To get you all loosened up and relaxed."

Because that's what being around Kelly does.

"There's no way it would be one hour," I say instead.

"Two hours."

"Che." I tighten my expression.

"What if they run off with you?" she says, even though she knows her concern is completely irrational. Her brows are cinching together and she's fiddling with the rose-gold ring hugging her index finger above the knuckle. "What if they decide today's the day and they kidnap you off to whatever state your dad's been in, no warning?"

I take her hand across the table.

"Cherish."

"What," she says, but she's not looking at me.

"It's not called kidnapping when parents relocate with their own child." I smile when she yanks her hand away. It always eases my own anxiety to see it on her. "Okay, I'm sorry. But that isn't gonna happen, I promise. They're going to say yes." She's still not looking at me, so I pull gently on her hand. "I will make sure they do."

"You're gonna tell them you don't wanna go, and that's it? You really think it's gonna be that easy?"

"Yep. Because I *don't* wanna go. And obviously that matters to them, or they wouldn't have let me come to your house in the first place."

"That's temporary, Farrah. Why would they leave you here? Even if we want them to?"

"Well, first of all, if you're going to convince someone that what you're asking isn't a big deal, it's probably a good idea to believe it yourself. How many kids have left the academy because they were going to boarding school?" I ask, and Cherish nibbles on the inside of her lip. "That's normal, right?"

But her mind's on something else.

"What?" I ask, and tug on her hand again. "What arc you *really* worried about?"

She takes a moment to collect herself and then puts on as brave a face as she can manage.

"You're really gonna ask . . . right?"

"What?" I squint at her.

"It's just. I know you haven't been having as good a time staying with me as I thought you would," Cherish says, looking at me from under a tented brow. Her puppy-dog expression is all the more endearing because someone like Cherish could only achieve it genuinely. "I thought it'd be fun, you and me, like one of the sleepovers we tried to make last forever."

She smiles, her dimple puncturing her cheek in the dimly lit break room. It shouldn't be pretty, but it is. Like a collapsing star.

"But I haven't been as sensitive as I could've been," she goes on, and I let her. "About . . . *why* you're with me. I didn't really get it until we went back to your old house."

She finally lifts her head and for a moment we just study each other.

"I just want you to know, I'll do better," she says. "If you stay."

"I know," I tell her. "And yes. I'm really gonna ask. Okay?"

She nods and pulls my hand to her side of the table.

Cherish isn't built like me. She isn't resilient. She's a masterpiece, but that also means that she's exhaustible. A facade of a world has been built around her; the slightest exposure to the real one is depleting. I have to remember that.

I have to coddle her back to calm.

"You don't understand how much we accomplished with those slumber parties. Before you, there was no such thing as a sleepover in the middle of the school week!"

Cherish shakes her head like she's never heard such a thing, but she's starting to smile.

"I couldn't even stay the full next day; I'm serious. Sleepovers ended abruptly at noon, no matter what. Nonnegotiable. None of this all-day lounging. You woke with the birds, had breakfast, and it was time to go home."

"My God." She looks like she's just watched someone stab a kitten. "Why would you do that?!"

I shrug, snorting.

"So what made them change their minds? How'd we manage to get you from serious lockdown to weeklong turns at each other's houses?" she asks, and I pause for a moment, but not because I don't know the answer.

You aren't protecting me, I'd told my mom after a tear-filled plea hadn't swayed my parents and my dad was out of the room. *Black parents being overly stern and restricting? You're not teaching me to be careful in the world; you're teaching me that you'll hurt me first. You always tell me no before they ever do.*

I wasn't crying anymore, but the tears were still on my face. I knew from my mother's calm disquiet what they must have looked like, paired with a mismatched steady expression. When she answered, I knew for certain that she could tell which were real and which was fake.

I don't say no because I'm a Black mother. I have to say no because I'm your mother.

I rewarded her honesty with a fresh sheet of tears spilling down my otherwise unaffected face.

To Cherish, I offer a smile.

"My parents love you as much as your parents love me. You know that, right?"

Cherish's cheeks lift despite herself, and she glances back down at her ring. I don't buy for a second that she's sheepish or that the question wasn't a fishing expedition, but her expression is adorable, and I need to have this at the ready anyway, in case I have to remind my parents how much our friendship means to them, too.

"They were worried about sending me here," I say, gesturing around as though all of the academy is in this break room. My other hand still holds hers, and I pull it a bit more toward me so she has to lean in. "It's one of the impossible paradoxes my dad's always talking about. Knowing what to sacrifice for, and when the sacrifice will cost more than the goal is worth. They weren't sure this education—any!—was gonna outweigh the fact of being the only Black girl here."

I almost say that that's never what it is, but the truth might be too complex for Cherish. Because being the only one is the part we say out loud. What *happens* to you when you're the only one, be*cause* you're the only one, the treatment you endure and the constant state of unease and hypervisibility—that's what we mean. Being bullied in a way no one thinks is bullying, because no one on the staff looks like you, and anyway they daily barrage you with microaggressions, too.

I don't say it, and it's not because it's too complicated. It's because if I mention how Cherish is the other Black girl who made all the difference to my parents, I won't be able to keep from saying that Cherish is always the only one. In her house, in the sanctuary everyone has with their family, she's the only

Black girl there, too. And that's the kind of thing you only get to say once—to great effect anyway.

"My parents worry about the same thing," she tells me. "I mean, I was allowed to have regular sleepovers before you." And she throws me a hilarious side-eye.

"One night is regular!"

"It's not, you were deprived, and I feel sorry for you, stop."

"Shuttup!" I toss her hand away and she grabs mine back.

"But when you came along, they were relieved," she says. "Just like your folks."

Just like my folks.

Like she could hear what I didn't say. Like maybe, despite saying not everyone's out to get *me*, when it comes to her parents, she can misinterpret harmless statements as a challenge.

Maybe she's asserting that she's loved just the same. She's protected, and considered, and guarded just like I am, and her parents being white doesn't change that. She's saying it doesn't matter who they are, as long as they know who *she* is.

A series of muted xylophone notes play over the intercom, signaling the end of the period, and doors calmly open, footfalls spilling out into the hall. Pretty soon, someone will come in and undo the pleasant emptiness I've been enjoying.

"You'll still come home tonight?" Cherish asks me, because there *is* a room for me in the smaller house on the other side of town. Even if they've betrayed me, my parents didn't go somewhere where there wasn't room for me, too. Which makes it a wonder they let me stay at the Whitmans' at all.

I hate anyone knowing I'm surprised. When someone throws open the door of the break room and loud voices spill inside, it covers the little gasp I make. Cherish doesn't hear me; I'm glad she's looking over her shoulder at the intruders, so she doesn't see the way a realization carves into my face.

Of course I know why my parents let me go to the Whitmans'. Why they arranged it before even asking me whether or not I'd want to.

It was jarring before I overheard our mothers talking. I was getting whiplash going back and forth between conflicted thoughts. One moment, it made perfect sense in a selfless, considerate, parental way that hoped I could be distracted from the drama, and the next moment it was confusing and excessive.

It makes sense now. Now that I know they've been faking it and my dad has been traveling, and all along, I've known nothing about it . . . it makes sense.

It was easier to keep me in the dark if I wasn't there to know there was a secret in the first place. It was easier to hide that they didn't want to save the house if I wasn't there to question why they weren't.

Control is why I don't send the empty apple juice glass careening to the ground.

Control is why I don't take it in both my hands, raise them above my head, and crash them into the table so the container can shatter in my palms.

My blood doesn't rush between my fingers in thick red currents because I am in control.

"I need your car," I say instead, and Cherish whirls back around to face me.

"After school? Or you mean now?" One of her eyebrows

curled high. "Your parents aren't expecting you until this evening."

"I know." I smile as I slide the key ring from her finger.

I SQUEAL OUT of the parking lot in Cherish's pearlescent bauble of a car a bit more aggressively than I intend to, but it's more determination than reckless abandon. There are no other hallmarks of carefree teendom on display. The sunroof isn't open, and the wind isn't whipping through my hair. I'm not filling the late morning air with the percussive chillstep I've forced Cherish to love.

I need quiet. I didn't use to; I could strategize on my feet, in the moment, but these past few weeks have taken their toll and finally knowing the truth doesn't change that. Not yet. It still takes concentration to decide exactly how this information must be wielded to produce the desired result. It even takes a moment to process the fact that this weakened state was my mother's intention. My parents' lies and betrayal have been a sinister kind, destabilizing me enough that realizing them has taken effort—not to mention retaliating.

I say "my parents," but something so sinister and perfect could only have been Nichole Turner's work. My dad's just a person, easy to ignore. He would realistically think all the stress and trauma of losing my home could be mitigated by letting me cocoon with my best friend. Only someone like my mother— someone like me—would know the torment it would cause, appearing to give me what I want, when all I ever really need is control. From her, this would be a precision attack. Only she could've devised this plot to buy them time.

I didn't grow up on this side of town where the boulevards are wider and the street signs are bigger, like they're advertising the fact that, by contrast, the homes are small. The yards are, too, and it means the houses are sometimes so close it looks like you can hear everything that happens at your neighbor's place. It's claustrophobic, not cozy.

I'm sure homes are made of relatively similar stuff, no matter which neighborhood, and there are trees here, too, even if they aren't white birch. It isn't as manicured and precise as when the residents pay a fee to keep it that way, and that means that there will be the inevitable eyesores.

It isn't lost on me that there are immediately more people who look like me. I'm still in the suburbs, of course, and there are still plenty of white people, but there is so much more. Which is supposed to make it feel like home. It's supposed to mean I'm rejecting them if I say I deserve better than this.

But I do. This is a downgrade. This isn't where I was raised. I didn't get the internal chip that makes me gravitate to our assigned seats. It isn't because I don't recognize the brutal terrors that necessitated that self-preservation. It's just that I am confident I could do worse. That if I uncoiled myself, if control ever began to mean something other than strictly maintaining a mask for the rest of the world—I am capable of terrorizing them back.

I turn onto the street where my parents live, and even though I tore out of school like I wanted to confront them, a wave of relief passes over me. I want to flip a switch and be over it now that I know it was my mother's orchestrated attack. I want to go back to being quiet and quietly underestimated in that way that also lets me go unsuspected, but I still need a few minutes more than I used to.

There aren't any cars in the driveways, and that includes theirs. It's the middle of the morning, but I don't actually *know* that my mother's been supplementing with her notary license, like she said. For that matter, I don't know that their cars being gone means they're working at all. I am choosing to believe something is as it should be because it serves me. Whether I like it or not, it's stabilizing, being able to trust my parents. I need that if I'm going to be sane enough to spar with them. With her.

I park at the curb because this sad excuse for a house has a one-car garage and a car-length driveway, which means there's only enough designated space for my parents' cars—and I want them to notice the way I keep out of it.

I can't get to the front door. Halfway up the path running parallel to the driveway and cutting even farther into what was already a modest lawn, I stop and just . . . stare.

There's nothing malevolent about it—it's just a house—but I despise it the way you can when you know it stands for so much more. The boring stucco exterior's the same as all the other houses on this street, although they each have some variation of color and accenting. Like everyone was allowed one special request during construction, and that's how you know which one is yours. If you didn't know what real customization looks like, and that it's not ticking boxes to adjust only preapproved features on otherwise identical floor plans, it probably seemed like a very charming development, as far as tract housing goes.

Now, even with whatever variation the original owners chose as their signature, my parents' place stands out from the very lived-in neighborhood because it looks vacant by comparison. There are no flower pots on either side of the door. There's no flag mounted beside the electronic garage door that faces the street like it's an attractive detail of its own, even though every single one is just a cheap-looking roll-up that is apparently impossible not to dent.

This is the first time I'm using the key my parents gave me, and I enter without announcing myself the way I always did at home. Even when I knew no one else was there, I'd fill the entryway with the sound of my voice, like I was greeting the house itself, welcomed in exchange by the familiar aroma. The perfume of home.

I guess there's a smell when I come into my parents' rented place, but it's not one I recognize. It smells the same way it did a couple of weeks ago, the first and last time I was here, but it still doesn't smell like us and I guess it's because *we* don't live here.

There weren't any furnishings the first time I walked through this house. Now there are decorations and pictures in the great room, and the kitchen shows convincing signs of life. The coffee maker and the food processor and the scale are all on the counter and accessible, even though they look crowded here. Once I leave the front of the house, though, it's like I've been on a sitcom set; it was designed to look lived in, despite the fact that no one really does.

The facade ends abruptly. The hall bathroom is totally sterile, aside from the fact that there's toilet paper on the roll.

They've been here for two weeks—and supposedly didn't know what would happen next, or when—but Nichole Turner didn't put out her ornate bowls. The two that hold lotion and soap are missing. She didn't put out the heavy matching frame, either, the one that has a picture of me in it because for some reason she prefers that to giving restroom patrons reading material. My dad says she likes bathrooms that can double as little living rooms, that look pretty and smell pretty, and that make you forget what people go in there to do. I'm not sure anyone has ever done anything in here.

My parents' bedroom is equally unadorned, but more upsetting.

There is no attempt at the lie in here.

In any of my childhood memories, as early as I can remember, there was always abundant color and light in my parents' room. It was always a sanctuary, with a place for everything, and a sitting place for everyone. This room is a fraction of the necessary size and couldn't have offered the feeling of retreat, but even the familiar sense of comfort is missing. It could never have compared, but it could have been less depressing.

They haven't put up the bed properly. There's a mattress and box spring on a metal frame with wheels, but there's no headboard. There are two pillows instead of two dozen. There's no full-length mirror, or bedside tables. My dad's reading glasses are just folded on the carpet on his side of the bed, next to a book on which his earbuds rest.

Sweat sprouts above my lip, and a hot nausea blooms in the pit of my stomach.

How could they live like this? How dare they, when giving

me back what I wanted was so much easier? It must have been. Nothing about the destitution before me seems preferable, unless the point was withholding from me, and being so willing that they'd sacrifice the basics themselves.

I don't walk around to see what lies on the floor on my mother's side. The satin-lined turban she wears over her hair every night is lying on her one pillow, because there's no drawer within reaching distance to store it in.

If I didn't know better, I'd be sick again with grief instead of rage. I'd be trying to make sense of everything they've given up, thinking they had to. I'd be reminding myself that they're okay because they're adults. Their whole world doesn't feel upside down because they don't have their *things*, I'd try to believe, when the space around me seemed to be screaming the opposite. I'd try to console myself that they know these weeks, this awful turn of events, are part of life, even if they were unexpected. I'd be struggling to hold on to the hope that even though my parents had clearly lacked the energy to make this place a home, they were all right.

Because what it looks like is that they've fallen apart, too. That if they aren't like me—if it isn't completely upending to have someone else assert control of their very surroundings—then at the very least, they couldn't make sense of falling through the social stratosphere so suddenly.

But I know what they've been up to now. Instead of hard times, this room looks like my parents didn't want me here so they wouldn't have to suffer the pretense of constructing a temporary home when they had no intention of sticking around.

I haven't looked in their closet, but I don't bother; I don't need to see that they've been living out of suitcases for weeks because they were that committed to leaving this town behind.

I don't go into the bedroom I never moved into, just shuffle lethargically back down the hall to the great room. It's only noon, but I feel like this rented collection of depressing rooms in an unspectacular neighborhood that isn't close to being what I want is misleading. At first you think it's impoverished, made harmless by everything it lacks. But it isn't. This place is a vacuum, a black hole, and it's been sucking the energy out of me, pulling me toward the edge ever since I stepped through the door.

My mother was right.

She *isn't* exactly like me; she's worse. Because there's a room here, but there was never any place for me.

My parents knew I'd be coming today. How did she think this house, in this state, would make me feel? And why this obvious escalation when all we've ever done is spar? My mother and I have become accustomed to our innocent game of tug-of-war.

But this.

This is punishment. It is wholly punitive, with no expectation or framework for atonement or rehabilitation. She offered me no warning, no guidelines before subjecting me to this. She would have, if it were about the two of us. Which means her provocation must be my father.

Can't you just . . . move a few things around for a while? I'd asked him.

What do you mean, Fair?

I'd intentionally asked when the two of them weren't

together, but the moment the question was out of my mouth, I saw my mother come casually around the corner. It was too late to take it back, and to try would've opened me up to an innocent interrogation of why I wanted to. It would prove I knew better, or at least I knew that I should. The damage was done.

Move what around? he asked, like he didn't feel his wife's hand slide across his shoulder—or like he didn't know what it meant.

I only looked at her after that. My father was wearing a confused expression, but not her. My mother's began at sterile but gradually transformed into something like amusement, quietly mocking.

She didn't interject. She didn't tell my dad that it was natural for a child my age, with the life experience I'd had, to think it was as easy as that. My classmates at the academy had "fallen on hard times" before, after all, in far more scandalous ways. Someone or other's parent had ended up on the news, walking silently past a group of reporters clamoring for a statement into their definitely illegal business practices, even though their lawyer intervened every time. One year, someone's family "lost everything"—but everything didn't include houses or boats or memberships. Everything was a feeling, a state of being. It was a sense of certainty that the world was as it should be, that reputations were intact. Everything was a status and a scorecard, and it only required patience. Whatever had happened only needed a few months or half a year to turn itself around, and there was always money to move from one place to another in the meantime.

How was I to know it wasn't the same for us?

I could take this pathetically staged living room apart, leave them the debris of a life they've only been pretending at. But control. Instead, I do what she did to me. Instead of destroying something they don't care about, *I* fall apart.

Plant my feet shoulder-width apart, and relax my shoulders until they droop.

Breathe deep and hold.

Three seconds the first time.

Now five.

Now ten.

With every exhale, I let my chin drift to my chest like I'm back in the water and the motion is coming from outside me.

I blink slow so I can tell when I get lightheaded . . . when my lids get heavy . . . when I'd rather keep them closed.

I give in, unlocking my knees so that I can feel my own weight, and then I stagger toward the couch. I embrace every suggestion of weakness my body makes; I draw it to the surface and sink inside.

This is where they'll find me, out of sorts and out of place, asleep on their couch because the bedroom isn't really mine. Because they lost what belonged to me and I have not recovered.

"DID YOU GET enough, Fair?" Dad kisses my forehead as he sweeps my bowl from in front of me and then hesitates, unable to take his eyes off me as though I might collapse again at any moment.

We're eating at the kitchen island because the dining table— the one I carved into as a sixth grader when I didn't understand the difference between a wooden cutting board and cutting my fruit on the wooden table—would dwarf this room. My parents never replaced it, so it and the series of carvings I made are probably in storage with everything else. Or shipped ahead to wherever they're moving.

"Mm-hm." I nod at my dad and fail to turn my lips up enough for a convincing smile. He's still hovering, worried that I only finished my food by sheer force of will. Conchiglie with meat sauce and ricotta is one of my favorites, and it's the first meal my dad's made for me in weeks, but I've hiccupped several times, always toward my chest, and without excusing myself. As though if they haven't noticed, I don't want them to.

"Do you wanna take some for Cherish?" my mother asks, and I wrestle back the grimace trying to overtake my faint smile.

"Sure."

Because even when she's withholding something from me, of course my mother implies that Cherish deserves even this.

"That girl can eat some pasta," Dad says, and my mother looks at him with an amusement that means the two of them are about to leap headlong into a series of memories I'm sure are meant to sound reassuring even as they make my blood boil. It's supposed to seem lighthearted, like Mr. Whitman covering his eyes as though it was Cherish's wedding day, but it's calculated.

When I'm not here, they probably don't even cook. They don't clean this cramped kitchen together, and they certainly don't reminisce about my best friend's appetite.

The point is that Cherish *deserves*, and I do not.

"Did you ask the Whitmans to keep me so I wouldn't know you were interviewing out of town, Dad?"

The question sounds involuntary, like I had to blurt it out to keep it from curdling in my stomach with the dinner I almost couldn't eat.

Ben and Nichole Turner both look at me, and it's delicious. It's like someone hit pause. For a moment, I'm not sure they're going to breathe or reanimate again, and then my mother's eyes creep over to my dad.

But I didn't ask her. I didn't accuse her of masterminding their betrayal; I didn't assert that it was intentional. This isn't a confrontation at all; I'm a confused teenager trying to make sense of the life falling to pieces around me.

She has to give him the appropriate number of beats, in case he knows what to say or how to, but not so long that it's obvious when she swoops in and saves him. Before she can—before she can say just the right thing to change my perspective and make me see how manageable or fortunate something is—and because this pause is proof I chose the right approach, I carry on.

"Because it's only been a couple of weeks, so if you got hired somewhere out of state, you must've known it was a possibility when we were leaving home. Right?" I mean to sound fragile, but I don't mean for my voice to crack. Some of this is genuine, but that can be forgiven. "Even when you were promising you'd still try to save the house, you were looking for work somewhere far from it." And then I'm timid in my accusation. Even gentle. "It means you guys haven't been honest with me. Right?"

Dad leans into his hands on the kitchen island.

"Not exactly, Fair," he says, and beside him my mother shakes her head a little.

When my dad glances at her, when it occurs to him—maybe

for the first time—that all this is Nichole Turner's fault, I notice. Because the logical question is how I came by this news. How did I know there was another job, and another state to begin with? Perhaps he's feeling a hint of betrayal, like me.

There's a current traveling all through my body, and my skin is dancing. It makes my breath come more quickly, but that's easy enough to explain. I'm upset, after all. There's a reason my eyes keep darting back and forth between my parents, and it isn't because I'm greedily devouring the tension brewing between them. For all I know, they're a "united front."

"I told her we were going to sit down with you," she says through an almost whisper. She's decided to follow my lead and take her chances with confession, but she's clenching her teeth, and the words come out thin, like they've been through Dad's pasta machine. "I really don't appreciate Brianne taking it upon herself—"

"Nichole," Dad begins, because he believes in her mask. He doesn't see the side of me she tried to warn Mrs. Whitman about, and he doesn't know I take after his wife. He honestly thinks they're a team, that sometimes it's his turn to manage things, and this is one of those times.

"I told her it was delicate." She's talking to Dad like in her irritation she's forgotten I can hear her. Like they're so used to having the place to themselves that maybe she doesn't remember I'm here . . . or else that's just how she wants me to feel.

"I'm sure she thought she was helping."

"She always thinks she's helping, Ben."

I start, my eyebrows cinching like a reflex before immediately relaxing. I've never heard my mom speak poorly of

Cherish's mom, or either of the Whitmans. To hear her tell it, Brianne is the most remarkably aware and surprisingly informed white person she knows, not to mention one of her absolute closest friends.

Is this perturbed outburst as unscripted as it seems, or is this for my benefit? Maybe this is just act two, and after trying to poison Mrs. Whitman against me, she's trying from the other end. Which begs the question: What is her goal? Is her first priority besting me, winning advantage in our ongoing tug-of-war, or is this moment just about recovering in front of my dad?

"Mrs. Whitman didn't say anything to me," I say, gathering their gazes with my interjection. I make sure my dad is paying attention when I tell her, "I overheard you in Cherish's room."

One of her shoulders slips.

"Oh."

It's a satisfying turnabout: stumping my mother, and learning something else about Brianne Whitman. She didn't just keep my mom's confidence; she clearly kept mine, too. She could've given my parents a heads-up that I'd heard the conversation, but she didn't. The only thing she did last night was give me a present of my own after celebrating her daughter's birthday.

"Well, I'm sorry I didn't get a chance to tell you myself, Fair," my dad says, rubbing his wife's back so I don't forget it's her side he's really on. "But the job opportunity actually happened a lot more quickly than that. One minute I was contacted by a head-hunter, and less than a week later, I was flown out to start the onboarding process."

His answer lacks texture. There wouldn't be enough detail

to convince me if it were anyone but my dad speaking, but I'm accustomed to the uncomplicated honesty of Ben Turner, and it sounds consistent.

"Frankly, I was a little shocked by the package. It'd take me another five years here to get what they're offering. And under the circumstances . . ." And then he stops. "I'm sorry, Farrah. I couldn't stop what happened with the house, and we didn't want to tell you that. I didn't."

There it is.

They didn't want to tell *me*.

There was something about telling *me* that would've been difficult for them. Something about the way *I'd* react, as though I wouldn't understand. Or couldn't, is what he's implying, as he stupidly tries to take credit. It was my mother I warned, who knew it had to be done, but with my dad claiming the blame, their failure recasts me as that foolish teen who didn't know what she was asking.

Can't you just move a few things around for a while?

My face goes hot.

This is worse than my mother ignoring my warning, and she must know it. This mischaracterization is humiliating because I'm the one who said those words, but they're being used beyond my intention. It's not unreasonable that I didn't know the difference between our situation and everyone else's. I didn't realize my family doesn't have magically robust reserves, that there's no extended family to give my parents what they needed or else to give my mom a new position with a salary to match her old one. I didn't realize those were privileges that didn't come with everything else we had. Now my innocent question is supposed to mean I was also unreasonable for being unable to imagine a world where other people may have what they require, but not me. All the years they told me I was just as capable and intelligent and deserving as everyone else at the academy, I should've known those were platitudes. That privilege dictates the demands of others are met; that is permitted. Only my demands are worrisome. That *I* am demanding is cause for concern.

"I could've dragged it out longer," my dad is saying, like two weeks is anywhere approaching long. "But, honey, we just would've ended up in an even worse position, that's all."

Ben Turner is oblivious. Like Cherish, his presence on the board never makes him aware of the game.

It's my turn now, and I don't plan to be any more merciful than my parents have been to me.

Clenching my jaw to fight back tears isn't complicated, but it *is* observable and people like my dad never doubt it.

It's about control; it always is. Not opting for hysterics when restraint will convince. So I say nothing while my dad explains all the things he couldn't have changed, implying all the ways it's my fault he had to consider trying while I look like I'm trying with all my might to stay strong. Like they've given me reason to think that's required of me now. Which makes it even more heartbreaking to watch when it doesn't work. When I just can't. Tears start slipping down my face, and my parents immediately part to come around opposite ends of the island and console me, or at least to hold me between them.

"I didn't let you stay with the Whitmans to keep you in the dark, Fair," Dad says after he kisses my forehead.

"We let you stay because we thought it's what you'd prefer,"

Mom says, but if she's trying to direct her husband, trying to conclude the explanation so that I have less material to manipulate in my reply, he doesn't get it.

"I was hoping renting this place would be a very temporary situation," he says, unintentionally diverging from his wife's message. "And I didn't want you to have to go through it twice."

I don't say that I didn't go through it the first time, either. I didn't pack up my room, or help load a truck, in the first place. I packed for Cherish's house, and after a nice dinner during which I was genuinely confused by how relaxed they seemed to be, my parents went back to my childhood home and dismantled it all themselves.

"I know it doesn't look that way, but this move is a good thing," Dad says. "I know it's not what any of us had planned, but it might be better. After your mom's layoff, we know it's not the same thing as security; we know we made mistakes, that we can't live right up to the edge of our means, that we can't afford not to save much more than we did. But it's not a lesson we need to learn more than once, I can promise you that."

It's the most either of my parents has ever said in front of me about anything remotely financial, and if my mother had said as much to me that day in the car, outside the Whitmans' house, when I told her what I needed done, maybe it would've meant something to me. That honest vulnerability. Tonight, it means nothing.

"I'm not moving," I say, before both my parents pull back and look down at me with different but equally concerned expressions. "I don't want to start over. I just did that. And you're right." I look at my mother, and her eyes are like saucers. Like she's a deer caught in my headlights. "This *is* where I want to be, with Cherish. We all seem to agree on that. So. I'll stay with the Whitmans."

"Farrah," Mom says, and her breath has to force it out. "The Whitmans didn't agree to you living there long-term. And even if they had, we're not asking for that. I'm sorry for what we've put you through these past few months; I know they've taken their toll on you. But we're not going to leave you here."

"It wouldn't be leaving me," I start, but I can see that despite my suggestion leaving them heartsore, and probably a little guilty, they're not even considering it. So I choose my words more deliberately, make sure every one of them can cut. "I know you didn't mean to disappoint me, or make me feel betrayed, or unsafe."

She flinches. It's slight, but I see it. My dad's mouth falls open a little, and then he curls his hand around the bottom half of his face and looks away.

"I know you miscalculated when you lost your job, and you never meant for all of this to happen. For all of us to pay the penalty for your ego." My mother blinks in rapid succession, but that doesn't mean she's forfeiting, so I don't let up. "And I know you wouldn't have asked the Whitmans just to suit your needs; I know it means you trust them." I let my shoulders fall, and my head with them. "I'm only just getting comfortable again."

"Farrah," my dad starts, but he's hesitating.

"I'm sorry, Dad. I know losing the house is just a change of plans when you're old enough to understand, and maybe that's why you didn't try as hard as you said you would. I know it shouldn't matter so much to me, the way it doesn't matter to you and Mom, but—I can't grow up that fast. I've been trying . . . but I keep getting sick over it. And being with Cherish helps. Like having her at the academy. I don't want to start over someplace else and be the only one again."

My mother's completely turned around, which can only mean she doesn't want me to see the way she's holding her fingers beneath her eyelashes, catching tears. I only wish I could see whether they're from sadness or frustration.

"No one wants you to grow up any faster, Fair." Dad holds my face with one hand and pulls me into his chest. "You shouldn't have to. And you have nothing to apologize for."

I hold him snug and nuzzle my forehead into him the way I always did when we were watching a movie that was supposed to scare me, and he rubs my back, slowly, up and down.

"None of this is your fault," he says, and I open my eyes even though I'm too close to his shirt to keep the gingham from blurring. "We can try to take it slow. Okay?" He pulls back and looks down at me. "The least we can do is not rush you."

"Okay," I agree.

When my mother finally turns back toward me, she pulls me into a hug before I can get a good look at her, and hooks her chin around my shoulder.

"We'll figure this out, honey. Dad and I will figure everything out."

I can't help but smile.

Dad and I . . . Just so I know, as far as Nichole Turner is concerned, nothing is up to me.

I take an arm from around my dad and put it around her waist, my fingernails scraping deep enough to reach her skin as my fingers curl into the fabric of her blouse.

VI

O *n my way now!* I text Cherish when I'm in the car with a Tupperware container full of Dad's pasta on the passenger's seat.

Good! I'm with the boys and you're my ride hoooome!

And then she sends a selfie of her and Kelly. He's scowling, of course, and she's straddling him, sticking her tongue out like she's taunting me by sending a photo of him. Which she is.

As if she can see my sneer, Cherish sends a follow-up picture, and this one shows her clearly catching Tariq by surprise when she leaps onto his back. She and Kelly were in the Campbells' TV room, separated from the terrace and pool area by a set of French doors, and Tariq is standing beneath a slowly darkening evening sky when she attacks. Whatever she and Kelly were doing was clearly not fun for the whole gang. Not that it ever is, or that they ever care.

I send back a kiss emoji and blast the music as I pull onto the highway to head back to my side of town. It doesn't matter what music in particular; I'm cosplaying a teenage girl, reveling in an obnoxious display of self-centeredness meant to declare that I'm carefree—even though it's safer to be constantly aware. Constantly observant, and interpreting; your outward behavior a decision based on forethought, not narcissism.

I do not believe that my mother would prefer a child like that, that she'd be *less* worried if I were myopic and one-dimensional. But her performance has taught me a valuable lesson. When I was very young, I thought part of self-control was adhering to the truth. Parents, after all, teach no lesson more intentionally than "Thou shalt not lie," and if children listen to what they say more than observing what they do, it will be years before we know the value of deciding the narrative for ourselves.

But I knew better. I studied her.

I saw the real her, the one hiding behind her eyes, so when she first recoiled at my behavior, I understood that it was a lie, a strategy in the war games we play.

I tried to teach Cherish. The lie I told the day with the nails and Jerry Whitman's renovation site didn't just get us what we wanted, and it didn't just keep us out of trouble, even though that was the point. It also turned into a kind of lore, a beloved origin story told at birthday parties, years and years later.

Control.

A bold, ambitious lie is a last resort, its tellings few and far between. That way it isn't just disarming, but convincing every time.

When you tell that lie, you commit to it, even if it means doing the thing no one believes you'll do.

If you learn to tell the lies no one else has the stomach to commit to—the brazen kind—it is amazing how well it works. The way it did when we were in fourth grade. The way it did tonight, with my parents. It can be addicting, too, but I'm not greedy.

From now, I'll be obedient. It's how you make sure they'll believe you the next time. When they agree to let me stay with the Whitmans, I'll just be doing what I was originally asked. When I was in distress, my mother goaded me with instructions to be gracious. She said to appreciate being taken in, and now I will. Now I'll want to.

I'll even deliver my dad's cooking to Cherish, like she needs anything else, and I'll put up with being around her ass of a boyfriend. Because, no matter what, I'd always rather be with her than not.

Everything is going to be okay now.

When I get to the Campbells', which is almost a compound, with a guard's office right before the very imposing-looking gate, I'm welcomed. The housekeeper does the same when she lets me in and tells me the kids are all still in the entertainment room off the pool. I'm almost there when I hear something crash. It's followed by an eruption of loud voices.

"You really think I care, Tariq? You think I'm scared of you?"

I walk a little faster, and when I'm in the doorway, I find Cherish, Tariq, and Kelly sprinkled throughout the space. They're standing far enough apart that, at first, I can't make sense of what's already happened.

Cherish is in the middle of the room, on the same side of the long, wide sectional sofa as Tariq, and she ducks when Kelly makes a throwing motion, even though whatever he grabbed from the floor-to-ceiling bookcase behind him wasn't headed anywhere near her. It bursts against the wall a good five feet from Tariq, too, but that's when I notice something's not right.

Tariq's got what looks like road rash across his forehead, and one of his eyes is surrounded by bloody and broken skin, like a purple doughnut is growing underneath. It looks like he crashed into something with his face—or something crashed into him.

I lift my hands as though to pause the scene, but Kelly goes right on yelling about not being afraid of Tariq when it looks like he's finally proven he's the one they should be afraid of.

"Cherish," I say, when the trio fails to take notice of my arrival, and as I expected, the sight of me sends Kelly into a lather.

"Are you *kidding* me? I thought you were going home, little hobo!"

"Kelly, calm down," Cherish says, and there's a wobble in her voice like she's been crying, or since she clearly hasn't, like she's about to. "You're scaring me." It's a whimper, and it's supposed to explain why she's standing closer to Tariq than she is to her boyfriend when the two boys have obviously been fighting.

He pays her no mind.

"You cannot be this stupid, man," Kelly is saying to me, and it isn't that he doesn't look disgusted the way he always seems to when I'm around; it's that he looks . . . something else, too. He has a similar rash of red across his face, like maybe the boys started scuffling somewhere outside, around the pool. Where the skin is broken, it's beaded with red and accented with dirt, but there are also little spots of paler pigment where the skin has been scraped away. One of his eyes is running so it looks at first like he's crying, but only from the one, and maybe he thinks with all that, no one can tell that he doesn't look angry. Not at me.

I've just arrived, and while Tariq looks worse for wear, either boy could've started the fight. There could be a reason for this confrontation that's got nothing to do with Kelly being a thorn in my side; there could be some relevance to Cherish's presence, and where she chose to stand.

It might not be Kelly's fault.

I don't care. I don't have to, since neither Cherish nor Tariq is capable of seeing past his explosive behavior. The destruction he's causing.

I don't have to worry that they'll see what I see.

I can use that. If Kelly persists, if his rampage isn't interrupted by my presence, if he makes me witness to it, it won't be an intrusion when I speak.

"You need to take a walk," Tariq advises his friend.

Kelly doesn't take the out. His jaw clenches, and at first it seems like they're going to have a staring match. Then Kelly reaches back to the bookcase and whips something against the far wall, defiantly.

A smile flickers across my lips. If I'd tried to carve Kelly out of our lives before, it would have seemed like a petty little feud. Two orphans sniping at each other like there aren't enough spoils to go around, because of Kelly's constant antagonization.

Neither Tariq nor Cherish moves a muscle or says a word.

Kelly is intentionally terrorizing us, and although I'm the person everyone will expect to fear him, I'm the only one not on the verge of tears—which means the moment has finally come.

While Tariq stands with his fists clenched and his chest heaving but his mouth closed, and while Kelly takes his time hand-selecting the next item he'll destroy, I decide.

This needs escalating if it's going to be the end, and the reason Kelly thinks I can't be the one to call him out is exactly why it's going to work. It's going to look like an act of courage to Cherish and Tariq, after long suffering his unnecessary abuses. Kelly will be his horrible self, and our friends will finally see that it's reckless to care indiscriminately. That sometimes you have to choose.

It takes self-control to be intentional with compassion, to focus it so that the object of your affection feels its intensity.

Now Cherish and Tariq will understand, and Kelly will disappear.

"Kelly!" Cherish pleads after the next crash, because she doesn't understand that her distress is the point.

"Why are you breaking his dad's stuff?" My voice wobbles, and even though I stepped forward, I immediately step back. They're all watching me now. "After everything Judge Campbell's done for you, this is how you thank him? By destroying his house and attacking his son?" I demand, even though I didn't see the fight.

My interjection breaks the dam, and a fresh wave of anxious tears overtakes Cherish. Tariq is less accustomed to my salvation and his face is blank when he looks at me. Maybe he's exhausted, or maybe until now—until I spoke for him—he didn't realize I was here. He didn't realize he needed me to be.

Kelly's eyes are trained on me, as I expected. It's interesting. He isn't huffing; there's no snarl carved into his lips, no wildness coursing through his eyes like I'm prey. Tonight he just looks at me like I'm intruding, but I trust the others not to notice. Their own distress will overshadow it.

If he were literally anyone else, I would make note of this unexpected dispassion; it would be cause for further study. But I have no use for Kelly.

"I hope he lets you rot next time," I say, and then I add, "Because there will be a next time," so that the focus stays on him. I don't want my friends to mistake this for retribution. What I want is for Kelly to react. "It's inevitable with ingrates like you."

When Kelly starts toward me, Tariq finally jolts into action. He heads him off, coming between the two of us just in time and knocking me back. The boys struggle, and Tariq throws a punch, half his knuckles connecting with the corner of Kelly's forehead. It doesn't look like a solid hit—in fact it looks like the kind of pathetic attempt that results in a full-body cast for the unfortunate soul who threw it—but it stops Kelly. Inexplicably.

A punch that couldn't have stopped a fly stops Kelly.

It's inconsistent with having instigated the scuffle they must have had to produce the abrasions on their faces.

I let my breath catch. I trigger concern that if Tariq had taken one second more to get between us, there's no telling what Kelly was going to do.

He wipes the site of impact with the heel of his palm and

then examines it briefly, just so Tariq knows he didn't do any physical damage. When Kelly nods, both his eyes are glassy now.

"'Cause I gotta be a monster, too, huh?" His eyes are locked with Tariq's, but he's so close to me that I can't smell the subtle difference between Tariq's sweat and his.

"You *are* the monster," I say, my voice a bit stronger now that someone finally got between us. I can take a shuddering breath and say what I've been holding in, know that now they'll hear it. Tariq's action won't be heroic now; my words will serve the double purpose of shredding Kelly and being an indictment that anybody let him get this far. They should've known his cruelty toward me would escalate. "Who else would bully someone for doing the exact same thing you've done for years? I take that back; it's not the same. I was only in danger of being uncomfortable; you were going to jail, Kelly. Who the hell are you to say anything to me? Or to be here in the first place? You're the one who refuses to go back where you clearly belong."

He's staring at me with wet eyes, one of them bloodshot in the corner.

"Maybe now you'll get what you deserve," I tell him, and that part is just for me. It's an acceptable risk to take, given the night's events. Because I can't imagine he comes back from this. After tonight, everyone will have to see him for what he is.

Not charming; not edgy. Dangerous. He's entitled, like he wasn't rescued. Like Judge Campbell didn't take mercy on him in that courtroom when he was thirteen and on his way to a long stay in juvie. Because thank God, Judge Campbell, a man who looks exactly the way you'd expect a white man named Leslie to look, had a Black son Kelly's age. He gave him the kind of sentence a white boy would've gotten for stealing and destroying property, which meant community service and anger-management courses, and he said in the courtroom, in front of everyone, that there are consequences to poverty and they shouldn't be borne by the children of people who are given few options.

It made the news. A year later, the judge was granted guardianship of Kelly by his mother, who has three younger kids who do not have a wealthy, benevolent judge taking an interest in shepherding them down the right path. She said Judge Campbell saved Kelly's life, and it's very observably true, even though right now I assume he'd regret it. Being like brothers with his son was supposed to be a good influence on Kelly, not a trauma for Tariq.

When Judge Campbell appears in the hall behind us, no one hears him until he speaks.

"I think it's time to say good night to your friends, guys," he says, like he doesn't see the scene before him. Like there isn't a mound of broken pieces that used to be his awards. "I think you've both upset the girls enough."

And just like that, the tension breaks. The electricity snapping in the air between the two dissipates, and both Kelly and Tariq are standing with their chins down, avoiding Judge Campbell's gaze despite the fact that he sounds completely and illogically calm.

What's funny is that at least one of them was raised by a Black woman, and there's no way this subdued disappointment should be even remotely chastising. As for Tariq, all it would take is him saying he hasn't done anything wrong. Cherish and

I would vouch for him, even though I wasn't here for the entire fight. Even if it weren't true. But Tariq doesn't say anything in his own defense, and it only upsets me more.

I am done with Kelly, and Cherish better be, too.

We slink out of the house in silence, and she doesn't say a word until I'm driving the two of us home.

"RahRah, it was awful."

"What happened?" I ask, now that interrogating the situation won't muddle the outcome. Still, I need to couch it in a warning. Anything related to Kelly from this point on needs to remind her how unsafe she's feeling. "What set Kelly off like that? Has that happened before? Cherish, you have to tell me."

"I've never seen him like that," she says, like she's coming out of a trance. Her voice sounds almost far away, and she's got the same uncharacteristic, stunned look she had in the entertainment room.

"What *happened*?" This time I mean it. Kelly is over; it's only natural for my attention to turn to understanding Cherish's role in the evening. How the three progressed from the two photos she sent me, from she and Kelly groping each other and Tariq being pushed poolside to the scene I entered.

Instead of answering, she suddenly becomes aware of the Tupperware at her feet, and picks it up.

"Oh, that's for you, from my dad," I say, so we can get back to the matter at hand.

That is clearly not going to happen when, holding the plastic container as though to study it or its contents, Cherish starts crying.

"Che," I whimper, and I reach over to stroke her arm before taking her hand. "Babe, what's the matter?"

And I pivot. Because I have to be gentle with Cherish. She isn't like my mom and me. And because, after tonight, she has to know for sure: we're all we have.

"You don't have to answer that, Che. I'm being insensitive. Of course I know what's the matter. You liked Kelly. And I'm really sorry all of this happened. I'm sorry you had to see that side of him."

Cherish nods, weakly, at that, and keeps hold of my hand when she adjusts in the passenger seat, holding the Tupperware protectively against her lap with her free hand. When she turns her head toward the window, I take a deep breath.

"Everything's okay, Che. I'm here."

VII

It's going to be a nice change of pace—Cherish being teary and tired, and me taking care of her and feeling well. Not only am I myself again after dinner with my parents, but when Cherish and I hold hands the whole way home from Judge Campbell's place, I feel better.

I'm prepared for the obligatory days spent in heartsore hibernation as my Cherish cries Kelly out of her system. Staying in bed, in the room we share, and listening to her try to make sense of the person she tricked herself into thinking he was, saying nothing or very little while she expresses shock and confusion over the person he's revealed himself to be.

I'm even ready for the limited contact I'll have to have with Tariq. It'll be temporary, while knowing he and I can still be together might be too much for Cherish to bear.

It's better than I could have hoped for—making Cherish my new home and being rid of Kelly all on the same night.

Only I don't get to enjoy it.

I go to sleep big-spooning Cherish and wake up with my guts in a vise. There's a fire under my skin, and it's clearly not a sudden development, because the sheets beneath me are soaking wet. At first, I'm worried I lost control of my bladder. I sincerely hope I haven't capped off a perfect night by pissing my best friend's bed.

I haven't. At least I don't think I have. Sweat is gushing from my pores, and the wetness is everywhere, like an aura, or an outline of my entire body. My bladder could not have held enough contents to do this damage.

My scarf has slipped clean off and is on the pillow above my head, and my hair is wet either from the sweat-drenched pillow or from the sweat flooding from my scalp. Or both.

This is disgusting. Everything is wrong.

Cherish isn't in my arms anymore. It looks like she rolled away, probably to escape my sweat-scape, and while she hasn't woken up, she's on the absolute edge of the bed. I get three seconds into a half-baked plan to somehow change the sheets without waking her, and also without knowing where the Whitmans keep their linens, before the reason I woke up in the first place barges back to center stage.

I'm gonna be sick.

I don't have time to turn on the bathroom light, and I shouldn't need to. I know where the toilet is by now—I just don't know how I miss it. The first wave of vomit bursts out of me like water breaking through a dam, and I hear it splash against the floor.

I moan because my throat keeps pulsating even after the stuff escapes, and I can't get the curse word out.

Now the bathroom reeks, and the nightmare isn't over. More is coming, but when I try to get closer to the toilet, to thrust my face into the open bowl this time, my hand serendipitously finds the pool of chunky bile, and I lose what little stability I had. My chin crashes into the porcelain, and I both hear and feel a crunch on impact.

My eyes are squeezed shut but the world lights up.

I hear a splash, so at least *some* of what comes tearing up my throat next makes it into the toilet.

I give up. Hope this is all a dream.

My face is throbbing in pain, there's vomit on the floor and in my hand and under my knees now, and my throat feels raw from whatever undigested chunks of food are forcing their way up and out.

Food poisoning. It has to be. From Dad's conchiglie and meat sauce.

And then I'm back at their house, remembering standing in their sterile bedroom and the packed suitcases I didn't see.

They lied to me. And I figured them out.

I called them on it. And now I'm sick.

I burp into the toilet, my guts heaving and my throat gagging, but nothing more comes out.

I can't speak, so I just moan.

My parents didn't do this on purpose. They ate the same meal I did, and they sent leftovers for Cherish. If anything, they're curled up around toilet bowls right now, too, one in the master bathroom that's barely large enough to deserve the name, and the other in the one in the hall. I guess it'll feel more lived-in now.

But if they *had* done it on purpose, it would've almost been the perfect cover. I've been sick to my stomach for weeks. It'd just look like more of my homesick, world-turned-upside-down confusion, and only they'd know it was something else. Only my mother would know.

I can't escape the fetid smell anyway, so I just lay my head against the cool toilet seat and breathe.

They didn't do this. I know that because my parents might be liars but they aren't cruel. They've only ever used traditional punishments—grounding me from social gatherings or personal electronics—and those have always been accompanied by long talks. My mother is cunning, but I haven't ever actually seen her do any of the things I know she's capable of. Which is why I've never told her the truth about what happened in the fourth grade, even though I wanted to. I could never decide whether she'd be proud or feign disapproval—or something worse. Because now I wonder whether she would have told Brianne Whitman the truth during her little character assassination attempt, knowing how much the story means to the Whitmans.

"No," I finally manage, and it croaks out of my sore throat.

If my parents had given me food poisoning on purpose, they'd want me to learn a lesson, and the only way to know that I had would be to talk to me about it. There's no such possibility with secrecy.

The blinding light is outside my head now, and the bathroom is bathed in it.

"RahRah!" Cherish discovers me at last. "Oh my gawd, Farrah, wait here!"

As though I'm going anywhere.

Relief swallows me up. My Cherish knows something's wrong; she's going to take care of it. Knowing that, I fall asleep right there.

The next time I bat my eyes open, Brianne Whitman is kneeling beside me in what looks like a satin robe. I feel her cool hand against my forehead.

"Run a bath, but keep the shower running, Che," she directs.

"It's all right, sweetie." Jerry Whitman's somewhere in the room, too. "She'll be fine."

Cherish is crying.

I moan, try not to smile, but I can't help it. They'll just think I'm delirious. I probably am.

"Honey, I can't lift her."

"I'll get her in the tub, and then you girls get her undressed after."

"RahRah . . ."

I can hear the tremble in her voice now, and when Jerry Whitman gathers me up, groaning under my deadweight, I try to open my eyes a little to find her.

"Che," I manage, still fighting back the smile I can feel has tugged my lips higher on one side. It hurts, and my chin is swelling up already, so I sound even more pathetic.

"Cherish, honey, please give your father some space. She's okay, baby."

His back must get rained on when he leans in to lower me into the tub as gently as possible. Thank God for fit dads with impressive core control.

"I'm gonna step out," he says when the water is already swelling over my shins. In a moment, it'll cover my knees. Luckily I'm only wearing a nightshirt and underwear, so there isn't much for Cherish and her mom to wriggle me out of.

"Go," Brianne answers, like he's been called to war. "We'll manage from here."

"Should I send someone up for the mess?" he asks, almost like he's hesitating.

When his wife answers him, it sounds like she's made a serious decision, rather than elected not to have her hired help wipe up my stomach bile and half-digested conchiglie in the dead of night.

"We'll manage."

Cherish is still whimpering when Brianne instructs her to get me out of my clothes, and when my best friend leans into the shower, she doesn't even think to put a shower cap over her bonnet first. She's only managed to get my soaking-wet nightshirt from under my butt, which is now completely submerged, when one side of her head interrupts the water falling from above.

"Mom!" She's fully crying now, and if I had any strength at all, I'd reach for her.

I have no idea what's happened to me, or why I'm so sick . . . but it's worth it.

Cherish can't stop crying.

Jerry and Brianne Whitman came running like I'm their own child.

He lowered me into a bath, and she stayed to take care of me.

I can't see Brianne, but I know she's upset. Her agitation is bleeding into her voice, and she's losing patience with Cherish. That's the most overwhelming part of all—the way Brianne is snapping at Cherish now. Cherish, her universe, her heartbeat. Because of me.

"Cherish, stop crying, please. None of that is helping Farrah."

"I can't—" But whatever comes after in Che's almost unrecognizable shrieking voice is completely undecipherable. Neither I nor her mom can make out what she's blubbering about at first, and it's a good thing Mr. Whitman didn't wake the housekeeper to witness this embarrassing scene.

"So turn off the shower for a moment and get in, Cherish! It'll be easier than trying to undress her bent over that way."

Another whiny series of shrieks that are clearly in protest.

"Then your hair is already wet, and it shouldn't matter. I hardly think that's as important as getting your best friend cleaned up and back in bed so she can rest. Now, Cherish."

The showerhead stops pouring water over me, but the bath is already full enough to cover my stomach. It's going to be next to impossible for Cherish to get the now heavy, clinging nightshirt off me on her own, but her mother isn't helping.

I can't keep my eyelids open, and when I manage to bat them, there must be water on my lashes and in my eyes because it's like driving in the rain. Everything's distorted, blurry and bleeding into something else. Cherish disrupts the water when she steps in with one foot, wedging it between my legs to steady herself, and I see only wet and blurry brown stems and a red pajama shorts set. Whatever Brianne is doing, it's outside the bath, and I can't hear her over the sound of Cherish grunting near my ear while she laboriously peels my clothing off my skin.

"Mom, some of her vomit got in her hair," Cherish says, on the verge of sobbing again.

"You were going to have to wash her hair anyway, Che."

"It's the middle of the night!"

"Maybe you'll think next time."

That's the part that doesn't make sense.

I roll my head to the side, trying to find Brianne, but even if I could keep my eyes open, there's a fogged and frosted window between us.

Brianne doesn't speak to Cherish that way. Cherish is a masterpiece of her parents' design, and it isn't as though she's ever been made to undress a full-grown human with vomit on their clothes. It isn't like she should have known how to avoid cross contamination—but I'm not one hundred percent certain that's what Brianne said in the first place.

The bath that's supposed to be getting me clean of my bright-orange vomit must be serving the dual purpose of sweating out my fever, because I realize it's sweltering in here.

But Cherish is going to wash my hair.

She's been given permission to leave my underwear on because they're free from throw-up, and it's almost like we're back at my house, in the pool together, preparing for baptism. Even though she's still dressed, she hugs me to her and clumsily rear-ranges me so that my head rests against the basin instead of the tiled wall. I'm not sure how this'll make it easier or less messy to wash my hair, but I guess we'll see. Only Brianne interjects again when she grabs the detachable showerhead.

"Part her hair, Cherish, you know how to wash hair. I'll get the clips," she says, and then it sounds like she turns away.

"I'm tired!"

"So Farrah should wake up with a knotted mess because you're tired? Because that's what's gonna happen if you try to wash it all at once like I didn't teach you how to simplify wash day."

And then I feel Brianne's thin fingers in my hair. I know it's her by the faint waft of floral that precedes her touch.

"Here, sweetheart, I'm sorry. I'll help."

When her fingers pause, separating my hair, I hear her kiss Cherish's cheek.

"It's okay, baby. I know you're tired."

Apparently the agitation is gone. I can hear my friend snif-fling, and occasionally the swift work Brianne is accomplishing in making six sections of my hair and clipping all but one of them down stops, and I know she's coddling her daughter.

She's taking care of us both now.

My chest and shoulders are goose-pimpling without the shower running over them, and I'm exhausted, despite not be-ing able to throw a tantrum the way Cherish did. Thankfully, they only jostle my head for another fifteen minutes or so, rins-ing the conditioner out without undoing the twists they made of each section, before wrapping my head in a fresh terry-cloth turban and working together to get me somewhat on my feet. They get me out of the bath somehow and back into the bedroom.

Mr. Whitman must've changed the linen, because Brianne and Cherish have to turn down the covers to put me back to bed.

"What happened to her?" Cherish asks when the two return to the bathroom for what I assume is going to be a long and backbreaking hour of cleaning, at least.

"It's probably just something she ate," Brianne answers, and I can tell by the echo of her voice that she's near the toilet. Bent down, probably, and beginning to clean the putrid mess I made. "I'll let her mom and dad know in the morning."

"It couldn't have been from their dinner."

"Well, of course it could, honey. How would we know?"

"Because I had the same thing she did," Cherish insists.

It's quiet except for the sound of a scouring pad or maybe a brush scrubbing the bathroom tile and the grout groove in between. Mrs. Whitman must be concentrating, or more likely sick to her stomach, because she doesn't respond to her daughter.

I didn't know Cherish had eaten my dad's leftovers already. When we got home, I didn't expect her to do anything but collapse in a crying heap on her bed, but her parents called her name as we were going upstairs, and I went ahead without her. It was only a little while before she came up, too, and then Brianne was in our suite at some point. I'm having déjà vu, listening to their voices reverberate in the bathroom on the other side of the wall—only the last time they were intentionally hushed.

I've started to sweat again, but at least it's not like before. Whatever's going on with me, it isn't food poisoning, and it's not completely out of my system. I'll have to give in at some point, but I want to stay awake a little longer. I want to enjoy the way they're all responding. The way everything they're doing and saying revolves around me, and the way they don't know I'm conscious enough to know it.

"This can't happen again," I think I hear Brianne say when it seems like they've been working in silence for a long time.

"Do I put a trash bin next to her side of the bed?"

"I'm talking about what happened at Judge Campbell's, Cherish."

My eyes actually open completely now.

My head is muddled and I'm probably borderline delirious, but that feels like a strange and disjointed segue.

"It's done," Brianne says, in a tone that—from my post-puke stupor—is nothing like I've ever heard from her. "Am I making myself clear?"

She means Kelly. By "what happened at Judge Campbell's," she means whatever Kelly and Cherish were doing that drove Tariq poolside, not whatever came after that resulted in Tariq's black eye and Kelly's destruction of property. She's telling her daughter that she's not allowed to see Kelly anymore, which makes perfect sense—except for the timing of it. I just assumed that's what she and Mr. Whitman wanted with Cherish when we got home last night . . . so why is she saying it now?

"Cherish. Am I clear?"

"Yes."

No whining, no hissy fit. No pleading or declaring her

mother unfair. Cherish agrees with shocking calm, even if her voice betrays a hint of apprehension, or worry. Which is impressive for a one-word reply.

"Good. Give me Farrah's toothbrush."

My eyes have fallen shut again, and I can't do anything about it. They're heavy like an iron curtain, so I only manage to ribbon my eyebrows at the second confusing segue.

But there's no question I'm delirious. I know because the same rainy windshield effect that was happening in the shower is happening now, even behind my eyelids.

There's a good chance I've been falling in and out of sleep, hearing snippets of conversation and thinking they're immediately following other pieces, when really I've missed the connective tissue in between. There's no way for me to know without asking the two people I'm eavesdropping on, and I couldn't if I tried.

I'll ask Cherish tomorrow. Assuming tomorrow comes.

I hear my toothbrush clatter against the inside of the small waste bin under the sink.

"There should be new ones in the top right drawer." Brianne waits through the sound of a deep wood drawer sliding open. "The very furthest right drawer, Cherish," and then—when I think she's exasperated again, the way she was when they were bathing me—I hear her laugh.

"What?" her daughter whines. "Stop laughing at me, Mommy."

"I'm not, baby," she manages, though her twinkling laugh continues until there's a golden swarm of locusts amassing above the bed. A moment later, the sound of her kissing her daughter, probably against the temple, like she so often does, with Cherish nestled under her shoulder. "You're just adorable."

"Why?" And I can tell she's smiling. "Because I don't know where things are in my own bathroom?"

In reply, Brianne lets her head fall back—I know she does—and the swarm hovering over my head expands.

Of course that's how she responds to evidence that Cherish is ridiculously spoiled. It's not like it happened by accident.

Reindeer playdates don't just happen.

Reindeer, with furry antlers, might still draw blood.

I furrow my brow, unsure what I was thinking just before that.

I'm so tired. The back of my neck feels clammy and uncomfortable against the pillowcase, and there's an itchy, throbbing discomfort inside my head that's localized exclusively on the left side. Worse, there's a rumble in my gut, and it's followed by a series of pops and small-scale explosions.

I know what's coming.

I could test my vocal cords, see if I've built up enough energy to make them hear me.

It'd take even less stamina to roll to the side and cast my impending vomit on the floor beside the bed, since Cherish hasn't placed the bin like she suggested.

What isn't easy is getting to her side of the bed.

Making my own momentum so that by the time the wave comes, rushing up my throat and out of my mouth in a torrent of orange, my head is on my best friend's pillow.

VIII

*D*ays pass. I'm mostly unconscious, fever dreams swimming to the surface and mingling with outside stimuli so that what's probably the bathroom faucet becomes the waterfall in my pool, and what's probably just Jerry Whitman's normal speaking voice becomes aggressive growls from who knows where. They get mingled with whimpering that sounds like it's coming from Cherish, and sometimes I moan, trying to console her, only to wake myself just enough to know she's not around.

The sickness has officially exhausted its intrigue by the time I come to and find Brianne gently wiping my forehead with the softest hand towel. It's cool and damp, and there's a radiant glow around her because the sun is pouring into the bedroom. It might be morning or midday; it's impossible to tell now that it's basically summer.

I prepare for a struggle, but when I try to speak, my voice has miraculously returned, and it scrapes out of my throat with little effort.

"How long was I out?" I ask.

"Two days. I'm afraid you girls missed the last couple days of school," Brianne tells me with a smile. "If you were gonna skip the end of the year, I wish you could've at least enjoyed it."

"Are my parents coming?" Now that I can speak and control my eyes, it feels a little dramatic to ask for my mom and dad like I'm expecting my last rites. I can even sit upright, which I find out when I pull myself up on my elbows and then against the headboard.

"Do you want me to call them?" she asks, still tracing my face with the refreshing towel. "I didn't want to worry them, when we're taking good care of you."

It sounds like she means she hasn't told them I've been sick at all, but in the bathroom, she told Cherish she'd call them the morning after I first threw up. Except I can't be sure what I heard, or when, or whether it was real or imagined. Every memory I have after driving home from Judge Campbell's place is fuzzy and subject to reconsideration.

Not that it matters. For all I know, my parents would've overreacted and taken me to the hospital, and probably back to their place after that. And like she said, the Whitmans are taking good care of me.

"What do you think? Solid food today?" Brianne asks, folding the damp towel in her hands and sitting with her back perfectly straight so anyone can tell she didn't quit ballet like

Cherish and I did. Or maybe her posture comes from playing the piano with the restrained passion and rote precision of a debutante in a Jane Austen adaptation. Either way, the sun is bathing her in warm light, and there's a sparkle in her eye as she looks at me, awaiting my decision.

"I'm starving," I confess. "I haven't eaten for days."

"Don't be silly, of course you have. Jer or I have made sure you've gotten all your nutrients in liquid form, even if it took ages." She picks up a feeding syringe from the bedside table.

A blushing warmth washes up my neck and into my cheeks.

"That must have been a lot of trouble," I say.

"Not at all." Her hand collapses into her lap, syringe included. "But it did bring back memories of feeding a very good-natured, but very weight-resistant little Cher-bear."

She's smiling wistfully. That must've been Baby Cherish's nickname. I've never heard it before, so she must have outgrown it. I know her parents didn't by Brianne's sigh.

"So. How do you propose we break your solid-food fast? What do you want more than anything in the world?"

The first thing I think of is my dad's conchiglie, but it's involuntary. It also almost makes me dry heave despite the fact that I know it isn't what made me sick. My brain will no doubt hold it responsible until I know what did.

"Anything but pasta," I say through a grimace, and Brianne gives one big nod.

"No pasta. Got it. How about some thick, delicious burgers?" she asks, eyes big and knowing. Maybe burgers are a staple of Cherish's after she's recovered from something. "Dad can throw some on the grill, and I can get you some ginger ale, just to be safe?"

I just smile a little. She's in Mommy mode, and talking to me like I'm Cherish.

I don't correct her.

"Definitely burgers," I say. "And coleslaw."

"Oh, that is a very good choice," she replies, wagging a finger at me. "I am on it. Okay, you get a shower and get back to your beautiful self, and I'll text Cherish to bring home ginger ale and coleslaw fixins—and maybe something sweet, just in case!"

"Where is Cherish?" I ask, trying not to let my eyes or shoulders slip.

"Oh, she just needed to get some air. She's been joined to you at the hip this whole time, and I insisted she get out in the summer sun for a bit," she says as she stands and starts gathering the debris of the past several days from my nightstand. "I think she and Tariq were gonna get brunch, but don't worry, she should be ready to eat again by now!"

And Brianne Whitman kisses the top of my head.

"I'm so glad you're feeling better, sweetheart," she says, before bouncing out of the room.

It's dimmer when she's gone, quite literally, and I can actually see the stale air hanging in the bedroom. I get up and open the windows, even though there's hardly a breeze to feel.

Before I hop in the shower, I strip the bed, and myself, shedding what I hope is the last of this illness, and spritz some of Cherish's rosewater room spray so that when I get back from the bathroom, everything feels a little lighter.

The shower is divine. Between being conscious and coherent enough to stand up on my own and the exfoliating gloves Cherish convinced me are far superior to a loofah, within moments I'm feeling like I've shed a disgusting husk and am close to reclaiming my former glory.

The shower doors frost automatically when the handle is latched from the inside, but I let steam encircle me, laying my forehead against the tile wall.

I can almost hear Cherish whimpering and crying again. I can hear her grunt and grimace as she tries to undress me from an impossible position.

I can hear Brianne snap at her, her tone cutting even if her words aren't. The not-so-hidden message in them clear even when I was in a delirious stupor.

You are both my daughters now, and I will not choose between you.

I feel her nimble fingers detangling my hair again, and alone in the shower now, I let my head fall into the stream of water. The conditioning product she worked through my coils flushes down the length of the twists and comes out of the Bantu-knotted ends all milky white, leaving my hair feeling soft and supple. Like it was an intentional hair masque and not a result of being too out of it to rinse before now.

Once all of me is clean, I'm energized. I want to be dressed and coming down the staircase while Jerry and Brianne and Cherish look on with relief, but I also want to look my best, so I take the forty minutes to diffuse my hair once I've terry-cloth-dried, oiled, and applied one of my best friend's curl smoothies. All told, it's an hour-long process and I use most of the contents of the bamboo container—which is to be expected with hair as dense as mine—but that just means my resurrection supper should be nearly done.

Except when I come back into the bedroom to dress, it's exactly as empty as I left it.

No Cherish.

I would have definitely waited for *her*, or more likely come and joined her in the bathroom while she got ready, but she might be helping out downstairs, so I text her.

Which is when I realize that I have no idea where my phone is. And since my last memory of using it was en route to the Campbell compound after dinner with my parents, half a week ago, I have no idea where to look.

I start with the drawer of the nightstand on Cherish's side of the bed.

The inside of it is just as magazine-cover ready as the rest of the Whitman home. I know someone keeps our bedroom and bathroom in pristine working order, even if I never see them, but I'm surprised to find that there is not one single junk drawer in a house with this many rooms and pieces of furniture, and that includes the nightstand in the teenager's bedroom.

There's a white box inside, and beside that, a notepad that flips open and has a magnetic closure, and one of those little pencils people use to record their golf scores. It's a little infantile, with a cartoon character I recognize from my and Cherish's elementary school obsession with its show. Stickers overlap on every centimeter of the cover.

At first I think it might be a diary, and from the looks of it, one from early in our friendship. Back when I spent days studying a young Cherish because at first I didn't understand what I saw. If I asked what she thought back then, she wouldn't remember. She'd never be able to tell me factually; instead she'd tell me what she'd like to think she thought back then, overlaying nostalgia and current ideologies on the memory without meaning to.

I take the pad with me to lock the bedroom door, and then I lean against it and flick the cover hard enough to disrupt the magnetic bond.

Once it's open, there isn't much to see. Just . . . tally marks.

Little clusters of five, neatly organized in tight rows and columns.

On the first page at least.

I flip through the pages and there's really nothing but tally marks. No words, no secrets. No memories or confessions. No hearts and initials and arrows stabbing through. Nothing but marks that get increasingly sloppy and sometimes oversized, like whatever attention to precision and orderliness Cherish began with was frustrated the longer she made the marks.

I know they're hers. I don't know what they mean . . . but I know Cherish made them. And I know—I *know*—they're about me. They have to be. The character on the cover almost requires it. It means it's about me, and that it's a code she didn't want anyone to understand. Not the ninja housekeeper I've seen around the house but still never actually witnessed cleaning the always well-kept home, and not anyone else.

I want to take it. I want to move the notepad and the amputated pencil that used to make marks as though it had a perfectly sharpened point and now looks like one of my mom's old lip liners whose stray peaks extend past the lead and threaten to shred her lip if she dares to use it again.

Control.

Of course I won't take it. There'd be no explaining it if I moved the notepad from her nightstand. I couldn't make anyone understand that there was a code in what by the end resembles chicken scratch.

I'm not even sure Cherish knows it.

I don't take the notepad, but I leave a mark.

I chew off the collar creeping around the blunt shard of exposed lead, ignoring the bitter taste and then wiping the writing end clean with my finger, even though it marks me. Spitting the debris I can feel scratching my gums onto the bedroom floor, I find the last entry.

Several mismatched strokes, symbolizing three.

I add one to the end.

I make it match. Because I want Cherish to know I've seen them and understand—but only if she's clever enough to work it out.

Whatever she's keeping track of, I want her to know that I know.

I put the notepad back.

The white box is much less interesting. It's a jewelry box, and inside, resting on a generous velvet cushion, is a somewhat plain solid silver cuff. I pick it up and turn it over to find *Eloise Whitman* engraved on the inside before replacing it on its cushion and putting the box precisely where it was beside the notepad, whose position I memorized before touching it.

Her grandmother's hand-me-down bangle is hardly as intriguing as the mystery of Cherish's tally marks, and I still need to find my phone.

I look in my own nightstand second and find the device next to *The Whipping Boy* and the feeding syringe I slipped in there after Brianne left the room. I hadn't noticed my phone, but it's on its side, against the side of the drawer, so that I couldn't have seen or felt it without looking.

Almost like someone didn't want me to.

Cherish's tally marks come back to mind, but I can't be sure why. I can't formulate a theory about how they might be related to my sort-of-hidden phone, but I still don't know what they mean—which means they *might*.

What I can't understand is how it hasn't been vibrating against the inside of the drawer and making it impossible for me to sleep. I haven't heard a rumble or notification ding, not once, and delirious or not, I've heard people talking in the bathroom.

It makes more sense when the lock screen flashes on and the Do Not Disturb icon is up at the top.

Not everybody is out to get you, the Cherish in my head chides me, and I smile.

"Okay," I tell her. "Point taken."

I may have overreacted. Of course they only wanted me to rest. And it isn't like they hid it; it's just been silenced and put in the first place I should've known to look.

The point was to find Cherish, but I'm immediately distracted by the number of calls and texts I've missed from my parents.

My mother's phone.

My dad's phone.

Their landline, which they insisted on getting because with me living somewhere else, they wanted to be triple-sure I could always reach them. Which is why they've taken my silence over the past several days as an intentional slight.

Fair, I know you're under a lot of pressure, honey, but you have to talk to us.

If you want this to work, you've gotta communicate, Farrah.

Of course Dad's message is gentler; Nichole Turner's is more like a veiled threat. Until two days pass without any response.

Fair, she texts, *I'm sorry if I underestimated how difficult we've made this for you. Take the time you need, sweetheart. Your dad and I have been talking about how this homestay situation might work . . .*

There's a voicemail, too, which was sent today, but I don't play it.

Sitting on my side of the bed, I take a nice, deep breath and let it out slow, watching the particles float in the sunshine that streams into the room.

I can almost see them—my parents—huddling around the house phone that lives on the island in their unimpressive kitchen. The way they look at each other but can't find anything to say. Or maybe they're ready to tell the truth.

I'm not losing my daughter for you, Ben.

That's where my mother would start. No more swapping supporting roles for each other, the way they always do. No more of the "united front" they've presented all my life, the one she told me is important to my development.

She thought I was intentionally trying to get between them. That even at six or seven, I was "playing both ends to the middle." If I was, it was the way any intelligent child might, but she looked at me with a sternness that said she wasn't talking to a child.

My dad told her I was too young to understand, but Nichole Turner never broke eye contact with me, and she didn't simplify things, either.

I know she was proud. I was smart, like her. Shrewd, like Dad called her.

She entrusted me with more adult conversation after that. She didn't tell me to go play outside or in my room when she was on the phone or had company. And while she still never told me what she really thinks of the way my dad needs her to fix everything, I knew she wanted me to know. It was obvious in the way she'd press her lips shut as though to say there was plenty to hear but I'd have to read it on her face or in her body language. It was just the way she had to communicate with me, to keep up that "united front" she'd claimed they were. But we were more alike than they were, and she trusted me to know that. So she wouldn't be able to forgive him for making her betray me the way they have. She wouldn't be able to stand him if it cost her our special relationship.

I couldn't have answered her texts and voicemail any sooner even if I'd wanted to . . . but now I want to see how far she'll go. I want to know whether reconciling with me is important enough to finally show herself.

I clear the notifications without responding.

Finally, I hold the camera above me and lean back across

the bed, playfully seductive, before texting it to Cherish with the message, *Waitin' on you in the bedroom like* . . .

I only have to wait a few minutes to see that she's read it.

A few minutes later, she still hasn't replied. No undulating dots to signify a message being composed, either. It just quietly changes from Delivered to Read, and that's it.

I've been out of commission for days at a time, cutting the end of school short for both of us and probably trapping my poor Cherish in the sick, stale bedroom with me out of worry, and the first sign I'm back to my normal self gets nothing?

It'll make sense if she's waiting for me downstairs, with Jerry and Brianne, anxious to see my transformation with their own eyes. Ready to celebrate having me entirely back.

I head down to an empty kitchen whose island counter is the width and length of my parents' whole dining table. There's evidence of a recent presence, a mountain of cubed watermelon, half a lemon, its rind scrubbed off on one side by the nearby zester, a sprig of cilantro, and a few wayward blackberries left on a cutting board, knife unattended.

Even spills and messes know better than to disrupt the photogenic calm of the Whitman home. Various juices had dripped from the board and half seeped underneath, the rest forming a well-behaved puddle to the side of it. It almost looks staged. Like a delightful cookbook spread that tells a whole story in a picture—that this food was prepared with love, by a family member, which is always more impressive when there was the option of leaving it to the hired help. You know the family is somewhere just out of frame, literally enjoying the fruit of their labor, and now I can actually hear that taking place.

Brianne and Jerry Whitman's voices are faint, but I can hear them through the open door off the kitchen and I follow them to the outdoor great room.

A second dining table resides there, this one topped by thick glass and weatherproofed. Overhead, there's a canopy of large canvas squares outlined by sun and sky, the metal frame they're fastened to also home to unshaded light bulbs. Cushions adorn every seat, a host of them residing on the indoor/outdoor bench large enough for the entire family.

"Well, look who's up and operating on two legs!"

I offer Jerry a sheepish smile. It's such a dad thing to say, complete with mock awe and arms waving, barbecue tongs in one hand and his thick gold wedding band glinting on the other.

"I hope your appetite is as healthy as you look," he says, turning back to the stationary grill, beside which there's a metal countertop stacked with meat. It looks like he's added links to the menu, and there's a ridiculously huge jar of homemade sauerkraut nearby, like it was too anxious to wait in the fridge.

"Look at *you!*" Brianne beams at me, either as though she didn't see me an hour ago or as though I look remarkably different after my shower.

"I feel like a new person," I say.

"I'll bet," she says.

When she takes and squeezes my hand, I glance down to see, and when she keeps hold of it, it stops me asking where Cherish could be. It doesn't matter.

"Well, you're back to your beautiful self; that's what's important," she says as though agreeing with me. "And I went ahead and made a little fruit salad." She gestures toward the largest silver serving bowl I've ever seen. "Since I don't want you to have to wait for the coleslaw that apparently may never come."

"Drama." Cherish's voice appears out of nowhere, joined immediately by her presence, and the way both her parents coo and almost straighten up with delight, you'd think she's the one who recently survived the plague.

She holds up a tub of store-bought coleslaw with a kind of petulant grimace-smile on her face.

"Baby," Brianne whines, "I asked you to buy *fixings*, not coleslaw itself."

"It literally tastes exactly the same as yours, Mom, relax."

"Okay, ouch. And it's the sodium and sugar content, you know I don't like—"

But I tune out their sitcom bickering when Tariq steps out of the house behind Cherish. I haven't seen him since the night I had dinner with my parents, but I can't be sure he hasn't featured in any of my fever dreams. I feel like I've seen him recently, but maybe not *this* exact Tariq. Like maybe he's changed over the course of a few days somehow, and the Tariq in my dreams is closer to who he used to be.

"Hey, Mr. and Mrs. Whitman," he says, and the corner of his mouth twitches like he'll smile, only he doesn't force it. Like Cherish's disrespect, it goes completely unchallenged, and he receives salutations much more enthusiastic than he gave.

"How's everything, man?" Jerry first slaps hands with the boy before casually transitioning between at least two other gestures that end with them putting their shoulders into each other's chest.

I almost snort. I don't know how guys always know what to do next in these complicated rituals, and I certainly didn't expect Cherish's dad to do it that smooth.

I *almost* snort because something gives me pause. Something looks strange about Tariq's hand, even though it's moving around too much for me to get a good look. It looks like he's wearing something across his knuckles, but I can't be sure.

"Stick around," Mr. Whitman tells him, gesturing to the grill, and I hold my breath for his response.

"Yeah, I could eat," Tariq says, and instead of nodding, he pushes out his chin to one side and then the other like a boxer pantomiming a bob and weave, to Jerry's amusement.

I glance back down at his hands, but he's got them under his shirt, holding the hem away from his body in one of those mundane but inexplicably sexy poses guys strike.

He's doing it on purpose. I know, because the next place he looks is right at me. It's as though one minute he didn't notice me, and the next his gaze is fixed.

"Hey, Farrah," he says, and then absentmindedly wets his lips.

Something falls into the bottom of my stomach—but not my stomach. I know enough about anatomy to know that's not what's directly above my pelvis, but I don't know how watching Tariq's mouth can give me a sensation that deep.

It's a while before I can breathe out a simple "Hey, Tariq."

It doesn't seem like the adults take any notice, but Cherish is watching me from beside him, and there's something off about her look. Which is when I realize she hasn't said a word to me.

I crunch my brow at her in an unspoken question, and she blinks and turns to Tariq.

"You want something to drink?" she asks him, like she didn't just punch me in the gut, and when the two of them turn back toward the house without her even glancing back, the deep gut sensation Tariq gave me a moment ago turns into a stone.

My heartbeat picks up immediately, and my neck is hot, but I keep my composure. Jerry and Brianne Whitman haven't noticed anything out of the ordinary. They seem oblivious to the way Cherish has snubbed me, so I wait a beat and choke down an inhale before I let myself casually walk back into the house after her.

"Che," I say, while she's still standing before the open refrigerator with her back to me.

It's like I don't exist. Her shoulders don't tighten; there's no slight tick in her neck like she almost turned to acknowledge me and then decided against it.

I spoke not five feet from her, and it's like Cherish didn't even hear me.

She closes the refrigerator door and coolly walks out of the kitchen, leaving Tariq and me alone.

I'm on the verge of hyperventilating at this point, the palms of my hands clammy against the island counter, which is miraculously clean. The detritus from Brianne's "little salad" has been cleared away, the cutting board cleaned, and the blood of sliced fruit mopped up. If I hadn't witnessed the carnage myself, I might not believe this counter had ever been used. But it isn't unwelcoming and sterile like my parents' place. Instead it's easy to believe that food just magically appears, fully prepared, in this kitchen. In this house, everything you need simply appears, without cost or consequence, and—aside from Cherish—there's never any mess to reckon with.

"Che," I call when it's much too late. She's been out of the room for several beats and is probably halfway up the front staircase by now, but maybe the illness isn't totally out of my system, because it took all that time to process this.

Or maybe being in my right mind isn't enough to keep Cherish's behavior from destabilizing me.

My Cherish. The Cherish I've chosen as my home. The one person I love even when I hate her. Even when the thought of her name makes me think of nails pointed skyward and blood pluming underwater. The one person I chose, the one I trust, who trusts me, even when I hold her down in the pool.

It sounds like I'm there right now, water packed against my eardrums so that if there is any sound in the kitchen I can't hear it.

My hands are pressing too hard into the countertop, because my arms are starting to shake.

Cherish doesn't walk away from me. She doesn't act like I don't exist.

My eyes roll up toward the ceiling as though I can see through it. I can't hear her, either, but I know she's in our bedroom, standing in the dead space where I'm not, because she didn't plan anything past the intentional assault of refusing to acknowledge me.

She isn't prepared for this. Not really.

She won't know what to do next, whether to force a confrontation or broker a reconciliation.

She needs me to react.

My breathing starts to calm, and sound returns. Sensation, too, because I can feel Tariq's hand against my back now, and I had no idea he'd come so close.

"Are you still kinda sick?" he's asking me.

Because Cherish must've told him. My parents don't know I've been deliriously ill, but my crush does.

"Do you need to sit down?"

His palm is warm, the heat bleeding through the brushed cotton of my summer-thin shirt and into my skin. Beneath his touch, I let myself buckle, just a little. Just enough for him to notice.

He holds me more securely now, his hand sliding across my back so his arm is against the whole of it, and his other one around my front, like I'm not already leaning on the counter.

"I think I just need some water," I say, rationing my breath so that the words sound flimsy.

He's hesitant to leave me, but after a moment of pause, he moves quickly to get a bottle from the fridge before supporting my weight while I climb onto a barstool.

"Better?" he asks, and puts the hand that was across my torso on the counter in front of me when he bends his knees slightly so he can look me over.

I was right about his hands. The knuckles are raised with thin scabs and it's why it looked like he was wearing something over them. His skin is a handsome berry brown, but they're dark purple, and then bright red where the scabs are cracked, and the healing is clearly coming slow.

"What happened?" I ask, my fingertips hovering over the skin I don't dare touch.

"Oh." He makes a fist with the hand on display, and then as though he'd mistakenly thought the gesture would hide the damage, he pulls it off the counter. There's a smile on his lips that he keeps trying to pull down, and I pick it up without meaning to. "Nothing. You should see the other guy." And he gives a kind of grunt laugh and pushes his dreads out of his eyes, only to have them fall right back across his line of sight.

"Oh, I see how it is," I say, abandoning my previous weakness to convince Tariq I'm impressed. He smiles big and tilts his head back a little as though feeding on the attention.

Except I've seen him throw a punch. And if he was in another fight, why doesn't it look like he took any?

"So who was he? This other guy?" I ask, my eyes still wide and doe-like, my lip still curling up on one side. I casually extract lint from his shirt and then brush the material like it hasn't occurred to me that his chest is just beneath.

It doesn't work. Instead of being taken in by my nonchalant inquiry and physical contact, Tariq flicks his eyes to mine, and then somewhere else. After that, he shrugs and gives a kind of smirk I don't think I've seen on him before.

"It's just an expression, Farrah," he tells me, a grill gleaming on his bottom teeth.

I feel myself go rigid.

None of that was right.

"You should see the other guy" might be an expression, but bruised and scabbing knuckles are most definitely real.

Something was on the receiving end of them. I'm not being silly—so why is he trying to make me feel like I am? And since when does Tariq wear his best friend's grill?

Who is standing in this kitchen with me? Because it isn't the eternally mellow, sometimes painfully reserved, and always adorably gentle Tariq. It isn't the respectful and respectable Jekyll to Kelly's Hyde, and it isn't just the residue of delirium that's making me suspicious. In fact, if I thought there was any possible way for Kelly to have stepped into Tariq's skin, that's what I would swear happened. I'd think there was some kind of astral possession at work, that Kelly was somewhere else, controlling Tariq like a drone.

I want to ask Cherish why she didn't think it was strange that he's wearing her boyfriend's gear—which is when I remember that she ignored me. That's what I should be worried about. I've gotten the confirmation I wanted about Tariq's hands. I don't have any more time to wonder about him today.

Unless his behavior has something to do with the way Cherish is acting. His bruises didn't happen today, so I'm unsure how they could be related, but I also couldn't possibly have upset Cherish. She was gone before I was even awake.

"Hey," Tariq says when he's leaning close enough that I can feel his breath against my cheek. "You wanna go for a walk later or something?"

I turn my chin so that I'm looking in his eyes.

"I've missed you the last few days." He can't say it all without glancing down, and I almost smile. He's himself again, at least for a moment, so I nod.

"Yeah," I say. "Maybe."

Brianne's voice gets louder and she's obviously closer to the door.

"Be right back," I tell Tariq, and then slip out of the kitchen before she gets there, taking the stairs two at a time when I get to them, and then regretting it at the landing. My lung capacity isn't what it should be, and I have to hold on to the banister and breathe deep outside our bedroom door.

Before I collect myself, it opens, and Cherish looks surprised to see me. Like walking away was more than an attempt to get me to follow her.

Like she meant it.

She starts toward the stairs like she's just going to pass me— like it doesn't matter how heavy I have to breathe—and I grip her wrist.

"What's *wrong* with you?" I plead. "Why are you being like this?"

When she doesn't answer, the fire in my chest threatens to go wild. She's never been like this before—I didn't even know she could be—and I don't know what self-control is supposed to look like in this scenario.

"Che!" I pull down on her wrist to make her look at me. "Tell me what I did! What could I possibly have done to you while I've been sick out of my mind?"

She tries to wrench her arm back without answering me, and I tighten and twist, pulling it up between us now so that it hurts to resist.

Her expression goes from anger to something like heart-break in an instant. It knocks me off-center. I don't release her, but my mouth gapes in confusion.

"Cherish," I almost whisper. "Tell me what's wrong. Please. What did I do?"

"You're doing it right now," she replies, and she shakes her head before turning it away because there's a tear she didn't mean for me to see. She's not strong like me. Eventually she was bound to break.

My hand springs open, dropping her wrist.

"I don't know what you mean," I say, and she cradles it like she *wants* me to feel bad.

"Yes, you do."

"Cher-bear." I let my shoulders wilt, ignoring the way Cherish's brow cinches. "I've been virtually on my death bed. I've been sick for *days*—"

"And only on my side of the bed."

My mouth snaps closed.

She keeps saying things I don't expect.

"You didn't think I'd notice?" she asks accusingly. "I always notice, Farrah."

Nothing resonates but the way she says my name.

Farrah. Not RahRah.

"I've noticed the way no one told your mom and dad, too. Have *you*?"

"What are you doing?" I ask, my chin low.

"What am *I* doing?" she throws back at me, but quietly, and it's all the time I need.

"What were you doing with Tariq all day?"

"What?" she asks, her forehead crinkling.

"Is this about what happened to Kelly? What Kelly did?"

"Farrah, we're talking about *you!*" she hisses.

"I know he betrayed you, Cherish, but that doesn't mean everyone will. It doesn't mean *I* will." And then I pause. "Not everybody is out to get you."

Cherish isn't me. I adore her, but she and I are very different people. It's easy to disrupt her, to make it difficult for her to think. Just now, her face is caving. Under the anger that turned to confusion that became defeat, her resolve is crumbling. There's no use turning her face away now; I've already seen her tears.

I take her wrist again, and she doesn't resist when I pull her into my arms. Her chin's against my shoulder, like her last act of defiance is refusing to put her head on my shoulder, but I rub her back anyway.

"Sometimes I'm not even sure you love me," she whispers.

My hand stops.

"You don't mean that."

It's me who ends up laying my head on her shoulder, because I need her to believe me. Because this part is true.

"I love you, Cherish," I say quietly. "You have to know that. I'm not sure I love anybody *but* you."

"Sometimes I think . . ." But she runs out of steam. She doesn't finish, but her breathing calms, and I know she's stopped crying.

None of what she said matters. It's my Cherish. She wasn't looking for answers, just to know I still care.

"Look at you two," Brianne calls up from the bottom of the stairs. "You're just precious! Come and eat before I eat you up instead."

I kiss the soft skin of Cherish's neck where Brianne can't see and hold both her hands.

"Come on," I whisper, and she nods against me.

"My darling girls," Brianne Whitman coos, and she waits while we come down the stairs like a pair of Cinderellas entering the ball, and I wonder. If the fairy tale were true, and there could only be one of us . . . which would she choose?

Mr. Whitman and Tariq have set the patio table and displayed the grilled meat. When Brianne leads Cherish and me back outside, the two of them are huddling together over the latest patties, whose fat drips off and sizzles on the briquettes, sending up coils of smoke. It looks almost sinister, the way the white wafts in the limited space between them, and Jerry taps the backs of Tariq's wrecked hands with his perspiring bottle of foreign beer. They're both grinning, and whatever Mr. Whitman tells him—advice maybe on how to care for the scabbing knuckles, or else something more approving by the way their mouths split open a bit wider to let free a laugh—Tariq nods and gives a satisfied shrug.

He looks directly from Cherish's father to me, and his expression softens.

It's like watching another face slide over the last. Like beneath his asymmetrical dreaded fringe, there's been a polyhedron, and it can swivel and swap out one face for another, the same way mine can. Only Tariq has never seemed the type.

He can't be. I wouldn't have missed it all this time.

He gestures almost imperceptibly with his head, but I keep hold of Cherish's hand and sit her down on the opposite side of the table before asking what she wants on her burger. I make both our plates and go back inside to retrieve ice for our drinks, making sure to keep the trip brief when Tariq unsubtly follows me to the kitchen.

When I take my seat beside Cherish again, and she's taken a series of small bites that only serve to keep anyone from noticing the way she's not eating much at all, Brianne is on the phone.

"Hey, Nicki," she says, like it's good to hear my mother's voice, and she looks over at me. They all do. All three of the Whitmans cast their eyes on me like I'm Nichole Turner's avatar. "Everything's good. How are the two of you?"

It's like choreographed silence. Knowing she's on the other end of the call, we all pause in conversation and in eating, as though we don't want her to know we're here.

"The girls are good!" Brianne exclaims suddenly, beaming over at us. She's seeing us at the top of the staircase again, I'm sure, our arms tangled around each other in a scene that doesn't betray the tension of the moment before.

Suddenly Brianne is standing, edging between her seat and the table without scraping the patio with their movement.

"Sure, I'll go check," she says through a smile, and she winks at me before she carries on chatting to my mother while she wanders into the kitchen and farther into the house.

She's going to look for me. Obviously. I was sitting directly across from her, an arm's length away at most, and when my mother asked if I was there—the way I know she did—Brianne said she had to check.

That's how well she knows me already. She's been my best friend's mom for most of my life, but it's only been a few weeks that Brianne's been like one to me, and she can already read me the way she can read Cherish.

I must have given some glint of hesitation. Communicated with a gaze the way my mother does sometimes that I don't want to talk yet. I haven't listened to the voicemail or responded to the text messages, and Brianne Whitman can't have known that, but she must at least know how I feel. The way she knows all the other things that by rights she shouldn't. The way she knows how to care for Cherish, and how to see the world—the real one—even though because of what she looks like, she doesn't have to. She's always doing the impossible. Reading my mind isn't too great a feat to believe.

Jerry Whitman smiles at me before he takes his first bite of a gratuitously stacked double burger, and I giggle at how wide he has to open his mouth and the way Tariq has competitively crafted his own, and look at Cherish to share in my amusement. Instead I find her face blank.

She's watching me, and for a moment it's almost possible that she sees me.

"So?" Jerry begins, wiping his mouth before taking a swig of his drink to make room for words. "What do you kids have planned, now that summer is upon us? Tariq? I'm sure the judge'll be taking some time off to spend time with you boys?"

Tariq nods big.

"Yeah, me and Dad are gonna sail."

"That's awesome. I know he's been wanting to do that for a

while," Mr. Whitman replies, full of vicarious enthusiasm and boring follow-up questions about crew sizes and charts and whatever else people arrogant enough to take on the open ocean say.

"Doesn't Kelly have his sea legs?" I ask at an appropriate opening in their exchange.

Tariq flexes his right hand, but I only notice because I always do. Everyone else just echoes the subtle smile he puts on.

"He wants to hang out with his little brothers this summer. It's cool. We'll catch up when Dad and I get back."

"It's great he makes time for them," Jerry Whitman says, a bit more sober. "It's gotta be a tough line to walk, being a big brother and a stand-in dad at the same time."

"Yeah," Tariq agrees. "If he didn't take care of them, who would?"

"That's because of your dad," Jerry says, tipping the mouth of his bottle toward the young man like an invitation.

"I know."

"If the judge hadn't stepped in . . ." And he trails off like he's quieted by the memory. Like he was in the courtroom the day Kelly came before Judge Leslie Campbell. Like he witnessed the moment of transformation that was in reality a much longer sequence of events, involving a still hard-shelled young Kelly continuously running away from their home. And the Whitmans would've witnessed at least some of that, as close friends of the family. They would've seen the hard moments and all the ones in between, the way Jerry Whitman's friend made space in his family for a boy the system is set up to flay and forget, and the way the judge never blamed Kelly for the way he fought back.

Their conversation's passed me by. Mr. Whitman and Tariq carry on, talking more about Judge Campbell than anyone else, and I keep seeing Kelly's face the night he and Tariq fought.

Maybe Kelly isn't going sailing because Judge Campbell's finally come to his senses. Or if he's still not ready to turn Kelly away, maybe Tariq's hands are bruised because his father decided that at the very least Tariq should be able to defend himself.

The one thing I don't understand is the grill gleaming inside Tariq's mouth. I'm not convinced I can trust the new side of him that's on display today—but I know who can explain it.

Beside me, Cherish reaches toward the oversized bowl of her mom's fruit salad, and I grab the silver spoon and heap another serving on her plate before reapplying her store-bought coleslaw to my own.

"Yeah, you were right," I say, before turning the spoon over in my mouth and pulling it out clean. "Literally cannot tell the difference."

"Right?" she says, and even though it almost sounds timid and she's only looking at me through the side of her eye, it's something.

"Don't tell Mom I said that."

I'm crunching on the shredded carrots and cabbage that are a delicious mix of tart and sweet, but my peripheral vision is enough to see the slight expression drain from Cherish's face.

"I am having another burger," I announce as I stand a bit to reach the still smoldering pile at the center of the table.

"Good girl," Jerry encourages. "You have a couple days' worth of calories to make up for, at least."

"Trust me," I tell him, settling back in my seat and gathering the condiments to myself. "I plan to."

IX

I never take that walk with Tariq. Everyone understands when I beg off to the bedroom to rest while they're playing a card game a couple of hours after dinner. Cherish is back to her old self, by all accounts, and is laughing and conspiring with her mom when I slide her phone off the kitchen island and into the front of my shorts.

Behind the bedroom door, I unlock the device by swiping my finger in the pattern I've watched her perform a million times. She's never changed it, and she's never made any attempt to keep me or anyone else from figuring it out. It's not horribly difficult anyway. The fact that the pattern starts off-center probably seemed unlikely enough for Cherish. No further security measures required.

I'm not betraying her confidence. We hand each other our phones all the time, swap devices to read texts and tweets and posts, and sometimes reply from the wrong one by accident.

That's just part of being as close as we are. The only reason I need it now is because I don't have Kelly's phone number. Obviously. And I need to find out if he did something to my boyfriend. If whatever he did has something to do with Cherish's uncharacteristic boldness.

I'll be able to tell immediately, whether Kelly lies or not. I just need to get him face-to-face.

Can I see you? I text him from Cherish's phone.

I'm surprised to see that the last conversation between them is from before the night of the boys' fight.

She really hasn't spoken to him since then.

"That's why you're so upset," I tell her, even though she's not in earshot. It didn't have anything to do with me, or something she's "always noticed" I'm doing. She's heartbroken and lashing out at the one person it's safe to push away. Because she knows I'm not going anywhere.

He's a lovesick pup. His response is immediate.

For real?! Of course, babe, thank God. Just tell me when and where.

I try to think of where they might have snuck off to before, if they have. I could scroll up and try to quickly find out, but I don't know how much longer I can have her phone without being noticed. And anyway, I know Cherish. If she's ever snuck out to see Kelly, she wouldn't go far. She'd be timid, even though no one can tell that about her but me. And Kelly would be used to risk, so it wouldn't bother him to come to her.

Somewhere on the Whitman property, then, far enough from the house to feel private, but close enough that she never really left home.

Gazebo. I text him. *Late.*

And then I delete the messages I've sent, and his replies, and I lock the device to sneak it back downstairs.

Toward the edge of the Whitmans' property, their private park becomes a rolling hill that naturally bestows both whimsy and privacy from the twelfth hole of the golf course it overlooks. There's a gazebo, with a lattice enclosure that stands waist-high, and simple, curved benches inside, and the structure marks the end of the line. After it, there's indigenous foliage in a neat line—only the sculptable kind that flowers, of course, unless someone is responsible for the precision placement of the blossoms—and there's wooden fencing discreetly woven between.

Someone like Kelly can figure out a dozen ways to trespass beneath the shingled roof either from the Whitmans' place or from the country club, I'm sure.

I wait until Cherish is asleep, and the house is completely dark, even though if asked, I'll just say I want to walk the grounds to clear my head, or my lungs. No one can watch me all the way to the gazebo; I'm not really all that concerned with secrecy except where Cherish is concerned.

Whatever the reason for her soul-crushing episode today, I don't ever want it to happen again.

I can see a tall silhouette before I've started hiking the incline toward the gazebo, even though Kelly's doing an okay job blending his form with one of the posts. He's checking himself on all sides, obviously, but that means there's a brief blind spot in every direction and he doesn't see me approaching from the Whitman house as soon as he could've.

I know when he does because he straightens up, and then his posture recoils sharply, and he's hunched again.

He's fidgety after that, but he manages not to rush out of hiding and down the hill to me, instead waiting for me to get all the way there.

Of course, it isn't me he's waiting for.

"Cherish?"

I don't answer at first. There's no unnatural light in the structure; the ones at ground level encircling its perimeter are clearly for up-lighting and showcasing the gazebo itself, which is blocking much of what's pouring down from the moon.

Kelly backs out of the gazebo toward the golf course so that the moonlight washes his brown skin in a pale shimmer, but it doesn't help him see me any better.

"Cherish."

This time it's a command. Like it'll break a spell and she'll materialize in my place.

"I'm not," I finally say. "Did you really think you deserved to ever hear from her again? After what we all saw you do?"

His face hardens, but when he tries to square his shoulders, he winces again.

I don't let my brow furrow. I don't acknowledge his pain.

"What, 'cause I threw some stuff? I'm supposed to be terrifying now?"

"You lunged at me, Kelly, or don't you remember?"

He doesn't say anything for a moment, but I can read his face. He's looking for a way to blame me. He wants to say that it's my fault the way it looked, but he can't.

He doesn't know that he can just ask me.

"You got her afraid of me," he says instead.

"I'd say you did that on your own. But I'm not surprised you can't take responsibility for your actions. You have no self-control."

"Yeah?" he cranes his neck forward, but the rest of him stays behind. "Then why aren't you scared?"

It's too late to wince or startle now.

"I see you don't need Tariq to hide behind when you trick me into meeting you in the middle of the night. You seem pretty confident right now."

I run through a short list of possible replies, but they all fall apart on the slightest inspection. They rely on his obvious but unconfessed physical impairment, but I couldn't have foreseen that, and he doesn't seem to realize that I know.

"Man," he mutters, waving me off and turning away. He's heading back whichever way he came, and I have to say something to make him stop.

"How did Tariq learn to fight?"

He stops, bright light spilling down his back, his white shirt luminous. He's got one arm wrapped around his own waist, except it's a safe distance away. It isn't resting against his abdomen, even though his fingers touch his side lightly, as though just enough to keep his arm in position.

Kelly looks at me over his shoulder before turning back around. He makes the effort to loosen his limbs, to let both arms hang at his sides, even though he can't unwind his shoulders. It hardly lasts a second before one arm is crossing his abdomen again and the other fist is closed as though there's no position of relief for that one.

He can't keep a secret for the same reason so few other people can. He lacks control. He's more concerned with his pain, with trying in vain to lessen it when it clearly isn't possible. Or maybe he doesn't think it's dangerous to look weak in front of me.

"Did you teach him?" I ask, and I let my eyes drift down to the backs of his hands just to verify they're unblemished. "He wasn't very good, from what I could see. He couldn't throw a punch. Not one with any impact anyway."

I match Kelly's cold stare after that. Whatever pieces don't fit yet, I have to look like I've already put them in their proper place; otherwise he won't talk. He's not on par with me, but he's not Cherish, either. There's probably something to that cliché assumption of street smarts, especially for someone who's been in police custody more times than he's been charged with an actual crime.

There's something else, though—another reason I wanted him here, to try to pick his brain like a lock, to see what information comes tumbling out when I do.

He's the only one I can afford to play with. He's the only subject—the only one who has something I want to know—with whom I don't have to take it slow. The only opponent who can know we're competing.

I can be completely honest with Kelly, because I don't care about him. I don't care why he's hurt, and I don't have to worry about what he might say when we're done.

He's damaged goods. Tarnished beyond repair. No one will trust him now. He isn't even supposed to be here.

There's nothing I can't do.

"Who said Tariq learned to fight?" Kelly asks with a wince that might be born of physical pain or something else.

"He won your grill, didn't he?" I ask, crossing my arms over my chest and coming to lean against the gazebo post closest to him. I step into the illuminating night easily, like I have nothing to hide from it, like Kelly and I are friends, or something like it, and I'm just being familiar, closing the space.

Maybe he's convinced. His head tugs back for a second and he smirks, but not like someone catching on. Like someone who's been caught.

"Yeah, well." He shakes his head, sneers. "I guess I took something of his first, right?"

My face is bathed in what might as well be a spotlight. I have to answer soon.

Kelly took something of Tariq's first, so Tariq got his grill. Only everything Kelly has is already from Judge Campbell and Tariq.

I see Cherish's face at the patio table when I ate the coleslaw.

Maybe Kelly got too close to Tariq's dad, and the son became jealous of the rescue.

Except Kelly doesn't want Tariq's father or anyone else's. He hasn't seemed to get any fulfillment from being Judge Campbell's not-adopted adopted son. He enjoys the perks and privileges, but he doesn't aim to please. He's not even smart enough to fake it.

Kelly's watching me, so I snort and shake my head.

"It's his own fault," I start, not knowing where I'll end.

"How's that?" he asks, like he's ready. He thinks he can

foresee my attacks now, the nature of them and the cause. He thinks he knows exactly what I'm going to say, even though I don't. But it helps.

"For thinking you were better than that. He should've assumed you'd steal anything he didn't nail down."

His jaw tightens. "You can't steal a girl, freeloader. I'm kinda surprised I have to tell *you* that."

I can't keep my mask from falling. My face goes slack, and the moon has spread its blinding light across it so there's no way that Kelly doesn't see.

That's okay. I already knew what I was going to do. What I've never had the opportunity to do before tonight, because I have always had to be careful.

Kelly can't escape seeing that I wasn't ready. He knows now that I didn't know what we were talking about, and that I didn't see that coming.

Because Kelly's talking about Cherish.

Cherish is what Kelly stole from Tariq.

My Cherish.

My Tariq.

Tariq who asked me to take a walk today, who hugs me like he wishes he were daring enough to do something more.

Tariq who's never given the slightest impression that he's interested in Cherish, at all.

Who spent all day with Cherish while I was sick in bed— and he knew I was.

Tariq who's never kissed me, even when Cherish and Kelly were clearly doing so much more.

I thought he was shy. I thought he was reserved, that I had

to take it slow with him—that he was more inexperienced than you'd expect a boy as gorgeous as him to be, that I should pretend to be, too.

I thought that made him the exception. Not that he didn't want me in the first place.

But this is Kelly talking.

His face is the only part of his body he hasn't had to coddle tonight. It doesn't have a scratch or bruise on it, but now it's wearing a smile.

"Is that news to you, Orphan Annie?" he asks, and when he starts to laugh, he has to bite it back. "You should see your face right now, you look so mad! I'm so glad you texted me."

He lets himself laugh this time, buckles forward a little but doesn't try to fight it, even when he audibly reacts.

He's willing to hurt for this.

"If I'd known that's all it took, I woulda told you a long time ago," Kelly says through a laugh that's gone breathy and broken, like there's a problem with his ribs.

He's bent over, so he doesn't see me coming.

I don't rush him the way Tariq might have, the way he did to get between Kelly and me in the Campbell entertainment room.

I almost want to tell him, it's got nothing to do with anything he's said. It's because he came to me wounded. It's because he's Kelly, and I can be completely honest with him. I can strip away my mask. I can do something I've always wanted, and it won't matter, because of who he is. Because someone else already hurt him first.

It's only a few steps in the bright-white moonlight and I'm in front of him, and he doesn't know how hot and panicked I feel. It's a terrible kind of exhilaration knowing I'm finally going to breathe.

It's still control when I let go, because I choose to.

Kelly doesn't know my chest and palms are sweating because it's my knee I bring up into his chest without restraint. I pull it up hard and fast like there's no such thing as hesitation. Like there's nothing but open air above my knee, instead of a body unprepared to part with the breath in his lungs.

The sound Kelly makes as he falls is like a seal barking. Like the Mediterranean monk seal, if you've had the great fortune to sail near enough to see them, during a Primer vacation with your best friend and both your families.

It's a sound I'll never forget, even though when I try to mimic it back to the fallen body before me, I know I don't get it quite right.

I bark again, and it's closer this time.

The air is mostly still after that, but there's a crackling sound, like a storm is coming, like there's electricity snapping in the air instead of short clicks that Kelly must hope will somehow turn into full breaths. Or words.

They might. So I hike up my knee the way I did before, only nothing breaks its momentum on the way up. It comes high without interruption, and then I bring my foot down hard onto Kelly's back.

From his hands and knees, he collapses all the way down and immediately rolls on his side, but I don't know why. His arm doesn't shoot out to grab my leg. He doesn't raise his hand in a silent plea for me to stop. His eyes find me but they keep roving, like they're looking for something inside his head instead of in the brilliant night with a high, crisp moon and static-filled air.

It's interesting, at least—the way he doesn't even try to crawl away. And the sound he's making, like a body that's forgotten how to function. His mouth is gaping and there's nothing blocking his airways, but even with an abundance of air around him and with what I'm sure are still working lungs inside him, he can't breathe. He's writhing on his side, but if I close my eyes I wouldn't know for sure that it's a person in front of me.

"That's enough for now," I say, but I'm only talking to myself. I make the energy sparking through my extremities coil back to the center and settle deep inside where it has always stayed.

Where it's safe.

Control. Even when I don't need it. Even when it's only Kelly.

That's the key. That's the way to ensure there will always be a next time.

I squat down in front of him and then get comfortable on my knees. The grass is soft and the ground is like a cushion beneath me. It gives so that I sink into it just the right amount. There are no wayward stones, no hard places. Even the Whitmans' soil is immaculate, like what they have is more powerful than money, and far less tangible. You can't see it; you can only experience it.

"It's nice, right?" I ask Kelly when he finally lets his head relax, the veins in his neck thick and spidery from the way he stayed so tense.

It's like his whole body's rebooting. His eyes aren't swimming anymore, but they're watering now, and he keeps squeezing them shut and then releasing them. Maybe it helps, but I don't see how.

He can breathe now; I can tell because the rest of his body relaxes, one region at a time, and then he remembers the rest of the pain. The arm that was beneath him snakes back around his abdomen, and then the other arm joins it for added protection.

I reach for the hem of his shirt and he doesn't shrink away. I pull it up, pushing his elbows out of the way. He grimaces but I hardly hear the groan, and when I see his skin, it's a kaleidoscope. Around his torso and across his ribs and around to his back, what should be consistent brown skin is covered in orbs that have gone purple and something that's more orange than red around the rim, sometimes even a green that I rub to make sure it isn't painted on.

With his shirt pulled up, I can see how much he's still struggling, either to breathe or with the pain.

"Tariq." He barely gets the word out, and it's broken up into too many syllables when he does.

I delicately return his shirt to its proper position and sit back.

"What about him?" I ask.

Kelly just looks up at me, curled on his side on the Whitmans' lawn, with wet streaks down his face. He doesn't bother saying anything else, choosing instead to breathe. I blink and look away.

"You should probably get going soon," I say through a deep exhale. "I have to get back to bed. Cherish will miss me.

Brianne might come to check on us, and she'll be terrified if I'm not there."

There's a strange sound again, and I look back at the crumpled boy on the grass in front of me.

Kelly's chuckling—or trying to. He's turning his forehead into the soft grass and letting his shoulders quake to make up for the air he can't spare on real laughter.

"You're so dumb," he tells me. When he gasps, it's involuntary, and then he coughs, and he pulls his whole body into his core, like there's a string tied around his waist and someone in heaven is trying to hoist him up.

I wait until the fit is finished, and then I trace one of the streaks on his cheek while he watches me with one eye.

"They love Cherish." His voice is low and hoarse. "Not you."

"Cherish and I go together," I say, and I don't let myself breathe for a beat or two so that my chest doesn't rise or fall. So there's nothing for Kelly to notice. Because I can be completely honest with him but that doesn't mean I will.

"Not"—he starts and then closes his eyes—"the way you think."

My neck tenses, and I exhale through my nose, as slowly as I can manage.

If he'd said we didn't go together, I would've known what else to say. Or I'd at least imagine bringing my fist down on the bull's-eye the colors on his side have made and watch the aftermath.

If he'd said we didn't go together, it would mean he doesn't know us, that nothing he says matters, because he's outside writhing on the grass and we're on the inside, and we are something he can't understand.

But he didn't dispute that Cherish and I go together. He said not the way I think.

"You don't know what I think."

He groans, squeezing his eyes shut and nodding like he's talking to the grass.

"There can be two exceptions," he says, but he gestures at me with his chin, like he means that's what I think. And then he shakes his head. Slow. "One."

I don't respond.

It's my eyes that roam now, even though I shouldn't let them. Kelly's regaining his composure. He'll be able to stand up again soon, to walk around, to focus on something other than the poor state of his beaten and bruised body. He'll read whatever I leave on my face.

"They only want one."

"You don't know the Whitmans," I tell him. The words come shooting out at their defense, even though I want to dam them up and hold my tongue. I don't want to say anything to Kelly that I didn't already decide. I don't want to lose control, only fold it primly and set it aside when I decide I can. He isn't even worth it, but I can't stop. "They want me here. Brianne wants me to stay, whether my parents move or not. She keeps secrets with me."

I manage to stop myself before I say that there's something even Cherish doesn't know. In the drawer on my side of the bed, there's a gift that has nothing to do with the daughter they already have. And I trust them because of her. Because of how they've always been with her, of how they use their privilege to shelter her in the only way Brianne says white privilege must be used until it's dismantled for good.

"You don't trust them because they're white, and normally that would make a lot of sense—but you don't know them. You don't even know Judge Campbell, after everything he's done. He had an exceptional son, and he still took you in."

"For something else." He forces the words out, as though no matter how much air he's taken in, it isn't enough.

I don't wait for the words to sink in, the way too much of what Kelly's said has tonight. I stand up so that I'm looking down at him.

"It's probably gonna take a while to get back," I tell him. "You shouldn't lie there much longer."

I turn on my heel without waiting for his reply, for some ridiculous request for assistance that I wouldn't honor in a million years, and I head back to the house. I go home to my bedroom, and to the bed I share with Cherish.

X

It's the rain that wakes me up. At least I think it is.

There's the sound of torrential rainfall, the kind that doesn't come for days, and when it does, it's because something snaps. Lightning, at last, when the air has gotten so still that it feels like the whole world is coming to a dangerous pause. Just when you think you'll never breathe again, when you're Kelly on the soft ground writhing while his eyes roved like they were searching for the air that wasn't in his lungs—the world cracks with light and the roll of a timpani drum the size of the sky.

When relief comes, it's unrelenting. It can't be stopped. It can't be sated.

The rain will fall until the world drowns. But it doesn't matter if you're already underwater.

I know it's a dream because I can hear the raindrops smacking the surface of the pool. Cherish and I are both below the surface, in a dual baptism without need of a priest, and when I finally open my eyes, I'm looking toward the turbulence, the way the rain attacks the water and causes waves.

It should join the rest, droplets being absorbed by more of their kind, but it slaps instead, little pellets that strike like bombs and then explode, or else prove themselves impotent and somersault away.

I want the dream to stay this way. I want this world where there's only Cherish and me, in a place no one ever thought to look for us no matter how many times we came. I can sense the rest of the house where I used to live, the way you can in dreams, and I can feel the white birch trees, but all I can see is the rain breaking the surface and Cherish's arms or legs as they churn slowly beside me so that we stay at the bottom of the pool.

We're holding our breath and we're somehow breathing deep.

It doesn't matter.

We belong together.

Not the way you think.

Kelly's still writhing on the grass outside the gazebo, and I try to bring my foot down hard on the bull's-eye across his ribs, but the water slows me down. The effort is frustrating, the way I can lift my leg with ease, but it grinds to a slow motion so that there's no force left by the time it strikes him. It doesn't matter that I'm still in the pool at my house, and Kelly's far away; I should be able to reach him.

Instead I try to take hold of Cherish, but her arms and legs are gone now, and neither of us is at the bottom of the pool.

I must've heard the rain outside the bedroom window, the

difference in the sound it makes against the roof, or else the glass, or else the drainpipe, or else the grass down below. I'm in bed, where I should be, and I remember climbing in beside Cherish and nestling against her back so that I could hear her breathe, and for a moment I think I've woken up.

That's the best part of sharing a room. No matter what she's like during the day, no matter how she looks at me—even that expression she gave me that seemed to wonder what was wrong with *me*—at night, we're at peace. If I use a phrase I know will burrow under her skin, if she spends the day away from me when I'm delirious and ill, when we sleep, all is forgiven. I make sure to sync our breathing, and she wraps herself around me when I come close, no questions asked.

But Cherish isn't in the bed. She's standing over it.

She's standing over me, even though this isn't the pool.

I can't see her face, but I know it's my Cherish by the shape of her hair.

One two three four fiiiiive, she whisper-counts, *one two three four fiiiive*.

The numbers come one after the other, immediate and brief except for the last. The last one she draws out like she's dragging it across the others.

Like she's making tally marks, the way she does in the journal I found.

What are you counting? I ask her, but her shadow face doesn't change. She doesn't lean closer or turn away; she just recites the numbers again.

One two three four fiiiive.

This time I feel them, four fast, one slow. Five is deeper

than the rest, because it has to reach farther. It has to be sustained.

I've been feeling something all along, tiny, sharp pinpricks that don't connect. They accumulate now, the sensation taking on weight once I know what they are. They become distinct when they join with Cherish's count.

I can look down now, at the naked side Cherish hovers over.

At first it's ugly and bruised like a bull's-eye, and then just as suddenly, it's not. It's my side, not Kelly's. It's my unblemished skin, and Cherish is carving into it.

One two three four fiiiive . . .

One two three four fiiiive, I say as well.

One two three four fiiiive.

She isn't surprised when I count along; she just keeps carving with the short golf pencil. Four short sticks that streak thin and red around my torso until it reaches the bedsheet, and then one diagonal and deep that cuts across them all and makes sharp jags of my skin.

It's all right, I think while Cherish and I count. *It'll be my turn after.*

I am calm and patient, the way Cherish will be next.

Until the echo separates into other voices.

One two three four fiiiive.

Brianne is nearby. Her wrist sends her hand swaying through the air like she's conducting our chorus, her thin index finger counting out the beats between the tallies.

I recoil a little, knowing she is seeing this exercise that is meant just for Cherish and me—but I shouldn't. It's Brianne, who is like home now, too. She has kept a secret with me.

I decide that she is welcome here, while the thin red streaks run, and for once Cherish doesn't seem to mind.

One two three four fiiiive.

But there are more, even though I can't see them. I hear Jerry's voice, and Tariq's, and in the distance, I think that I can hear Judge Campbell's.

There are too many people watching, too many witnesses who are uninvited, but their voices are tangling with Cherish's and there's nothing I can do to pry them apart.

Now the tallies hurt. The blood pulls as it leaves the inside of me, and Cherish doesn't notice or else she doesn't care.

I don't want this anymore, but my limbs still move weighted, like they're struggling underwater, and the numbers come faster until they're too close.

Onetwothreefourfiiiive.

WHEN I WAKE UP, it's still raining.

One of the bedroom windows is open, and a breeze too cold for a summer night has swept in to chill the beads of sweat across my chest.

The nightshirt tangled beneath me feels slightly damp, too, and I twist in the moonlight, to see whether the wetness is clear. Whether the side of my abdomen is a scoresheet, and there are rows of tally marks, and streaks of red running toward the bedsheet.

My skin is untouched. The marks that Cherish made are gone, like the chorus of intruders that hovered somewhere around our bed.

On her side of the bed, Cherish is curled around a body pillow, facing away from me, one leg clamped down across the sheet and trapping the other leg beneath it. Our summer quilt that's only twice the thickness of a sheet is bunched at the foot of the bed, where it always is when we wake up.

I put my hand against her back and feel it slowly rise before I get up and come around.

She doesn't rouse when I move in front of her.

She doesn't stir when I sit in a small space she's left on the edge of the bed.

She doesn't wake when I tug at her bonnet and tuck one of the cornrows that frames her face back underneath.

I know that she's still fast asleep when I turn to her nightstand and open the drawer, but I watch her just in case. I lower my hand into the space that housed only two possessions— except I only feel one.

I pat around, but I'm looking inside now, too. I know the journal's gone.

Cherish has moved her collection of tally marks, dating back to grade school, kept in the journal covered with stickers of our favorite cartoon character so that I would know the marks have something to do with me.

I added one strike, just so she'd know that I had seen it, and she hid it in a new place.

Like I wasn't allowed to know. Like Cherish needs a secret from me.

All that's left in the nightstand drawer is the jewelry box that holds her grandmother's cuff, which Cherish has left for me.

She's taken the journal and the tally marks and left a family heirloom because she must think it's a peace offering.

I only take it because it's hers. I lift the box slowly out of the drawer, careful not to scuff it, and then I leave Cherish's side for a moment while I bury it in the backpack I never had a chance to unpack once school ended.

Then I'm back with her, standing over her side of the bed the way she did in my dream, when I couldn't see her face because of shadows.

"One two three four fiiiive," I whisper, and I trace my finger softly on her side. "One two three four fiiiive."

I only do it twice, and then I retract my hand.

She could almost be Kelly, if she'd buckled into this position because she found it hard to breathe. If she'd fallen this way instead of intentionally curling around a long pillow so that she could fall asleep. She's quiet the way I made him, and just as helpless, even though she's so much more at peace.

She doesn't see it coming when I reach for her. Not quick or hurried, but calm, the way I was outside the gazebo.

I take her by the shoulder and jostle her once.

"Cherish," I say, leaning closer to her face. "Wake up."

This time when I shake her, her eyes open, slow and lazy.

"RahRah?" she croaks, and I can't help but laugh.

The night always heals us. No matter what seems wrong during the day, everything's okay again in the middle of the night.

"Come on," I tell her, and I pull her out of bed and across the bedroom.

"What's happening? Where are we going?" But my Cherish giggles. "Farrah, I think I'm still asleep."

"Shh." I hold my finger to my lips and press us both against the wall outside the bedroom door, and now she's wide-awake, and her grin is spread across the width of her face.

We burst into a run, trampling down the staircase even though we're as loud as stampeding bulls now. It doesn't matter. Cherish knows where we're going, even though this isn't my house. There are no white birch trees, and no waterfall, but I've woken her up in the middle of the night and there's still her and me.

We leave the kitchen door wide open when we run across the outside dining space and careen into the light rain, the soft grass slick beneath our feet, laughter pealing out of us.

I wonder if Kelly ever made it back onto his feet, or if he hears us. I hope that he's still broken by the gazebo and that he can hear Cherish and me as we cross the Whitmans' garden and come to the edge of the pool.

"Baptize me," I say, when I've pulled her to face me, and I only give her time to nod before I fall backward into the deep end of the Whitmans' pool.

The surface breaks and then the water is an open mouth that devours me whole, and Cherish is a wavy figure up above me. Raindrops are beating against the surface, just like they did in my dream, and then wavy Cherish walks around the edge of the pool, and I swim to meet her where she can stand.

My feet never touch the bottom of the pool. After I swim to the shallow end, I flip onto my back and float before Cherish, waiting for her hands to settle on my chest. When I surface, I don't close my eyes against the rain. It's warmer than the water that surrounds me, and I want Cherish to lie down with me, to float on her back the way I am and watch the clouds illuminate even though it's the middle of the night. I want her to see it when the sky lights up; I want to squeeze her hand a little tighter when it catches me off guard. But I want to give her something, too, a reminder that we make each other powerful. That we let each other be. That we belong together, and whatever she is keeping tally of, there's nothing more important than the two of us. Not even what Kelly said about Tariq. Not even if she knows. Not even if there's something between them that I don't know.

Cherish begins the ritual. The rain is falling onto my face, but she still lifts her hands from the pool and lets the water drip from her fingertips until it runs out. She still draws her finger down my forehead before crossing it, and then I put my arms over my chest and take in a long breath so that I am ready for what comes next.

But Cherish doesn't push me down slow.

She doesn't baptize me the way we always have—the way I last baptized her.

She puts both hands on mine, and with a burst of power that doesn't match the girl who very recently was sound asleep, she shoves me back below the surface as hard as she can.

The thrust is too sudden, and it's too unexpected, and my mouth pops open even though I don't mean to breathe in. My eyes bulge and at first I don't have a choice; I resist like a reflex. I struggle underneath her hands because I've inhaled the water, and I need to come up for air—and Cherish's arms go slack.

She's willing to let me up. Which means this is a test. This is Cherish's way of asking me if I'll resist, if she's really allowed to be strong, if I trust her the way she always trusts me.

Control.

There's no way to stop my body needing to breathe. I don't know how to get control of myself without coming up first, but I refuse.

I grip Cherish's hands so that she'll hold me down, and I force myself to open my eyes, even though the rain is still disrupting the surface too much for me to see her face. She's obscured just like the Cherish in my dream, but just like in my dream, I know it's her. That has to be enough.

When there's a fire raging through my sinuses like the water that flooded my nose has turned to lava, or like the blood vessels inside it are coursing with flames, it's enough to know it's Cherish.

It's Cherish who shoved me into the water, so the pain that's tearing through my head and up behind my eyes doesn't change my mind.

My heartbeat is thundering inside my chest, but I can feel and hear it against my eardrums, and it hurts in a way I didn't know a pulse could, but I hold Cherish's hands so that I won't come up.

My body is screaming, sending messages to every part of me that we are desperate to breathe, and I can't inhale, so I force whatever air is left inside me out.

It's a relief, and a lesson. Everything inside me was sure I needed to let something in, that there was no other way, that terrible things were imminent if I didn't give in, but what I really needed was to expel even more.

There was something vital I was being told I could not live without, but I forced what little I had out, and still my body calmed. Still a tiny rest.

And all at once, I can feel the rain on my face again.

"RahRah!"

Cherish's voice is sharp and loud, like I haven't heard it in a long time. Like I haven't heard anything.

There's something sharp across my back, just below my shoulder blades, and it takes me a moment to recognize it as a step.

I'm not where I was a moment ago, in the center of the shallow end of the pool, with Cherish standing over me. She's beside me, I'm propped up on the pool steps, and my nightshirt feels tight because she's got some of it balled up in her fist.

"You have to breathe," she says, and she's patting my cheek.

I don't know why but it finally makes me cough, like I should have when I first went under.

I buckle forward and clear my lungs, while Cherish wraps one arm around my back.

"You're okay," she whispers, and lays her wet cheek against my forehead while she rubs my arm. "You're okay; just breathe."

"I didn't resist," I say, and once I try to use my voice I realize how hoarse it is.

"You didn't," she confirms. "I pulled you out."

When she pulls back and finds me smiling, she tries to bite hers back, but she shakes her head and lets it break.

"You're awful," she says, before pulling me into her chest, both of us sitting on the step, half in the pool and half in the rain. My body still feels limp and I let her hold me.

"Do you really think so?" I ask her.

"It wouldn't matter if I did. You'd still be mine."

I only smile in response.

"Nothing can change that," she says. "Not ever."

I hold her more tightly even though my arms feel like rubber, and the pain I felt in my sinuses is beginning to ache again. It's throbbing itself back into my attention, reminding me that my body thinks something traumatic just happened even though I know better.

"Not ever," I repeat, and then we're quiet. There's the pitter-patter of the rain on the surface of the pool and on our skin, and the low rumble of distant thunder. There's the warmth radiating between the raindrops, and the way the clouds above us are holding light.

"I don't remember the first time I saw you," Cherish says.

"You don't?"

"Mm-mm." Her hand moves up and down my arm. "I remember the first time you smiled at me, but it wasn't the first time I'd seen you. It was like the first time you saw me. It felt like the first time I realized I could be seen. Like you weren't just a figment of my imagination."

I could see a small Cherish, with perfectly diagonally parted ponytails, except her hair was twisted, and fastened at the top and the bottom by bobbles the color of the academy uniform. She was sitting with a gaggle of girlfriends, looking serene. Like no one had told her to feel out of place among them, even though her legs were the only ones that were brown, so that they would've looked dark no matter her complexion, and even though her lips were the only ones so full. She was so perfectly calm and confident where she was, and I felt every single set of eyes that landed on me like they all had edges.

No one told me to feel that way—but I did get a long talk about how to behave, as though I was known for acting out of turn. I did get daily reminders to wait my turn to speak, whether I'd opened my mouth yet that day or not.

No one said I didn't belong; they just treated me like I had to prove I did. And the first time I saw Cherish, she looked like she had a right to be there. So I walked right past her, the way I walked past everyone else, and when I saw her parents for the first time I decided she *was* like everyone else. How could I trust her?

I only studied her because I had to know whether there was someone else who could construct a mask that convincing. I had to know whether Cherish was a stunning performer, a rival where there had never been one before, or whether she was silly enough to really feel that safe.

I watched her for a week and she wasn't perceptive enough to notice. She didn't play at obliviousness only to send discreet signals that she was aware of my surveillance.

Cherish was genuine. She was that soft. Armorless. And like anything without a protective outer shell, pliable.

So I smiled at her.

"Your whole face lit up," I say. "Like I'd never seen. Then I knew your calm hadn't been the same as happy."

"I thought you couldn't see me," she says again, "or you didn't care. And everyone kept asking me about you, if I knew who you were, or if we were related."

I guffaw against her.

"But then you smiled at me, and I didn't care. I didn't care if they thought we were cousins, or even sisters, because I did." She laughs.

"You thought we were sisters?"

"Something like that. I knew we were kin," she says. "I knew I needed you. Before my parents explained why. I *felt* it. In a way they could only know. They knew a lot of things that made them amazing parents, always. But I didn't need them to tell me why you mattered so much to me. Why I needed to know you could see me."

"I still can," I say, but more quietly, in case there's any part of her as upset as she was yesterday. In case she moved the tally mark journal because there's something she doesn't want me to see. "Always."

She doesn't answer me with words, but she turns and pushes off of the steps on her back without fully letting go of me. In a moment, we're both on our backs, watching the sky and letting the raindrops fall on our faces while we hold hands beneath the water.

No one can tell me anything about Cherish and me that I don't already know. Certainly not Kelly. And no one can come between us. Not even Tariq.

She isn't just the home I've chosen; I'm the one who mattered. I'm the one who saw her. When she thought she was comfortable in the life her parents made for her, even with their hair- and skin-care classes, and their social awareness, and the way they've been intentional in raising a healthy, protected Black daughter. They made her vulnerable. They gave her a void, and I filled it. She needed me to see her, and no one can replace that.

I have to remember it. Brianne can't ever be what Cherish is to me, even if she puts me first. Even if she shows me the secret side of herself that even Cherish doesn't know exists, and gives me things that are just between us.

I will keep Cherish first in my heart, because I will always be that way in hers.

I want it to be night forever. This night, when Cherish thrust me underwater and I passed her test. I want to remember that I won this confession, no matter what happened in the moments I can't remember passing, between the middle of the pool and finding myself on the steps with her. It doesn't matter. Cherish and I belong together.

XI

*I*t's clearly afternoon.

The sun is beating down outside, but on the pile of pillows and blankets Cherish and I assembled beneath the window last night when we came back in, we're still comfortable. The glass is a hundred different kinds of energy efficient, so not even the rabid heat can come through. Just the sunshine, streaking across our wild and crisscrossed limbs. Just the spilling light that glows around us like a halo.

My parents would have woken us up by now, summer or not. For some arbitrary reason summed up in mantras like "Don't waste the day away," like leisure has to be constantly regulated or rationed or it'll become unwieldy. It'll turn against us somehow, however comfort can. But no one has disturbed us in the Whitman home, even though the morning's come and gone. No one's afraid of what might happen to us if we wile away the day fading in and out of dreams. No one thinks

Cherish and I'll spoil if we stay sealed away inside our bedroom. There's even a tray on the unmade bed with what looks like muffins and fruit, because someone came in to offer us food instead of a lecture.

"I'm tired," Cherish whines with her eyes still closed. "Turn off the sunshine."

My limbs are still wobbly when I stand up to close the blinds and pull the white summer curtains together. I'm as unsteady on my feet as if I were still in the swimming pool, and I wonder if that's because of what happened last night. I don't think I've ever blacked out before, but I've been tired a million times. I take a few steps more to prove to myself that's all this is.

"Someone brought us breakfast," I tell Cherish while I retrieve the tray and spy the clock beside the bed. "Well. Lunch. Do you think they know we were up all night?"

"We cleaned up after ourselves." She yawns, batting away the strawberry I press against her lips.

"Eat it," I say, trying not to laugh.

"Stop," and she folds her lips into her mouth and rolls her face into the pillows.

"Fine, none for you."

"Save me some," she says, but it's muffled.

"Too late," I tell her, and she can hear the fruit I've packed into my cheeks.

"RahRah," she whines, and sits up quickly, yanking the bowl out of my hands and snatching both containers of yogurt and both of the spoons.

We're laughing and wrestling things out of each other's grasps and making at least as much noise as when we "cleaned up after ourselves" last night. We'd tried to mop up our foot-prints, hunching over onto our hands and bending our legs so that we could scurry the towels around the kitchen and toward the staircase in the middle of the next room, but we kept trying to run each other off track, or swiping our arms out from under each other before collapsing into a bellowing heap.

We could have woken the dead, so there's no chance we didn't at least wake Brianne and Jerry, and we were making so much noise, we wouldn't have known. Just like we don't hear whoever's knocking on the bedroom door until they open it a crack to let their head in while they knock again.

"Mom," I blurt out at the sight of her, and for some reason I leap to my feet.

She's wearing a smile, but it's made up of politeness. I can always tell. When she looks at me, it doesn't change. And when her eyes find me, they just hold. All the laughter and ease in Cherish's and my bubble deflates, and my mother and I just stare.

There you are, she says, without speaking at all.

So you do exist.

And the longer she watches me, in this moment that seems to drag on beyond the normal rules of time—*I see you.*

"What are you doing here?" I finally ask, but even I barely hear it.

Cherish, on the other hand, squeals like my mother's arrival is a happy surprise.

"Mrs. Turner!" Despite how time stalled in my mother's gaze, it skips now. Cherish is on the other side of the room be-fore I untangle my feet from the mound of pillows and the sheet.

At her welcome, my mother comes fully into the bedroom and gives Cherish a hug.

"You girls aren't up yet?" she asks, before she kisses my head and pulls me into her arms.

"Not all the way," Cherish says, and plops back down on the pallet we made beneath the window, like she's inviting Nichole Turner to join. Like she doesn't know that Black parents who don't believe in proper sleepovers for sure don't see the whimsy in sleeping in.

"I didn't know you were coming," I say, and hold my mother's gaze for a moment before lowering back down beside my best friend so she remembers where we are.

"I haven't heard from you in quite a few days, so I thought I'd better come crash the party."

"I told her to call you," Cherish says, like they're on the same side, and she looks at me with a raised eyebrow that's playful but still serious.

"No, you didn't," I say, and she starts.

"Yes," she says, her eyes drifting and then returning like I'm the one lying. "I did. When you got sick."

The inside of my chest goes cold. It's bad enough what she just dim-wittedly confessed to my mother, but now I don't even know if she's lying. I have no idea if Cherish is being malicious right now or not, because I can't say for sure what she did or didn't say to me when I was ill. I have no idea what she's doing, or why, so I can't stop it. Just like last night in the pool before a very uncharacteristic baptism, I am at my best friend's mercy.

"When were you sick?" my mother asks, and she's subtly more alert. Her brow ticks up, but slightly. I could swear her pupils expand, just a little. Nichole Turner is just as gifted as I am at deciding what to wear on her face, but I know that just below the surface, there is rage.

And Cherish keeps talking because she doesn't know any better.

"The last couple days of school," she says, opening one of the yogurts she'd buried beneath a pillow to keep them away from me. "That's why we didn't go—I mean, not that I cared. Everybody was already gone. What I *did* care about was that she basically destroyed my bathroom. No, Mrs. Turner. I'm serious. Like, vomit, everywhere. And my mom made me clean most of it up. It was bad."

My jaw is starting to hurt, but I can't relax it. I am watching Cherish with an intensity that should burn through her. Her skin should swell with dozens of inflamed boils and then pop, leaving holes like Swiss cheese up and down her arms. Amber-colored blood and puss should ooze from each one so that it looks like Cherish is melting in a searing, painful mess. But my gaze can't even get her to shut up.

Now she's done, and eating like she didn't pull a pin and my mother isn't a grenade preparing to detonate. Cherish won't know when that happens, either. She doesn't know that it's happening now, quietly.

I know my mom better than my best friend does, so I know what the silence means. I know all the restraint that goes into what she says next.

"I didn't hear about any of that."

When she looks at me, there's an entire conversation passing in the taut space between our eyes. A tug-of-war. She is already pulling, the way only my mother and I can. She's issuing a silent command, compelling me to move, to give in. It's how I know she and I are alike, that Nichole Turner is just like me, even though she doesn't show it. Even though I've never seen her hand down a worthy consequence when her compelling is refused, I never doubt her. I never take her inaction to be inability, because I know it's much worse than that.

Nichole Turner refuses to prove herself to me. She has mastered self-control, and I am shrewd enough to see it. It's almost bright, the way it makes me want to squint, to seek some respite from the apparent calm of her gaze—but I won't.

Control.

Cherish is too far away to pinch, so I dig my nails into the palm of my hand and keep my mother's gaze until a tight smile breaks on her face.

"Your dad's downstairs, too, Farrah," she says, and Cherish just keeps eating like she's only now discovering how hungry she's been all morning. She has no reason to find my father's presence interesting—and on his own, neither do I. Except I know what it means that my mother brought him. It means she is setting things right, the way she does for him. She has brought him so that all the pieces are present, and she can put us back in line.

When she's certain she's made herself clear, her smile loosens. It looks natural now, even to me.

"You girls get dressed and come down, okay?"

She waits until I nod my agreement and then she stands up, and when she looks down at me before leaving, she clenches her jaw.

"I need to talk to Bri and Jerry," she says, but it's like she's telling me in particular. There's a threat in her innocuous words, and I hear it the way she wants me to.

When she's gone, I want to leap on Cherish. I want to slap the small container out of her hands, to shake her, to bury her in the pillows the way she buried the food.

My mother is here, so I won't. The freedom from the gazebo and the baptism and the haphazard, false attempts at cleaning up last night—the attempts meant to demonstrate that we knew we didn't have to succeed, that we could be brazen about our adventures in the middle of the night and no one would discipline us—are gone. Everything I've let uncoil is painfully rewinding itself. I thought I'd already put away the slivers of myself I set free in front of Kelly, but in my mother's presence, I see that I've been too lax. Now the rest of me curls too quickly and too tight. It's receding deep, back where it came from, and I don't know when I'll ever get to let it back out.

"She's here to take me home," I tell Cherish, and I don't hide the way I'm biting down on my teeth.

"What?" She looks up from the soft, pale yogurt she's scooped onto the edge of her spoon, as though any more would be too much. As though it doesn't have the lightest texture and a delicate flavor, or as though it's all she's used to. Anything else would be too strong. "You said you won them over. They were gonna let you stay."

"They were," I snap. "Before you opened your mouth."

She looks like she's trying to press the creamy substance between her tongue and palate, but I can tell from the way she furrows her brow that she's confused. Or she's pretending to be.

"All I said is that you were sick," she argues. She missed the entirety of what passed between my mother and me, but when I clip my words and refuse to say more than the bare minimum to show her my annoyance, Cherish can always tell. "I didn't know it was a secret, Farrah."

"Right," I say, calm but serious so she stays uncomfortable. "Because we don't have any."

I don't stay. I don't tell her what I mean. I leave her with her spoon hovering between the yogurt and her mouth, and I dress to meet my parents downstairs.

WHEN I FOLLOW the voices into one of the more formal sitting rooms on the main floor of the Whitman home, four adults are trying very hard to camouflage what is really going on.

This is a confrontation.

This is a refusal to be ignored.

This is my mother's brand of ambush, and it's too polite to be countered or refused.

My dad's sitting all the way back on the auburn leather sofa, his hand swallowing one of Jerry's short glasses. There's a set in three different rooms of the house, by my count, and Mr. Whitman's holding one himself. They're both wearing weekend attire, competing for most relaxed in a pair of respectable shorts, the kind that brush just above their knees and range in color from tour-guide tan to eggshell white. My father's paired his with a day-off polo while Jerry's chosen a V-neck that even from a distance looks soft and expensive, yet simple and noncommittal.

Brianne Whitman cannot be caught off guard. However long Cherish and I have been sleeping, Brianne looks like she's showered, gardened, had a leisurely breakfast with Jerry, jogged, showered again, run errands, and met my parents as they were all approaching the front door.

My mother's my reminder that something's wrong. I noticed her small earrings, the studs she wears with her hair up when she has to make a first or intentional impression. No fringe or bangs, her hair is swept away from her face, and she's wearing a gloss instead of lipstick, and a pair of flat, closed-toe sandals instead of her favorite summer espadrilles. This isn't what she wears to spend time with friends; this is what she wears so that the opposing party gets the subtle message that she means business and that she's capable of it. A Black woman in business can't afford to neglect either. My mother's been out of her primary field for a year somehow, but nothing dulls the knowledge that she must always be the most prepared. It's something I've heard Brianne Whitman admit to more than once.

This is my mistake. I gave myself too much credit. I left too much silence between the night at my parents' place and now. I thought that I was masterful in the words I chose, and maybe I was. Maybe they carried just the right amount of sting, but I should've known Nichole Turner would recover. Even with my father to focus on, she would clear her head sooner. It was never going to be a one-and-done discussion, and a new life with the Whitmans—and I'm almost glad.

I thought she'd chosen my dad, the way she always has, that she would coddle him through the entire process of moving to a new city and finding him a new home, and forget about me. I thought she'd expect that I could take care of myself, the way she knows I can, and I would slip away into the back of her mind for a while, just until my dad was comfortable in his new position, and he was stable.

I thought she'd forfeited our war games.

I would never have forgiven her, but I was prepared for that. I was resigned to carving her out of myself, the way I'm convinced must inevitably be done with most people.

But here she is. Nichole Turner is dressed for a conference with my teachers, or an escrow closing, or something where she's approachably no-nonsense, and whoever is depending on her knows they can. She's here to collect me and bring me home, and I appreciate it.

But I'm still staying.

I want my mother to refuse to give me up *and* I'm not going anywhere.

She should've chosen me before I chose Cherish. Before the Whitmans chose me. She should have imagined that they would.

"Are you sure you don't want something, Nicki?" Brianne hasn't sat down. She's been balancing out my mother's tension by floating around the room like a cloud despite the fact that my mother's perched at the sofa's edge. Finally, Brianne drapes herself over the arm of Jerry's chair, ready on a whim to rise again. "It's so good to finally see you two. I know things must be hectic at the moment."

I sit down just inside the wide threshold of the room's double doors, so that I'm outside the invisible borders set by the four adults, and try to blend in with the rest of the furniture. Cherish wanders in, and I tug her down beside me so our presence doesn't interrupt whatever Nichole Turner has planned here. I might not be willing to give in, but that doesn't mean I don't want to see it. It doesn't mean I'm not hoping she finally bares her teeth.

"The kids say Farrah was sick," my mother says, brushing past Brianne's frivolous pleasantries. "It sounded serious."

"It wasn't terrible," Brianne says with a shrug. Her ethereal poise is uninterrupted; she's even opted for cool reassurance. She manages to sound compassionate without validating my mother's concern. Impressive.

"To be honest," Jerry interjects, "it was pretty bad." And he does a shrug of his own in my dad's direction, as though inviting him to the conversation.

"Jer, you'll scare them," his wife says just a bit more quietly. She moves a small section of his hair though it wasn't out of place, but the gesture succeeds in lending the exchange a misleading triviality.

"What scares me is finding out something like that after the fact." Nichole Turner doesn't blink. She's looking at her dear friend with a resolute stare that makes no attempt at softening. "I can't imagine why no one thought to call us."

And then she looks at me. She lets me know I haven't disappeared into the background. I'm not eavesdropping. I'm here because she told me to be. Something's getting settled here and now, no matter how quiet I remain—so I choose a side.

"I would've been just as sick if I were with you," I say, and I don't blink, either, but Brianne laughs nervously.

"That's true," she says, though it's timid. Or at least it can be interpreted that way. "And we took good care of her, Nicki, just like we promised. Honestly, we were only trying to take some of the strain off Ben and you."

When she smiles between the two of them, my dad smiles back like a reflex, and ordinarily, I'd shift my focus to him. He's the easy target. He's the person who taught me there is such a thing. But he's not the one in control, and sometimes there's no escaping it. Sometimes you have to face down the strong one.

"I'm sorry, I know there's nothing more frustrating than feeling out of the loop—especially when it's your own kid. I take full responsibility for that, Nichole, I do." Brianne's humble and apologetic, and there's clearly an air of expectation, like the matter requires nothing more than a gentle touch. She's certain of her strength in that department, and I wonder whether this woman has ever tried to handle my mother this way before. Something tells me she hasn't; otherwise Nichole Turner wouldn't have thought so highly of her all this time.

She needs to know that acting out gracious contrition won't work here, but I can't very well tell her. I can't communicate to Brianne Whitman that it won't satisfy or obligate my mother, not now that she feels there's something wrong. Not when she might finally sense that the Whitmans are drawing close around me, adopting me the way they did Cherish. Or worse, that I'm adopting them.

I leave Cherish on the outside and come sit beside my mother on the Whitmans' leather couch. I can feel the way Brianne and Jerry watch me, soft smiles etching across their faces. It looks like I'm drawing near to my parents, to my mother, because I've missed her, or to let her know that I'm okay.

"I'm fine, Mom," I say, opening my arms and wearing a playful grin, as though teasing her or telling her she's free to inspect me. As though she's being overprotective and I'm goading her toward reason. I smile past her at my dad to remind her that he's there and they are not a united front. He hasn't matched her concern or her resolve, and I'm not the only one who can tell. I look between them to drive home my point, but only so much that she can tell. Then I tuck into her, so that she'll wrap her arms around me, and she does.

It must look heartwarming.

I couldn't have scripted my dad better. He reaches over and does his equivalent of a hair tousle, sinking his fingers into my thick hair and then massaging my scalp a few times so that it isn't mussed.

"Glad you're feeling better, Fair. Your mom and I were just worried," he says, like he's forgotten that until just now, neither of them knew. "Next time, don't forget to call."

"We'll make sure of it," Jerry says, and drinks what's left in his lowball glass. "We're supposed to be the grown-ups, I think," and the two men chuckle.

They're acting like that's the end of it, but I know it isn't. I drew closer because I'm sure. There's a stiffness to my mother's embrace, especially when my dad unwittingly hangs her out to dry. When his behavior confirms the message I was silently sending with my eyes, she looks at me out of the corner of hers, like it's my doing. Like I turned him, even though my focus has been on her.

"Ben and I have made up our minds," she says, and I don't leap out of her arms because I know what's coming. "We've decided to take you home with us."

A lesser person might point out my father's recently implied position, the way there's no reasonable interpretation of his words that fits with hers. They'd be right, but it wouldn't matter.

Your father and I are a united front.

She's already told me once; it doesn't matter if it's true.

We both know the problem with a turncoat is that they're easily turned back.

In my mother's case, she doesn't even have to do that. The upside of being his partner is that she can simply speak for him—the way I got in trouble for knowing she so often has.

Still tucked inside my mother's embrace, I don't look at a gaping Cherish, or fly into hysterics. I don't recoil from my mother's arms or begin spouting complaints. That's what the room is waiting for, though, because everyone goes still.

That's what she expected, or what she thought was possible. Like I'm not smarter than that.

She's testing my restraint. Loosening her hold of me as though encouraging me to flail or fling myself away. It'll be easier to sweep me up and out of the Whitman home then. It'll be understandable to hurry out, haul me over my father's shoulder like a misbehaving toddler whose tantrum can't be managed, so their parents just whisk them away.

I don't do any of that. I don't give her an excuse. If she wants it escalated, my mother will have to do it herself. I won't go willingly, but I won't be unreasonable, either. If I'm dragged back to my parents' sterile rental home, it'll be because Nichole Turner lost control of everything in her life a year ago, and she's trying to restrain the one thing she still can. It'll come with pitiful glances and compassionate conclusions about there being only so much she could take.

It *would* humanize her. Her breakdown would debunk the myth of the stalwart, inexhaustible Black woman, carrying the weight of the world without need of rest. In any other household, it might be worth it, but the Whitmans already understand. That's *why* it would work so well—because they are raising a Black woman of their own. Because they refuse to lay the weight of the world and society on her shoulders with the expectation that—despite or because of all the ways the world has tried to break or betray her—she alone can fix it. Instead, they spare her *every* burden, and because she's a Black girl, it's a revolutionary act.

So I elect to use them instead.

I look up at Brianne. Her mouth is open like she's ready to launch into some shapeless, half-baked plea, and I lock eyes with her before the useless words come tumbling out.

I need her to follow my lead. I need to show Cherish's mom how to compete with Nichole Turner, what works once my mother's guard is high and her mind is made up. I need to show her how to spare me, the way she's so accustomed to sparing her daughter.

But it's more than that. I need to know if the connection is real. I need Brianne and Jerry Whitman to be on my side, the way I think they are, and I have no time to test it. I just have to leap and hope they catch me.

"So I *don't* get a vacation this year?" I ask, and collapse my shoulders. I sink out of the embrace, and my gaze falls to the side, first toward Cherish, and then to the floor.

No eye contact. No signals or subtle cues. I have no guarantee that either of Cherish's parents understands that one of them has to take it from here. If they want me to stay, they have to finish what I started, and I can't explain.

Brianne is the one who speaks.

"I'm sure that's not what your mom means, honey," she says. "She didn't know."

"I didn't know what?" Beside me, my mother's voice shifts, like first she was speaking to Brianne, and now she's looking at me. But I can't say anything else.

"Oh." Brianne's sigh is perfect. It's like a gesture, a yielding even before the explanation has been heard. "Jer and I were planning to take the girls away," she says, and instead of looking at her husband, Brianne Whitman just takes his hand.

I watch their skin where it's made contact. This is where the agreement will happen, if there is one. If Cherish's dad understands what we're doing, this is where the performance transfers to him.

I hold back a smile, but I can't stop the way my chest expands when Jerry Whitman squeezes his wife's hand and then stands. He disrupts any attempts at interrogation by taking his and my father's glasses for refills. It's just a casual conversation now, with players moving about the room, but the room is also more chaotic. My parents' attention has to volley between Jerry Whitman's back as he refreshes the ice, uncorks the decanter, and pours new drinks, and Brianne Whitman's charmingly disappointed smile.

"It wasn't going to be anything fancy, and nothing too far," Brianne's saying. "Just something to keep the blues away while you two get situated in your new space. Just so Farrah doesn't miss you too much."

In her corner of the room, Cherish is ribboning her brow.

There are levels to this conversation, and my best friend is only privy to one. She didn't pick up on the silent struggle upstairs, and she's just as oblivious to the unspoken strategizing that took place between her parents and me. It's a side effect of her parents' revolutionary coddling, and as usual Cherish is none the wiser.

Maybe that's what's been missing for them, even with a daughter they so obviously adore—the ability to communicate without words. The ability to decipher more than the shallowest subtext. Cherish's obliviousness is a gift—but maybe that's why they want me.

"I didn't know we were going on vacation," she interjects, but it's just Cherish, and it's easy enough to diffuse.

"Well, we hadn't gotten that far," Jerry says. He's returned my father's glass to him and elected to sit next to his daughter now, loosing one finger from his drink to poke her playfully in the side. "We needed to be sure Farrah was even up for it, sweetheart, so we spoke to her first."

While her dad wraps his arm around her head and pulls her close enough to be kissed, my best friend stares at me, but her face is no more relaxed.

I know what she's thinking. It's something her father asked when Tariq was here. If her parents were planning a trip for all of us, why wouldn't he have said so instead of asking what us kids were planning to do?

Cherish is staring at me instead of them, but I don't speak. I won't. I adore her, but none of this depends on her playing along, or even understanding. I'll take care of it for both of us, the way I've always done.

"I guess you, me, and Dad can just do a vacation of our own," I say, and I put a lilt in my voice like I could get excited at the prospect of something I know they can't possibly supply.

"I don't think we have time for that," my dad says. "Not between moving and getting started in my new position. Frankly, I don't expect to have time to even get settled."

There's no money for it, either, I'm sure, but no one will force them to admit to that.

"I still have to job hunt in earnest," my mother says. It's like a concession, the way she says it a little more softly than everything that came before, or like she's making a mental list and accidentally spoken it aloud.

"I've been meaning to ask you about that, Nicki," Jerry says, Cherish comfortably sidled up against him, her feet drawn up into the sofa. She won't be any more trouble now. "I know a few headhunters in the area. I could send one your way. He's an absolute shark. I know he can get you tapped in with the right people. Find a place that'll offer what you're worth? It sounds like it worked for Ben."

His eyes flicker toward the end, and he recovers quickly, focusing on the daughter in his arms.

But a flicker is all it takes.

"A headhunter approached Ben," Nichole Turner says.

"Same guy," Jerry Whitman concedes immediately.

I stiffen, but my eyes roam. How did Cherish's dad accidentally derail our stunningly perfect play to end up here? And what is being confessed to?

"I don't think I mentioned, Ben, that I'd passed your name

to him," he says, and he's charming the way he always is. The words roll out almost casually, except for the way he's avoiding two pairs of eyes. Brianne's wearing a pursed expression I've never seen before, and I'm sure it means she doesn't mean to. My mother's feels more familiar. I've seen hers before. The night I had dinner at my parents' house, the night I coerced them into agreeing I could stay, when she thought Brianne had told me about my family relocating.

It's an expression that marries disappointment with something resembling disgust, like she didn't appreciate Mrs. Whitman taking something upon herself, but she wasn't entirely surprised. It says she should have known better, that she partly blames herself.

"Why would you pass his name to someone out of state?" she asks, but her voice is flat so that it doesn't sound at all like a question. She's making a statement, and Jerry Whitman can't justify looking anywhere but at her, even with Brianne's chest starting to flush with color.

Brianne Whitman is trying to hold a smile to her lips, but it's too tight. It's verging on a grimace, and she's looking above our heads while she twists a bracelet around her slight wrist.

"It's Cameron, isn't it, honey?" she says, and if she weren't standing where I could see her, her voice would be completely convincing. It's strange to watch the words come out of her mouth when the sound and the appearance are so mismatched. It's a disaster, but only because I'm looking at her. It's a talent that would be very useful in another scenario.

"That's right," Jerry answers, pointing to his wife as though the name was on the tip of his tongue.

"Well, *he* isn't out of state, of course, but he does have contacts all over the country."

"He'd better," her husband replies, once again adopting the tenor of a completely different conversation. "A good headhunter has to grant access to more than what's already in somebody's backyard; otherwise what good are they?"

That's Jerry Whitman's gift. It always comes across as charm, but today I can see the moving parts. It's an ability to assume authority over the narrative and the tone, shifting it right under the congregation's feet in a way that compels them to acquiesce. It'll either diffuse my mother's inquiry or require her to be more overtly confrontational.

Which is, admittedly, a somewhat despicable position to put a Black woman in, for a man who is as conscious and invested in our liberation as Jerry Whitman is.

"It just so happens that the people most convinced of Ben's talents were farther away than I guessed," he finishes, and it means my mother doesn't have to ask.

But it also means my dad might've been telling the truth.

Maybe it *was* a whirlwind connection, and maybe the Whitmans didn't pass along my dad's name until the situation was clearly untenable. Until the Turners' daughter was living under their roof.

Maybe there was no secrecy or betrayal on my parents' part—but the Whitmans still saved the day.

Maybe the fact that my mom's still looking at them like she's come to fully understand something just means she's a sore loser.

"Can I stay?" I ask her, quietly so that even though everyone can hear me, it seems like I'm trying not to put her on the spot. "Just until the vacation?"

I watch her jaw clench while she rubs my arm. Only I can hear the way her breathing is labored, the effort she's putting in to keeping it steady.

I squeeze her and smile up at her.

She's lost. She must know that.

Whatever she thought Jerry Whitman's misstep was going to expose, it's already forgotten. Everything, easily explained.

"Just until we get back from vacation?" I ask again, because I can push back one step at a time. I can ask permission as many times as I need to.

The Whitmans don't insist. I can get away with it as her teenage daughter; they are patient, smiles reestablished, and ready to accept whatever my mother decides.

"Just until after the vacation," she says. Her breath hitches before she's done, but all that matters is that I've won. "And then Dad and I want you to make the drive with us."

"Well, that sounds like fun," Brianne says, and smiles at me. "A summer road trip with the whole family."

I kiss my mother's cheek, while Jerry launches into a new conversation with my dad about the golf courses closest to our future home.

"Nicki, you and Ben'll stay for a bit, won't you?" Brianne comes close now, trading sides with her husband, so the couples split and pair off again the way they've always done. "You two can use a day, I insist. Let's just relax and make some dinner later, and have wine, how does that sound?"

"That sounds great, Brianne," my mother says, and there's a

pause before she says her name. It interrupts Brianne Whitman's smile—but only for a moment.

WHEN MY MOTHER weaves her arm through mine and says she wants to talk, I lead her out to the gazebo. I bring her right to the spot where Kelly collapsed, even though there's no place marker or evidence that he was here. I just remember. I know exactly where his body fell, where his head pressed into the soft grass while he was struggling to breathe. I can put him there, in my mind, and I only have to make slight adjustments so that we're standing on his back.

She studies me while I perfect our position. She knows I'm doing something, but she can't know why, and when I'm finished, I look at her and smile.

"What's the matter?" she asks me, soberly. My amusement isn't contagious. It doesn't catch on the corners of her lips, snag an uncertain smile, the way it's supposed to. The way it would on anyone but the two of us, who are capable of control.

"I smile, and you think something's the matter?" I don't tame my expression. I could, if I had to, but no one hears the sound of Kelly's body rustling against the ground, the noises he makes that for anyone else would be so difficult to place.

Nichole Turner only stares, and in a moment I realize she's not here, either. She's standing beside me, our arms still entangled, but like me, she's somewhere else. A different time, and—for her—a different place, too.

"You know, you never cried," she tells me. "When I brought you home from the hospital."

"Lucky you," I say, and nudge her with my shoulder.

"No." And the way her breath escapes with the word pulls some of the lift from my lips. "It terrified me. I never knew when you were hungry. When you wanted to be held. Nobody told me how important it is to hear your baby cry, especially when you're a new mom, and you don't know what you're do- ing. The crying tells you there's a need. And you didn't."

I should say something. I should interrupt wherever this is going before my mother's seriousness quiets Kelly for good— only I can't decide what. I filter through a series of sentence fragments, but I can't see the outcome for any of them. I can't tell what reaction they'd elicit, and what comes out falls flat.

"So I was a peaceful baby." My eyes hop around involun- tarily.

"I said you were quiet." My mother brings them back to center.

This is a criticism, and she knows that I know now. She lost in the sitting room, so she brought me out here to confront me one-on-one.

"I'm sorry I didn't cry more," I say, but there's no affect.

"You cried," she says, like I'm following the script perfectly, leading her where she already planned to go. "Eventually. But not until you decided to."

I clamp my lips shut when she leaves space for my reply. I refuse to speak, letting my gaze fall to the grass at my feet. Will- ing myself to hear the clipped breathing of a boy I brought down in the middle of the night.

I step to the side, and my mother has to follow because we're still arm in arm. When I slip free of her, it's so I can place both hands on her arms and turn to face her. Make sure she's exactly where he was. Turn her around so that my back can face the gazebo like it did when he was here.

She doesn't ask what I'm doing, not even when my smile returns. She just keeps looking at me like she knows. Like she's always known.

"I worry about you, Farrah," she says, when I've put her in exactly the right place. "I always have."

"I guess I can understand that," I tell her, and finger one of her stud earrings. "We're just alike. I guess the parent who sees themselves in the child knows exactly what struggles they'll face." Her expression tightens. "But you also know I'm smart, and capable. And ruthless. Just like you."

"Why do you do that? Why do you need to think I'm a monster, too?"

It's like the gazebo has a decloaking effect. The same way I was with Kelly, I feel honest and free with my mother, despite the lack of moonlight. We've both slipped out of cryptic, coded speech, and neither one of us is surprised.

"Why do I have to be a monster just because I scare you?"

"Come home," she begs me, and it doesn't seem to follow.

"I am," I say, before I can stop myself. I've started uncoiling again, and it's because of Kelly writhing on the grass, the way the moonlight bathes his white shirt and seems to make him glow. It's the way I hurt him so badly but I didn't make him bleed. The way I let myself, and still managed to scale it back. "You don't have to worry about me, Mom. I'm in control."

"I don't think you are, Farrah."

"If we aren't alike, then how would you know?" I say with a bite. "How could you know anything about me?"

The way her expression shifts is insulting. Nichole Turner looks at me like I'm a ridiculous child, like what I've implied is beyond reason and she's surprised to hear me say it.

"We're not alike, Farrah," she says. "Why would I have to be to see you clearly? I can see past myself."

Our eyes are locked but I say nothing.

"I'm always alert, even when I think I'm getting what I want. I don't mistake fixation for loyalty. I don't think someone showering me with attention makes it healthy, makes me safe."

"Am I a predator, or is someone preying on me, Mother? Which is it?"

"A smart girl would know it can be both."

"This is about Jerry's friend finding Dad a new job. A better job," I stress.

"And when you thought Dad and I were responsible for it, it was a betrayal," she says, and it quiets me. "When you thought we'd given up on the life you still want here, you twisted our words and feelings until we let you have your way. No strategic, chess-master level of interrogation now, Farrah? No wondering where this shark of a headhunter was when we were drowning for a year?"

Despite what they can clearly see with their eyes, people always say that dark skin doesn't blush. Before me, my mother's face has flushed, a fresh pink lifting beneath her skin, as though a light is shining from inside her. Her eyes go glassy and a rose rim begins to form around them. It's lovely.

"The Whitmans don't owe me anything," she says, as though to keep me from saying it first. "I'm just wondering why this fast-acting salvation didn't come before the bank foreclosed." She bites her lip and looks down where Kelly used to be.

She's embarrassed now.

"Maybe they wanted me to be their daughter," I say dryly, burrowing into my mother with the strength of my gaze. "Maybe everything that went wrong in your career is somehow their fault, not yours."

I should feel remorse. It's been so long since she was on top, but my mother *was* good at what she did. I know that. She was good enough to have her own team, even though she found out not long before she was laid off that one of her subordinates made more than she did. I shouldn't use live ammunition when this is just a war game—but she should've lost graciously.

My mother takes in an abbreviated breath, but it's too sharp and the smile she doesn't mean is pained.

"I wouldn't even know, Farrah," she tells me. "Whatever else you are, you're still a Black girl. One day you'll know how impossible it is to tell the difference between personalized terror aimed straight at you, and good ole run-of-the-mill systemic prejudice. That the only difference is, I can protect you from one."

I hold her hand and sit, forcing her to follow me down to the grass where Kelly lay. She doesn't know he was ever here. She can't hear him struggling to breathe, or see the colors decorating his abdomen, the bull's-eye that I didn't make.

She's just about to ask. I can tell by the way her brow crinkles when she looks between me and the blades of grass I'm delicately touching. She wants to ask, but she's near exhaustion, suspecting the unthinkable and not knowing how to phrase it.

"You've always worried about what *I* might do," I say, pulling the blades of grass between my fingers without pulling hard enough to pluck. "What would I need protection from? What is it you think might happen here? Do you think Brianne's gonna kidnap me? Wouldn't you make me come with you right now if that's what you thought?"

"I don't know what I think, Farrah," she confesses. "I just know I don't like it. And I know you can't see anything but the story you're telling."

"And?"

"And there's always more than one. We know that." And I know who she means by *we*. "We know there's always another narrative, and we don't have the luxury of ignoring it, even if we think it suits our needs." She reaches out and stops my hand. "Brianne Whitman wouldn't know to teach her daughter that, no matter how conscious she is."

I watch my mother until she slowly releases her hand and sits back, shaking her head like she knows she hasn't made an impact. She's losing again, because she still doesn't think enough of me.

"Who doesn't tell someone their child is sick?" she asks me, and I don't have an answer so I go back to stroking grass.

XII

o you still miss him?" I ask Cherish when I find her sitting alone in the garden. Half the distance between the pool and the gazebo, there are raised flower beds and a serpentine pathway made of rectangular mosaic stones. The path snakes between and beneath the lattices that create an overhang of sheltering ivy. It shades the garden furniture, raining down star jasmines along with their beautiful aroma. It's the single most relaxing place on the Whitman property—but Cherish isn't relaxed. She almost drops her phone, and then locks it as though I could've seen the screen from where I'm standing outside the ivy shade.

"Or maybe you don't have to." I come around the beds overflowing with tulips in a range of colors. There are other flowers, in other beds, but I've only come to water them with Brianne once or twice, and I've only asked about the ones I like.

"It's just me, Che," I say, nudging her with my shoulder

when I sit in the chair beside hers. "You don't have to keep it a secret from me."

"I haven't spoken to Kelly," she says. "Not since . . . that night. When you picked me up."

I already know she's telling the truth. Which means there's something else she's hiding.

"So . . . who are you texting that made you jump out of your skin at the sound of my voice?" I ask, and I already know the answer to that, too.

If Kelly is to be believed.

"You just startled me," Cherish says. "I thought you were one of my parents."

That doesn't answer my question, but I can't simply ask again. That would belabor it. Instead I start again, with an entry point she won't foresee.

"I know I wasn't really fond of Kelly," I say, wearing contrition like a veil across my face. "I'm sorry if I ever made you think you have to choose. You don't. If you like him . . . I'm sure there's something about him I could like, too."

That should please her. It should make her turn and look me in the eye, hope that I mean it, and that if I do, maybe there's a way to salvage whatever broke between them. It should make her hope out loud that if I'm willing to keep her secret, too, then maybe it doesn't have to be over. Maybe he didn't do something as bad as it seemed.

But Cherish doesn't even react.

"That's how it works, right?" I go on, a giggle lending the transition some levity. "When your best friend likes someone? Doesn't it always make you see the guy the way they do?"

She's thinking, but I don't give her long.

"Like me and Tariq."

She's a novice. She didn't respond at all to the mention of a possible reconciliation with her own boyfriend, but Cherish can't stop herself from straightening at the sound of Tariq's name.

"What about him?"

"Well, you're crushing on him, aren't you?" I say it easily, with a little grin. "I know you are; it's totally fine. You like him because I like him; it makes sense. It's cute. You're like a bratty little sister who can't help imitating me."

"What are you talking about?"

But she takes too long. Instead of it sounding like a plausible retort, like she's responding to nonsense, the beats that pass before she says it confirm that she absolutely knows.

"You are so bad at this," I tell her through a laugh, ignoring the sound of her counting in my head.

One two three four fiiiive.

"Bad at what?" She's getting defensive.

Good.

"At lying."

When she goes to move away, I grab her arm and yank her back, laughing and forcing her to relax in my arms. I pull her head onto my shoulder and clamp mine down against it to keep her there. If she resists, she'll hurt herself but it won't be my fault.

"Farrah, what is wrong with you? Get off!"

I release her abruptly and then recoil, my face contorted and confused. I move as though it's her response that's startling, as though her struggling was itself cause for concern.

"Cherish . . . what's the matter?"

Her chest is heaving, and I can almost feel the heat radiating from her skin.

One two three four fiiiive, one two three four fiiiive.

"Why are you so mad?" I ask. "Shouldn't I be?"

"I don't know what you're talking about, Farrah." She makes every word sharp and separate. "Why can't things ever just be normal with you? Why is something *always* the matter?"

She's building up steam. I can almost see it—the wheel of her brain picking up speed when it thinks it's on to something.

"One minute you're my best friend, and there's nobody in the world but us, and then"—she shakes her head, a heavy pressure building on her brow—"you snap. You come out of nowhere with something, like you always need to pick a fight."

I let her words hang in the space between us, just long enough that she thinks they've made an impression.

One two three four fiiiive.

One. Two. Three. Four. Five.

"You're bad at this," I say at last, and then I go completely still.

I know what's going to happen now, but Cherish can only see the move in front of her, never the one after the next. So when I'm unmoved by her attempt to derail me, she doesn't know where else to go. When she breaks—the way I knew she would—a tear slips down the length of her face. It's even more pathetic because she thought this was going to end any other way, and because she's always so upset when she doesn't mean to cry.

"I spent the day with Tariq when you were recovering," she says, shaking her head and swiping angrily at the streak on her face. "Is that what you're getting at? It wasn't a big deal, Farrah, I've known him a lot longer than you."

My eyebrow cocks.

"I mean we've been friends my entire life, literally longer than I can remember. We used to take baths together when my parents babysat him for the Campbells, when his mom got sick before she passed."

There are too many details, too much irrelevant backstory meant to cloud my judgment with knee-jerk compassion. She's talking too much, insisting I believe something rather than trying to relay the truth.

One two three four fiiiive.

What I'm not expecting is the way it hurts.

She's not any good at it, but my Cherish is still trying to deceive me. And the timing can't be coincidental.

Somewhere not far from us, in the house maybe, or elsewhere on the property, my mother is still here. The same day she said I can't see any story but the one I'm writing, my best friend lies to me. And with time enough for me to run back to my parents' arms.

Is that all this is? Cherish siding with my mother because she's afraid of the way I get along with hers?

"Our parents used to pair us up all the time," she's saying. "You know he's been my escort to every formal at the club. I'm just saying. You liking him isn't the first time I noticed Tariq Campbell, Farrah." Her eyes flick away and back. "*And* I don't have a crush on him."

"You're supposed to say he's like a brother to you," I say after letting a long silence stretch uncomfortably between us.

"What?"

"That's your line, if you wanted to make sure I didn't believe you. 'Tariq is like a brother to me, Farrah.'"

She doesn't move when I stand.

"And—if you were telling the truth—something like, 'I would never betray you like that.' Honestly, either one of those would've been more convincing."

I'm supposed to have the last word. I'm supposed to turn on my heel and rush back to the house, past our parents, and into the shelter of our bedroom. I'm supposed to fling myself across our bed because I'm devastated over what my best friend has done. Cherish has no reason to think I won't, but she says something to my back, before I get the chance—and it sounds more like Nichole Turner than her.

"You want too much, RahRah."

I halt, but I don't turn back around. I don't show Cherish my face. I'm stunned, like someone's knee has careened into my rib cage without hesitation, and I didn't expect it.

Cherish doesn't sound like herself. It's her voice, but there's not enough naïveté. Her characteristic simplicity is missing.

Onetwothreefourfiiiive, onetwothreefourfiiiive.

Just like with the tally marks, Cherish sounds like she knows something I don't—but that can't be. Just like those tallies can't mean what I think they mean.

Cherish hasn't struck a deal with my mother to push me out of the Whitmans' home, like she hasn't made a game out of hurting me. There's a journal filled with scratches, but that doesn't mean all these years she's kept a record of her score.

"Stop," I bark, and it sounds like a Mediterranean monk

seal. Or like a wounded boy getting the wind knocked out of him in the middle of the night.

I'm bent over the way he was, curled forward with my back to Cherish, but she can still see the way I pant. I'm breathing fast and heavy, making outbursts to quiet things that only I can hear.

Cherish is still behind me. I have to make it stop.

I swallow air and hold it, and make the count to five my own. *One two three four five.*

I am in control.

I've let Kelly inside my head, and he's confusing things. He's making me see a conspiracy where there can't be one; I'm hearing derision from the one person incapable of it.

She called me RahRah; that's how I know it's still her. It's my Cherish, and I'm overcomplicating her shallow remark.

She doesn't mean I want too much, the way someone would say you want more than your share. More than you are owed, or deserve, like you're of a lower station than them.

The day I smiled at Cherish Whitman, she knew what it felt like to be seen.

Cherish was invisible until me.

Cherish was a spoiled white girl who also happened to be Black, and it meant that the consequence of coddling, the incompetence it breeds, was dangerous. It meant that there was a void inside her, but because she was a Black girl, too, it meant that I could fill it.

I could make her whole.

That is what I did.

When I turn back, I find her there. Just my Cherish. A

breath of relief escapes involuntarily, and my face falls into a smile.

She even looks confused when I come back to her. Her eyes dart when I cup her face with my hands, but she lets me.

"You meant I want too much from you," I say out loud. "I expect too much."

Her brow furrows and she turns her chin, but not enough to escape me.

"I'm sorry, Che. You're right." I hug her and breathe deep. "I'm sorry. You're right."

MY PARENTS DIDN'T stay to let the meal settle. They didn't wander out beneath the darkened evening sky with Brianne and Jerry and full glasses of wine the way they normally would.

My mother said she wanted to go organize some things at the storage unit, and she studied my face before kissing my forehead in a nonverbal goodbye. I hoped she could read the twinkle in my eye, that she'd noticed the way I held Cherish's hand through dinner, just in case she *had* tried to turn my best friend against me.

My dad gave me a bear hug and whispered, "Have fun," before following his wife out.

At the end of the day, everyone was on my side.

The Whitman house quieted down after that, with Jerry disappearing into one of his offices, and Brianne filling the dishwasher so that whoever appears to perfect the home won't find a messy kitchen first thing in the morning.

All that time—ever since my mother interrupted Cherish

and me in our bedroom—I'd been wearing the Whitman heirloom bracelet, and no one noticed. If my mother did, she didn't know why it mattered. She didn't know it meant I was claiming the Whitmans—but I did.

After everyone went their separate ways, I replaced it in my backpack and changed my clothes.

"I'm gonna go for a swim," I'd said to Cherish, and then I'd waited.

She was sitting on the bed with her knees drawn up in front of her, staring into one of the books off our assigned summer reading lists like she didn't have anything better to do. At my statement, her feet shimmied on the made bed, as though to demonstrate she was comfortably—and permanently—settled.

"Okay," she said.

"Tell Tariq I said hi." I only said it to watch her tense, and she did, her eyes staring over the rim of her book, but not high enough to look at me. "I'm kidding, Che! Don't be mad." And I climbed up the length of the bed to plant an intentionally sloppy kiss on her cheek.

"Freak," she muttered, wiping her cheek while I licked her forehead. "RahRah!"

"Be back in a bit!"

I didn't say anything about the phone tucked almost underneath her. It doesn't matter; a phone is good for plenty of things beside calling or texting her childhood friend.

All of which it keeps a record of.

I find myself thinking of it the entire time I'm in the pool. How it feels weird to be down here by myself. How it's weird that Cherish didn't join me. We both love to be in the water, but together, not swimming laps like an athlete. I'm bored almost immediately, but I refuse to come back to the bedroom too soon, so I glide back and forth, turn on my back and watch the sky, and do it all again, five times.

One.

Two.

Three.

Four.

Five.

My hand reaches for the edge of the pool after the last lap and finds it. I'm preparing to hoist myself out of the water but something's already taking up the space.

I sense a presence looming, and when I open my eyes, I'm too close. Something's in front of me and it's broad and dark and imposing. My elbows buckle and I fall back into the water before I recognize Jerry Whitman, squatting at the lip of the pool.

"Nice form," he says with a smile, when my head's back above water. "Did I scare you?"

My forearm burns, and while I tread water, I glance down to find my skin a little inflamed.

"Lemme see," he says, reaching, and I reach back so he can pull me through the water to the side. He twists my arm gently. "Uh-huh. I think you scraped it on the way back down."

I make a timid sound when I try to agree, and then apply the slightest resistance to his hold so that when he lets me go I can protectively coil the wounded arm against my body the way Kelly kept doing.

But Jerry doesn't let go. He must not have felt my attempt,

which must have been as timid as my wordless reply. Instead he pulls again, this time as though he might lift me completely out of the water with one hand. The grip he has to make on my wet arm is tight, some of my skin pinching and the abraded part of it burning as though the scrapes are elongating because of his hold. I help instead of complaining, using my free arm to push myself up until between the two of us, we've managed to get me out of the pool and seated on the lip.

He's squatting again, hovering and turning my arm despite the fact that it's entirely overcast by his shadow and he can't see it any better than I can. He must, though, because he clucks in regret.

"That can't feel good," he says.

"It's okay," I promise through a smile, though it's unlikely a child can ever reassure the parent. I'm almost certain he'll blow cool air over the disrupted skin if this goes on much longer, but when I try again to retract it, Jerry Whitman lays his palm flat against my arm.

I suck my teeth, and he looks from my arm to my face, though he doesn't otherwise adjust.

"Does that burn a bit?" he asks, and I nod.

"Yeah. A little."

Another second and he removes the hand that seems to radiate heat by comparison to my cool, damp skin.

"I was afraid of that," he says with a chuckle, and then he lets me go entirely. Almost immediately, he lifts his hand again, index finger raised as though he's considering something before he points at my wrist. "Were you wearing a bracelet earlier?"

"The one with the engraving," I agree enthusiastically. Instead of cradling my stinging forearm against me, I plant the heels of both hands against the rim of the pool as though the topic excites me. As though I'm unaware he wouldn't be asking unless he were already sure. As though I can't tell by the way he's asking that he thinks I shouldn't have been. I will not lie to him—not after the way he and Brianne kept me when my parents tried to take me home. Or if I lie it will only be the way parents expect their children to, the way siblings use each other as scapegoats. It will be harmless. "Cherish thought it'd make me feel better," I tell him, "after being so ill and hideous for two days."

I smile but I don't bare my teeth. I keep my lips closed, and instead hunch my shoulders high as though my head is sinking into my chest, I'm so touched by my best friend's gesture.

"It's so beautiful," I say. "Of course I knew better than to wear something that precious in the pool."

"It's an heirloom bracelet," Jerry Whitman says, but not chastisingly. More evidentially.

"I love the name Eloise."

I should have waited a beat. With anyone else, I would have. But I trust Mr. Whitman, especially after today, so I'm not listening to him. I'm not giving him a chance to speak, and instead of performing penitence, I'm trying to impress upon him how special I understand the jewelry to be.

It's the kind of self-involved Cherish would get away with being—but I'm the family's new addition. I have to be much more conscientious before I can get away with flouting the house rules. I have to be perfectly well-behaved, a pleasure so that my invitation is extended again and again.

"I didn't feel right accepting it," I say as confession. "It must mean a great deal to all of you."

"It does. It was my mother's, and Cherish has always understood the gravity of inheritance."

This time I wait, but so does he. I'm not sure I've ever been so squarely in Jerry Whitman's sights, or else it's the kind of gaze that feels singular. It's impressive. I could see this stare cutting through any manner of Cherish's dissents or tantrums, stilling her into silence because Mr. Whitman is being so quietly direct. I find myself studying it, noting the anatomy of the presentation from his unwavering eyes to the athleticism that allows him to stay squatted beside me without tensing or his muscles trembling.

I should react, but I've never seen Mr. Whitman be the least bit disciplining; I'm not sure what he expects in return.

Control.

I wait a moment more. He will know I'm unaccustomed to this side of him, that I require some manner of instruction or explanation on how to proceed.

But his brow starts to furrow and then irons out almost before it's noticeable.

I've been matching his gaze too long. He's noticed—which can only mean Cherish wouldn't have.

Now I curl my arm protectively close to my torso and let my eyes fall, sweeping over the pool and out across the darkness of the yard rather than studying the stone beneath me. He'll know I'm not Cherish, not exactly. Even if I'm unsettled, I wouldn't cower.

He takes in a breath before he speaks, giving me a chance to return my gaze to his attentively.

"I'll have a word with Cherish."

I don't flinch, don't give any suggestion that I am threatened by this course of action.

"Family heirlooms are for family," he says.

It's night and even the light is creating shadows, so I don't know if Jerry Whitman sees the way my face goes slack.

Control.

I go still, the way he did a moment ago.

Control.

Even the good make missteps. That's what I tell myself when it threatens to uncoil in the deep of me. When the release that I let spill out over Kelly wants to unspool in my belly, when I wonder what it takes to knock the wind out of Jerry Whitman and I immediately know that it has to do with his daughter.

Control.

Because it would serve no purpose past this moment to tell him what happened in this pool last night, or in mine the night he and Brianne had to come retrieve Cherish and me. It would leave him breathless, knowing that there's an empty space inside her, that it's of his creation, and that only I can fill it—but there'd be no going back.

Control.

Tight.

Tight.

Wind it back like a fishing line.

Even the good make missteps, and Jerry Whitman is good.

Control.

I will not share our secrets. I'll only tell him what he already knows.

"Cherish knows that," I say, in a reassuring voice that nearly pleads on her behalf. "I guess she just considers me family."

A moment later, and one corner of his mouth ticks as though it wants to smile. When it doesn't spread, he looks almost smug in the uneven darkness. It could be a smirk in this light, a challenge. Like he knows more on the subject than I do, despite the fact that Cherish didn't know she was empty until she saw me smile.

"Genetically, Cherish and I are probably more family than she could be with Eloise."

I laugh. I have to. I spoke again without meaning to, and they aren't the kinds of words that can be taken back. I have to be a silly, thoughtless teenager who doesn't understand the impact of what she's said.

Jerry Whitman turns his face from me and I almost hear Kelly laughing, the broken way he bore the pain so that I'd know he was willing to hurt to prove me wrong.

They only want one.

My legs are still in the water, and even if I try to kick Kelly down again, it'd be too slow and heavy the way it was in my dream. He'd just keep laughing because he doesn't know what the Whitmans and I did together today, that I am as in sync with them as I am with Cherish now. He doesn't know that they've already disproven whatever he wanted me to believe that night.

Kelly is wrong—but I have never been this clumsy before tonight, and I wonder if my mother's got something to do with it. She came and disrupted me, even if she didn't get her way—or else she did and I just wasn't smart enough to see it until now. Until I've said the single most offensive thing imaginable to the adoring father of my best friend.

Nichole never fails. She never falters. If she'd really come to take me home, she would have and no unrehearsed display of unity between me and the Whitmans would've changed that.

She didn't come to take me home. She came to ruin this one. To get inside my head, pretending she didn't understand the waltz we did around Kelly's phantom body, letting me place her exactly where he fell, so that I'd uncoil it again. She got me to call it back to the surface and I couldn't tuck it away.

Cherish's father stands, but he's always angled away from me, the light from the house splashing across his face where I can't see it. His shoulders rotating once when his hands slide into his pockets.

I don't know what to say. I don't know how to tell him I'm not myself, that this is sabotage and I am not to blame—until I do. Until, as quickly as my breath went sharp and shallow, it settles.

I know how to show him that I'm not myself, that I couldn't be. *Thank you for loving our daughter the way we do, Farrah.*

It's what he knows best about me. That I love his daughter. That the real Farrah—the Farrah who is in her right mind, who can be held responsible for what she's saying—would never speak ill of Cherish. So I do, mildly, because he'll still feel bruised and defensive over what I've already said.

"She *has* been kind of inconsiderate lately," I say, my words slipping free as though on tiptoe, venturing but timid. "Not just about family heirlooms."

Jerry doesn't turn completely, but his chin almost meets his left shoulder when he glances back, his weekend attire completed by the absence of product holding his hair in place. There's a sharpness to the way it curves away from his brow.

"She doesn't mean to be, though," I reassure him. "That's not how Cherish is. When she hurts you it's never because she meant to. She just broke up with Kelly! I think it's got more to do with that than losing respect for Whitman family tradition." And then I confess as though unaware anyone else can hear me, "Or really wanting to steal Tariq away from me."

I don't wait for him to face me before shrugging the way self-conscious teenagers do when they're trying most to convince themselves, and when he does, I'm looking between the pool and the sky at nothing. I'm as confused by Cherish's behavior as he is. I'm helpless.

"It's okay. It isn't like Tariq and I were really together. She probably doesn't think it counts since she knows we didn't do the kinds of things she and Kelly did." I pull my lips to the side because it's awkward talking about intimacy with a dad, even when it's a relief to get something off your chest.

I wish I could see his face without looking. I want to know whether or not Jerry Whitman is preparing to scoop me up the way he did at the renovation site, even though Cherish isn't hurt this time—and even though she's the reason I am not myself.

"Come on," he finally says through what Cherish calls a dad sigh because she thinks Jerry's adoring brand of bemused exasperation is common. "Brianne'll never forgive me if I don't get you out of the water and get that arm dressed."

He gestures toward the house with his head and without removing his hands from his pockets. He doesn't extend a hand to help me up because sometimes he coddles his daughter and sometimes he reminds her that he knows she's capable. It's loving in a way that bolsters her confidence and doesn't feel like a gift because it isn't. It's an acknowledgment.

I show him that I understand, smiling through a firm nod before easily getting to my feet.

"Where's your towel?" he asks, walking ahead of me because I don't need a chaperone in what is now my backyard.

"I forgot to grab one," I tell him, without confessing that I'd hoped Cherish would bring one down to me when she noticed. "Should I wait outside while you get one?"

"Since when is that an option?" he jokes. "Am I not supposed to know about the last time you girls made a post-swim mess in the kitchen?"

"We were very mindful not to wake anyone," I say, almost as dismissively as Cherish would.

"Church mice, the both of you." Jerry feigns sincerity, holding the door and bowing his head at me while I pass. "Have a seat and I'll get the supplies."

I obey and sidle up to the kitchen island while he disappears around a corner. It must be a drawer in one of the nearby alcoves, because I hear it open and shut, and Jerry's back a moment later.

"Impaling small feet on long nails aside," he begins, half

lowering himself before he's maneuvered the stool beneath him. "Cherish never hurt herself much more than a skinned knee or scraped chin."

He's got a bottle the size of a nail polish container between his thumb and forefinger, and he's shaking the thing to mix its contents.

"This stuff still works better than a plain old Band-Aid, and no goopy mess festers underneath."

"It's just a couple layers of skin missing," I say, twisting my arm so I can see the wound myself. Under the kitchen lights, it's an angrier bright red than it looked by the pool, and there are more abrasions surrounding it like little inflamed satellites.

"It turns out skin is sort of important," Jerry tells me, setting the bottle down on the island and fiddling with a nail kit I hadn't noticed before. Opening the clear sleeve, he unsheathes what looks like a set of small pliers. "So we're just going to give you an artificial layer to stave off infection."

He catches my eye and then tilts his chin as though he can read my mind, or as though having done so, he won't embarrass me by divulging what he's found there.

"No, Fair-bear, this isn't going to hurt, no need to worry."

My lips lift while my shoulders dramatically relax so that he knows I trust him. That I have chosen to, and that it means something. It is not an honor given lightly, and in the whole world right now, it's one only on offer to the occupants of this house.

"Ready?" he asks, his brow high and what must be the cuticle trimmer raised as though for my approval.

"Ready," I say, and then squeeze my eyes shut playfully, as though afraid to watch.

The trimming end of the instrument is cold against my skin—or the layer below the skin that scraped free on the edge of the swimming pool. The sensation makes me straighten up and open my eyes, and Jerry checks in again.

"Okay?"

"Yes." I nod and perform calm, glancing absently around the empty kitchen while he works. I don't ask why he's trimming the impossibly thin and almost indiscernible frays of skin at the edges of my wound. It's not something I'd think to do or have ever done before dressing a severe scrape, especially not a tender one, but Jerry Whitman is known for his attention to detail. There is a process for all things, a proper way to prepare, proceed, and complete a task. Even when his renovations threatened unwieldiness and petered close to breaking his intended budget, he always reined them in. He always knew what could be trimmed to salvage a profit.

Cherish had no idea how it worked. When we were in middle school and her dad decided his passionate hobby had run its course, she was completely unimpressed. I asked why he'd lose interest when his last four flips had sold well over his projection, and not only was she unaware; she acted like it was weird that I knew that. She must've thought everyone had a head for real estate and renovation. She thought profit was a guarantee—which her parents probably found adorable. Except it meant she couldn't ever marvel at her father's prowess. If she couldn't even witness it, it certainly wasn't something she could study. Which meant she would never adopt his skill, make it her own, improve upon it and outshine him, the way parents must hope their children will.

My breath clips, a sharp and sudden abbreviation I hear almost before I can process that I made it.

My wound is stinging, hot and angry beneath the hand I've protectively shielded it with. I've retracted it from Jerry Whitman's reach, my eyes searching our scene to determine what's happened in the time I've been inside my mind.

He's still sitting on the stool next to mine, but he's twisted at the waist, holding a cotton ball to the mouth of a bottle of alcohol that he tilts three times in quick succession before motioning for my arm.

For a moment I have a silly hesitation. I want to keep my arm snug against my torso with the opposite hand guarding it—until I hear Kelly's crippled laugh. Until I'm behind his eyes and it's me contorted on the lawn outside the gazebo, my arm pinned to my side because of the bull's-eye hiding beneath his shirt.

I return my arm to Jerry Whitman before I've deduced what happened because of the pressure above his brow. He's concerned, concentrating on the dressing while I've been distracted.

"A little too close," he says, pressing the damp cotton against what feels like an opening, the acknowledgment serving as an apology. "We just wanted to trim the strays away, not make it worse."

I make an involuntary sound between wincing at the pain and agreeing with him.

"Maybe we'd better just get on with closing this up," he says, as though he'll soon be suturing a gaping wound.

I nod.

"Okay," he says now that we're decided, and sets all else down before reaching for the first bottle I saw him shake. "We're in the home stretch now."

And then he pauses, holding my gaze in a way that stills the air around me. My hair is still wet, like my suit and the towel I'm sitting on over the stool, but the occasional breeze of conditioned air I've been feeling disappears.

"Do you trust me?" he asks, tipping his forehead like he's preparing to let go of my bicycle for the first time instead of apply some liquid bandage to my hurt arm.

Jerry Whitman's question is an invitation, not just to trust him, but to entrust myself to him. To his family. To be less strict with my mask when I'm with them.

I may never get this chance again.

Kelly may never be on the grass outside the gazebo again, and I might never get to uncoil myself the way I did with him. I may never get to bring my weight down on the broken side of him, to hear him bark again. But that doesn't matter anymore.

Jerry Whitman is waiting. He won't proceed without my go-ahead. My trust.

Fair-bear.

I uncoil a little.

Control is a warning in my mother's voice now. It's a strategy in her offensive, to keep me from being truly at home here.

Instead, I uncoil a little more. Not too much, but enough to let them know I've decided. Enough to prove to Kelly, and Nichole Turner, and Jerry Whitman that I trust him.

That I choose them.

That this is home.

"Yes, *Dad*," I say, and petulantly roll my eyes to match the emphasis I've laced around the word—the title. "I trust you."

XIII

T *his isn't going to hurt.*

I'm edging out of sleep, but I don't want to. My mind is trying desperately to rip me back into consciousness, but I fight. From inside my dream, I try to rein myself in even though the pain is arresting.

This is like nothing I've ever felt.

I don't want to wake up. I don't want to go back to it because from the brink of waking, it feels like what Jerry Whitman did to me—only worse.

I fight to stay even though it's an inferno where I am. Inside the dream, I'm on our bed in the room I share with Cherish, but it's ablaze. All around me, the air is thick, yet somehow there isn't any smoke though every direction is bright with flames. The expansive room is full to the point of claustrophobia with fire, hot and smothering and alive. It dances while it devours, lapping at the vaulted ceilings, curving down toward me at times, and then rearing back as though it is saving me for last.

I am lying on the bed, my wounded arm tucked between the mattress and my side—but I'm not afraid. I am quiet inside the wreath of flames that have covered the wall behind me like living wallpaper and left the bed untouched.

Where is Cherish? I don't ask it aloud, but I listen for the fire's response.

Fire pits crackle, small and contained. This is different.

This blaze roars. It bellows. Sometimes it screams.

It wants me to scream back, to cry out, but I won't. The way I didn't when Jerry painted my wound a thousand times over with liquid skin.

I did not cry out.

This isn't going to hurt.

Except that it was agony. From the moment the silky brush and liquid compound touched the rawness of my wound and the still-stinging edges of freshly trimmed skin and the cut he'd accidentally made, I wanted to plead with Jerry Whitman to stop.

This isn't going to hurt.

So I didn't show it. All the time I could feel the bristles, could feel the liquid adhering to the shreds of remaining epidermis too small for the eye to see. All the time I felt the liquid move into the cut, seep into the shallow slice, I didn't make a sound.

It was a test. It had to be. When I anchored my gaze on Jerry Whitman, looking through his pupil and into the stabilizing darkness, he was watching me. Waiting for a reaction. Waiting perhaps to see if I'd meant the words I'd said.

This isn't going to hurt.

So it didn't. No matter how it felt. No matter how the ravaged area burned and tightened, the way it felt like tiny teeth were sinking into my raw flesh.

He said it wouldn't hurt, so it didn't.

The dampness that had been pool water became sweat, the effort of swallowing my pain and my tears sending it boiling to the surface until I felt it slip down between my shoulder blades. It beaded along my forehead and above my lip, but I tensed, and reached further into the dark of Jerry Whitman's eyes.

When he was done, he smiled and cupped my shoulder.

"All better?" he asked, and I mirrored his expression.

I never broke, not even when I was climbing the stairs to bed and I could hear him setting the kitchen right again. I didn't complain to Cherish before we turned in. I only changed from my wet suit in the bathroom and stole a single glance at the spot.

I didn't let myself gasp at the way it looked like he'd skinned another layer, not added one. How I wouldn't have had to see it if we'd bandaged my arm with gauze.

Sneaking her grandmother's bracelet back into her bedside drawer was the last thing I did before joining Cherish in bed. I know I'm all but awake because as I lie alone, curled at the foot of the bed, surrounded by the shrill screams of a fire that has raged but kept a distance from me, I am remembering it all. As though this is waking, and that was a dream.

The pain has followed me here; I cannot escape it.

Rah!

I pull up from the bed with a start and search the flames.

"Che?"

RahRah!

"Cherish!" I'm up on my knees and the fire responds by stretching higher, as though wherever she is, it wants my Cherish hidden.

The fire screams, and it is beginning to sound like me.

RahRah, please! Wake up!

The light is sharp when it cuts through the inferno and the dream breaks. The bedroom explodes into view around me, and I am looking around wildly, aware only that I am burning.

"Mom!" Cherish is at the door, yelling out into the house, and then she's running back to my side, her eyes wild and worried.

I am still screaming.

I am still burning.

My arm is hideous. I cradle it but I don't dare touch it now. The rim of the wound is somehow both swollen and shriveled, and alarmingly black, as though there really was a fire. It feels tight and tearing. No matter how closely I study it, I cannot stop myself from believing there is something unseen chewing into and under my skin.

"Get it off!" I beg Cherish, and when I stumble out of the bed, the damp sheet tangled up in my legs, she runs to help me.

We make it into the bathroom and I turn the faucets on full blast. I don't know whether the water should be cold or hot; I don't know what will soothe the nightmare of this.

I'm emitting something like a panting growl, and Cherish involuntarily replies with a humming whine, her face a constant replay of tension and collapse, her eyes wide. She will never get a handle on the situation, never be clearheaded or cunning enough that I can fall apart.

Control. Control. Control.

I keep the arm stiff and angle it away from the rest of me, and from Cherish, lest she do something ridiculous and try to touch it. With the skin bubbling black around the rim and the rest of the wound swirling red and orange like magma, I can see the layer Jerry Whitman applied, like cellophane on top of it all.

"I have to get it off," I say through the low rumble still escaping me, snatching a towel from the ring hanging closest to me. I wet it and first press it against the area to saturate the liquid bandage before trying to scrub it from my flesh. Immediately, I crumple forward and howl with regret.

"RahRah!"

I cast the towel at Cherish, who grips it tightly enough to wring the excess water out of it and onto the bathroom floor while she rocks from one foot to the other, too confused and afraid to successfully cry.

"Cherish? Farrah?"

Brianne is in our bedroom now, and Cherish, who was already horror-struck but at the sound of her mother's voice turns frantic, rushes out as though the woman will need a guide.

"Something's wrong with her arm," she's crying when they appear. "She was crying in her sleep, she wouldn't wake up—"

"Farrah, let me see," Brianne tells me, but at the sight of the ugliness she recoils.

It's only wet because of my attempt, but at first glance it must look like my forearm has exploded in a mess of tar and rainbow sherbet puss.

"I have to get the skin off," I say, using a shaking, hesitant fingernail to test the cellophane surface for the smallest breaks that I can use to peel the stuff away.

"Farrah," Brianne protests, because she doesn't know I only mean the liquid skin her husband applied.

"Is it supposed to do this?" I ask her, and when she has the same wild, worried expression as her daughter, I turn to Cherish. "How does liquid skin usually work?" I demand. "How do you get it off?!"

She's shaking her head and now her mouth gapes.

"Cherish!"

She jumps, and the tears come.

"Jerry!" Brianne cries, turning to run from the bathroom. She's no more help than her ridiculous daughter.

No.

Control.

Somehow, control.

They're all going to descend on the bathroom again to nurse me back to health.

But this time is different. I can't wait that long. This pain is searing, stinging, burning. I could tear my own skin away, if that would stop what looks like a bacteria spreading, like necrosis devouring my arm. It can only be the middle of the night; it's already widened the wound at an alarming speed.

"Cherish!" I grip her arms and sink my fingers in. Deep. I

try to pierce her flesh, to ground my pain like it's electricity and I can channel it through my friend to purge it from myself.

Control, I tell myself. But I can't.

"How do you usually get it off? How do you take off liquid skin?"

She can't focus when she's in pain. Just like at the renovation site, her brain shuts down. She's a wounded animal whose only recourse is to bleat until a savior comes along and rescues her.

I sink my fingers deeper. I dig into her nightshirt, pretend her flesh is something inanimate, like there will be no consequence to gripping until my fingers and thumb meet in the middle, where her bones must be. Like there are no nerves in the unfeeling thing I am boring into.

Onetwothreefourfive.

"Please, Cherish," I beg, and push my forehead into hers while she struggles to loose herself from me.

One. Two. Three. Four. Five.

"Cherish." I am kneading my head into hers, until it's like there's nothing soft between us. We are bone against bone.

She screams, but she can't get free.

I know what she's trying to say but she can only mouth it. Her words can't get around the sobs.

"It's hurting *me*," I tell her. "Please! How do you take it off?"

Cherish shakes her head, and I shake the rest of her.

"How do you take it off?"

"RahRah, I don't know," she cries. I try another approach, let my fingertips ease up ever so slightly. She knows the instant

I give her relief and she tries to wrestle out of my grasp again, this time gritting her teeth when I resist and punching my forearms—despite my wound. "I don't know!"

I release her and pull my arm back where I can protect it.

"I don't know what you're talking about. I don't know what liquid skin is!" Cherish crosses her arms over her chest, hands splayed to cover the damage my fingers have done to her arms. She looks like someone being laid to rest, except for the confusion and anger on her face. "I thought you were still dreaming!"

One two three four fiiiive.

"You're lying." I stumble back a step. "I know you're lying."

"Rah! I don't know!"

I shove past her, sending her hard against the counter on my way out of the bathroom.

She calls after me, but it isn't to confess. She's pretending she's the one being hurt. She's pretending she doesn't know I know. That I didn't see her tally marks. That she isn't the one keeping track.

I have to find Brianne and Jerry. I have to get this off, make it stop.

The bedroom door is open, like Cherish's mom threw it wide in her harried haste, like it might seal and lock behind her otherwise—but I hear her.

I stop. The top half of me sways forward when the motion comes to an abrupt halt, as though I might topple head over feet.

They're close—but they aren't coming.

Their voices have made it up the stairs, but I'm alone in the bedroom, listening to them from just behind the open door.

I know the timbre of a hurried conversation. A hastily delivered summary so that Jerry knows what's going on, when there isn't a moment to waste.

This isn't that.

I can hear their voices but not their words. There's too much blood surging through my ears, my own pulse drowning out everything else I should be able to hear.

Control.

"Control."

I've never had to whisper it aloud before. I've never had to close my eyes—but this is like nothing I've felt. This pain feels unnatural. In my arm, in my head, in whatever part of me makes sense of everything but can't. My hands are at my head, like I need pressure applied there, like I'm bleeding even though no one can see. Or like if I can make blinders for myself, if I can focus, I can regain control. Because it feels unrelenting. All of it. Like it's been building to this for weeks. Every strange thing compounding the previous, escalating steadily. The vomiting episode after dinner with my parents. Cherish's combative behavior. The tally marks. It's warped me until I actually believe the Cherish who needs me to know she's alive is trying to hurt me. Worse. That she wants me scarred, that being sick wasn't enough.

Control.

That is the one thing that cannot be true. That isn't.

"Did she wake Cherish?"

That's Jerry.

"She was screaming in her sleep." Brianne has regained her composure, the way she always does. She's relaying the details to her husband, and not for the first time. She's told him this before, and now she's adding emphasis to her telling, so that he understands the severity of the situation.

But they still aren't coming.

"Cherish is scared," Brianne says, and between her even tone and the contemplative quiet that follows it, it is being factored into whatever is delaying them.

I close my eyes to keep quiet. A throbbing that began in my forearm has traveled through my veins and is against my right temple, threatening to drown out all other senses. But I have to wait. I have to hear what they say next.

In the bathroom, Cherish is crying. It isn't feral or dramatic now that she's alone. It's perfect the way she says my name once, as though I'm still there with her, so that when her parents return, they'll expect to find us huddled together on the bathroom floor.

"Cherish being scared isn't the worst thing," Jerry tells his wife in a way that makes me think she took the next step and he reached for her, asked her without words to reconsider. "Sweetheart." Her hair must be what muffles his words. "What's the point if she never sees what she's done?"

Control.

Cherish did this.

Control.

What she's done.

"Control," I whisper.

Cherish has done something, and even her parents know.

"One two three four five."

This can't happen again.

"One two three four five."

But I shake my head and take a step back. Because I was sick the same night Kelly fought Tariq for Cherish. I got sick the same night Cherish didn't get what she wants.

Her parents made her take care of me. They made a girl of whom they require nothing but existence undress me and wash my hair. A girl who had no idea where her own spare toothbrushes were kept. Because, Brianne had told her, this couldn't happen again.

But it obviously has. Whatever liquid skin is meant to do, it isn't this. Whyever it burned when Jerry said it wouldn't, Cherish has something to do with it. She wouldn't go swimming with me—but that doesn't mean she didn't watch. It doesn't mean she wasn't close by when I scraped my arm. She would've known what would happen next. She had plenty of time. While her father squatted down next to me and studied my arm, while we talked about the bracelet . . .

She noticed.

If Jerry noticed it on my arm throughout the day, there's no reason Cherish couldn't have. But she left it for me. She took the tally journal from the drawer but left the bracelet—and then punished me for taking it?

"No." I shake my head, squeeze my eyes shut to quiet the distracting pain, groan against the way it stabs and then courses from my arm throughout my body in a tidal wave. "She wouldn't do that."

However reverent Jerry Whitman is over his mother's belongings, Cherish wouldn't hurt me over something she doesn't even want.

Tariq.

I remember the way she dropped her phone when I startled her in the garden, and I know. I know what she's punishing me for. I know what she wanted today, what she thinks I'll take from her again. I know why she's upset every time she hurts me.

She hasn't left the bathroom, not even to see if I've found her parents and gotten help. When I come back inside, she's sitting with her back against the wall, her feet planted on the bathroom floor, her knees in front of her. She looks like she's hiding underneath the sink, her temple resting against the exposed bowl of the basin. She looks up at me sullenly but doesn't say a word. So I do.

"One two three four five."

Cherish's brow crimps briefly, and then it flattens and she's just looking at me again.

"One. Two. Three. Four. Five."

"One two three four five," she parrots back to me as though to appease me, her eyes darting away from me and then back. "RahRah—"

"One two three four five," I say, and I bring my hideous forearm in front of my body where I know she has no choice but to look at it.

"I heard you." Cherish sighs—and then she screams.

The hardened magma-colored monstrosity protrudes where Jerry Whitman accidentally cut the skinned flesh, allowing whatever Cherish added to the small container of liquid skin to slip inside of me and erupt back out in a small volcano of shiny red crystals. A moment before Cherish screamed, I pinched the protrusion between two fingernails and tore.

I feel it separate in a flash. It almost doesn't hurt. The small volcano and its crystals snatch some of the cellophane away with it, and after the pain, there's the slightest relief.

Cherish is gaping at me, incredulous. Like she can't believe what I've done. Like what she's done to me makes sense, but not my getting free of it. She doesn't care that the cellophane layer was cinched too tight, that it was pulling my skin so taut that it was buckling, blackening. That if it isn't the liquid skin, then it's however she tampered with it—or with me after the fact.

"One two three four five," I tell her, and then I hook my fingernail into the opening I've made and rip again.

I don't flinch. I don't close my eyes or break my gaze. I watch Cherish watch me as I undo it.

"One two three four five."

I dry heave, the third time. It's a reflex that doesn't seem connected to the tearing I've done, but my guts clench anyway. Something warm and thick rushes down and around the curve of my arm. I know when it drips and hits the bathroom floor because I feel droplets land on my bare feet.

"Mom!" Cherish is screaming, her hands flat against the floor, her fingers splayed as though we're in the grade school yard and I'll outline them in chalk.

I want it off me—for both of us. She's scared, like Brianne said. That's why I'm not angry. She's scared at what she's done, and it means Cherish doesn't have the stomach for this, even if she's the reason it's happening. It isn't a decision she made because she'd measured out the impact and the likely reactions and decided it was worthwhile. That isn't how Cherish works. It isn't the way she's equipped.

I don't know why she's the one I always forgive. I don't know why she's the one I love even when I hate her. It's involuntary like the multiple attempts my body makes to vomit while I tear away the skin without looking.

I don't know how to explain that it's the void in her, the way that even when she plots against me and succeeds, I know she isn't built for this. She can't be. She didn't know that *this* was going to happen—not this, specifically. That's why I'm willing to undo it.

"Onetwothreefourfive."

I am tearing away the pain she caused me, but the damage is done and she needs to see. It adhered too well to me. Tearing it away is taking strips of me with it. I can feel it even though I won't look away from Cherish. My feet catch splatter, but I only know for certain that it's blood when she finally scuttles from beneath the sink and tries to stop me.

It matters that she comes. When she's sloppily hurrying from her hiding place, her eyes jumping between my forearm and my face, I almost stop. I almost buckle at the sight of her wide eyes and contorted mouth, even though I'm not listening to whatever she's pleading. It may be the first time Cherish has knowingly come toward something that frightens her, and I know that I am good for her.

She tries to get a grip on me, but her hand slips instead and I am still free to tear the skin. Both her arms windmill around trying to secure one of mine, and the palms of her hands are smeared with my blood. When she can't get a hold on it, Cherish does what is unthinkable for her; she grabs my wounded arm instead.

"One two three four five," I say, but I think this time it's just a whisper. I'm sick to my stomach though I've seen very little of the carnage. I feel light-headed, but not much else, and it's as though my body has finally decided to put a cap on the amount of pain I am allowed to feel in one day. "One two three four five."

It isn't a timid hold, as though she wants to avoid touching what she did not want to see. Cherish's grasp of me is getting tighter, and even though it's hot the way the inferno felt, the pressure is such a relief. It's interrupting the now blinding pain the way a tourniquet interrupts the bleeding.

Face-to-face, she sees the way the focus is leaving my eyes. They are threatening to close, but I don't want this moment to end. Not the hold she has on my forearm that's dulling the pain, and not the hand she moves to slip around the back of me when she realizes I'm going to faint.

I let my knees buckle a little.

Control.

"I've got you, RahRah."

"I know."

The bathtub is cold behind my head, just like the floor should be beneath the rest of me—but I can't feel it. In a moment I don't think I'll feel anything at all.

"I've got you."

Cherish isn't screaming for her parents anymore. She's here with me. She's using a blood-slick hand to hold the curve of my cheek, and when I can't keep from smiling, she hiccups a fatigued sob.

"What's wrong with you, RahRah?" She's cross-legged beside

me, and she leans all the way over so she can lay her forehead against mine.

I smile again, close my eyes, and press back against her so she doesn't go away. I'm not angry when I remind her that I know who started this.

"One two three four five."

XIV

We're quiet when Jerry and Brianne find us. They don't try to whisk Cherish protectively away, no one chastises her, but neither reacts to the ruin of my arm as though it's my fault, either. It's a comforting calm, the way they orbit us. If this were Nichole Turner's house, she would have barged in and required control. She would have dissected the scene, rotating its parts until she'd deduced who had done what, and what was required of each of us now. She would have stood above us, looking down, locking eyes with just me until she didn't have to say that I was the reason things had gone wrong. But the Whitmans don't do any of that. They don't single me out, don't separate us or intrude. They only come down to where we're seated on the floor, offering guidance to Cherish as I slip further and further toward unconsciousness. They gently relocate us to the bed because regardless of what's happened or why, they are cognizant of our comfort. It matters.

"We'd better use gauze to bandage her this time," Jerry says, both he and Brianne careful to speak softly.

"And some antiseptic," his wife adds.

"I'll give you a hand," he says, and then: "Cherish, you keep an eye on Farrah."

She nods at her father as both her parents leave, and when she turns back to me, she looks surprised to find my eyes open. I let my lids slide a little lower to put her at ease, and remove some of the focus from my gaze.

"You have to keep an eye on me," I tease her, but I don't have to exaggerate the amount of effort it takes to push the words out. We're on the bed, still untouched by the fire that I'm beginning to hear whinny from the other side of my mind. There's a crackling sound, dim but approaching, and I squeeze Cherish's hand to keep the dream at bay for a moment. I push my shoulders back into the headboard we're leaning against and lay my head against hers. "Che . . ."

She hasn't said anything directly to me since the bathroom. Her reflection watched me through the mirror while her mother took her to the sink to wash my blood off her hands and her father draped a quickly ruined hand towel around my arm, telling me to hold it vertically against my body while we moved to the bed.

"Say something, Che," I whisper to her now, and even though she nuzzles me back, she won't speak.

It's for the best. I don't know how much longer I can stay awake, and there are things I have to tell her while it's still just her and me.

"Then just listen. I don't want Tariq," I say, and I feel her

tense beside me. "I don't need him, I swear. If it's a choice between you and him, you should have known that you can have
him. I would have given him to you, if you'd asked."

She's holding her breath, and if the adrenaline weren't leaving my body and stripping every ounce of energy along with it,
I'd twist both our necks so that I could see her face.

"I want you to know that, Cherish. I'd give you anything.
You never had to take it from me."

I can feel her stiffening next to me, and I speak more quickly,
while I know she still has no choice but to listen.

"You can't. You can't take something out of my hand. And
you could never hurt me as badly as I can hurt myself. Okay?"

Silence—but it's stiff, like Cherish. It's stuck, suspended in
the space between us. Like this moment had to happen and she
couldn't move even if she wanted to.

"I know you understand that now, Che. I'm only telling you
so you don't ever try again. No more tally marks. No more journal. Okay?"

It's work to turn my head; I have to push against Cherish's to
do it, and instead of holding steady to support me, she wavers. I
want to see her face, but I don't make it that far. Instead I see
her chin, pointed straight ahead, as though she can see the fire
that's come back to wreath the bed. I'm looking at her neck. It
only takes a moment to find her heartbeat, her pulse jumping
beneath her skin like it wanted my attention. Like it will always
answer, even when she won't. Like it's reminding me that she is
real, the way she didn't know she was until I smiled at her.

I want to say the words again because I know she doesn't
always grasp things on the first pass—but I must be careful not

to frighten her. I have to remember that despite anything she's done, Cherish is WGS. She's demanding, not diabolical. Petulant, not premeditated. And afterward, she will always be preoccupied with the way *she* feels. She'll always be most concerned with herself, and she'll never be self-aware enough to know it. Antagonist or not, she'll never even comprehend that she could be, and there's nothing she could've done to avoid this fate. As a child of the Whitmans—because they have the means to fashion a bubble in which it's true even for a child who looks like Cherish—the world revolves around her. How would she begin to frame or understand events outside of how they impact her? How would she understand her*self*, except as being central? At the center? No matter what I say, it will always be impossible for her to understand that she might deserve a repercussion based on something she's done.

So no.

I can't tell her the truth more than once, and I can't require too much of her, because Cherish—my Cherish, with the void her parents ingrained in her—would not survive it.

"I don't want to change you," I tell the pulse jumping beneath Cherish's skin, leaping toward me because Cherish still hasn't turned to face me. "I love you just the way you are, Che. You have to love me that way, too."

Her parents are coming back now, and the edges of the room are going dark, black like the edges of my wound were, like the edges of a picture as it burns. I stop fighting the fatigue and slowly let my limbs go limp.

"Cher-bear, why don't you dress her arm?" Brianne coos to

her daughter when she's close enough to stroke Cherish's hair. "I think she'd feel better that way."

Cherish doesn't respond. It's a small and silent gift, but I receive it—the proof that she wasn't just refusing to speak to me.

"Come on, baby," Brianne coaxes her, and then I feel Cherish shifting next to me before what must be Jerry's strong arm is holding me between himself and the bedframe so that I don't slump while his daughter gets up.

My breathing is slow and steady while they rearrange themselves, but I'm still here. I'm somewhere between wake and sleep, with the Whitmans' voices echoing around me just like the fire does. They both lap the vaulted ceiling and tumble back down, both ebb away and then flow back to comfort me. This bed is my island in the midst of them, and while Jerry and Brianne bob not far away, Cherish returns to beach with me. The mattress dips when she settles on the opposite side and follows her mother's instructions on how to carefully clean and then cover my arm. I can't feel it anymore but Brianne doesn't know that, and she is adamant that Cherish take gentle care with me.

"Farrah needs you right now," Brianne tells her daughter in a way that accompanies a delicate touch. Her fingers are neatly adjusting Cherish's perfectly hydrated and separated coils; I know without opening my eyes. She knows how to admire them without disrupting the curl pattern, how to give the tactile expressions of love that she herself receives without hesitation or complication because her hair is thought unfussy. Standard. It is a testament to Brianne's open-eyed, full-hearted definition of love that it required learning to respectfully dote on her daughter's hair. To become accustomed to the product and the texture so that Cherish was accustomed to the same tenderness Brianne had always known—and without being made to feel self-conscious. "It's so important that you're here for her, Cher-bear."

Cherish's hands continue to dress my wounded arm, her touch almost as delicate as her mother's voice—but she still doesn't speak.

"I know it can be hard to see people's struggles close up, baby," Brianne continues. "It can unsettle us, make us want to pull back or look away. But that's the thing we shouldn't ever do, sweetheart. No matter how hard it is to understand, we owe it to the people we love to witness those things we can't experience with them."

"There are things Farrah faces that you're never going to completely understand, Cherish." Jerry comes closer, and I know he lays his hand at the back of her neck, applying a bit of reassuring pressure, massaging her skin while she tends to mine. "And it isn't just because you'll never lose this house. But that's part of it. You've got a stability that isn't as easy to gift to someone as we wish it were. This world has intentionally made it that way for families like Farrah's."

"That isn't it."

Brianne and Jerry are just as surprised by Cherish's interjection as I am.

Her voice is low, but it isn't weak. It rumbles instead of wavering, and the register is so uncharacteristic of the Cherish we know that for a moment everyone else is quiet.

All I hear is the rustle of the bandage against my arm and Cherish's fingers. The dull tear of first-aid tape.

"Cher-bear?" Jerry says her name like it's a question. "What isn't it? Talk to us, sweetheart."

They're standing side by side now, beside the bed. I know it. Their knees are slightly bent so that they're eye level with their daughter, or they're squatted down the way Jerry was beside me by the pool. She isn't facing them yet. I feel both her hands on my bandaged arm, as though perhaps she's saying a silent prayer to conclude the ordeal. When she turns to her expectant parents, it's with my arm held in her lap.

"None of this is happening because Farrah's having a hard time."

There are spaces between her words, but Cherish isn't hesitating. They think she is because they aren't accustomed to the way she speaks when she thinks whatever she's about to say is a lost cause.

"It's not because Farrah's Black and that's hard—I mean it is hard but . . . that isn't what's going on. That isn't why this keeps happening."

Now their brows are cursive, but they wait a moment more. Maybe Brianne glances briefly toward her husband because he has a way with Cherish, a special bond they've always had. He's the one it came easy to. He's the one who rewrote the world as soon as he saw Cherish's face, without needing time to adjust. He put up no resistance, unconsciously or otherwise, because like his wife, he thought he knew from personal experience what oppression meant. There was nothing he had to put aside in himself to protect Cherish the way Brianne did. He gladly made everything a lie for her to be true. If Brianne does glance at him, it's why I hear Jerry's voice next.

"I don't think we can ever responsibly discount Blackness in someone's experience or treatment," he begins, and then even with my eyes closed I can see him raising his hands against his daughter's inevitable irritation.

"Dad," she says through a whine that sounds much more like Cherish than the low rumble from before.

"But I know you know that. So I want to know what *you* mean."

Now she loses her nerve. She's playing with my hand absently at first, and then she becomes attentive. She wraps all her fingers around one of mine, her thumb softly caressing the back of my hand.

Control.

I let my index finger tick, as though spasming, reacting to her touch from unconsciousness.

When she looks at me, she finds my eyes still closed, my face slack.

"Cher-bear?" Brianne presses, and the movement I sense is Jerry's hand quietly coming to lie against his wife's arm.

"It isn't what you guys think," Cherish says. She's stalling—or else she's reeling them in. She's waiting until they lean far enough to lose their balance, so that no matter what she tells them, they'll latch onto it. "This didn't happen because of anything that's happened to Farrah," she repeats. "This happened because something's *wrong* with Farrah."

The silence descends. The stillness, and suspended animation.

Jerry and Brianne Whitman were entirely unprepared for what their daughter just said.

Brianne is blinking quickly, as though batting something from her eyelashes, the way she's done on the very rare occasion when something in her auction presentation hitches. When there's a near catastrophe of an antiquity placed improperly and then stabilized mere moments before teetering to its end. She'll sweep her thin hand across her hairline, intentionally loosing and displacing a blond strand in a distraction that simultaneously reminds the in-house audience that her imperfections are charmingly slight.

"Farrah was in a lot of pain," Jerry answers for them both, but gently, as though only just now realizing how awful the ordeal must have been to make his daughter feel this way. "She must have had a bad reaction to the medicine I gave her, or it was expired and I wasn't paying close enough attention. I know that was frightening, but imagine how badly it must have hurt."

"She tore her own skin, Dad."

"I understand that, Cherish. I'm just telling you it's not that extraordinary when the human body experiences overwhelming pain, to want to get rid of what's hurting us."

"It's not just this," she insists—but she's holding my hand. They can see our fingers are entwined, and only one of us has the presence of mind to be responsible for it. "It's . . . everything. She wouldn't let go of me!"

"Cherish, she was out of her mind in pain, honey." Jerry is just as insistent. "I know you know that. She's your best friend in the world. Isn't she?"

Her eyes must snap to meet his.

"Of course she is, Dad."

"I know she is. And I know this has been hard for you, too. But like your mom said, this is what it is to be close to people. We have to be close enough to hurt when they hurt. The way she was for you in fourth grade. Right?"

Cherish deflates around the hand she's holding in her lap. I feel her shoulders sink, her eyelids falling partway to match.

As though she ever really wanted them to believe her. As though she would've forgiven them if they had.

As though she would've known how to make them, even if she wanted to.

This was a tantrum. I know that because she's still my Cherish. I'm the one unconscious—the one who supposedly scares her sometimes—but her hand is closed around my index finger because she can't help grasping me. Even while she flails for her parents' attention, tries her hand at the kind of manipulation I employed on her father mere hours ago, she keeps hold of me. Her need of me is observable, and it both gives her away and saves her.

She didn't tell them about the baptisms. She didn't mention the only thing that might have actually troubled them—the only thing that predates the Turner family breakdown. Even now, while her father reminds her of the myth of us, when she doesn't know that I can hear her, she doesn't revisit the night at the security office when they came to pick us up to tell them that the guard was telling the truth. That's how I know she doesn't mean it.

This isn't a betrayal; she's acting out. Just like Jerry told her, she's tired. Standing beside me, feeling the impact of all the waves that are only actually crashing into me, is taking its toll—and I should have considered that, too. I should have known how hard it would be for Cherish to see hardship, let alone experience it vicariously through the person she loves most in the world.

I should have taken better care of her.

I will.

Her parents are distracted by their concern for me, understandably preoccupied with teaching Cherish to make room for the only person they'd ever expect her to compromise for—a sibling. Another Whitman child.

I'm the only one who can make things right, because I'm the one Cherish has been hurting. I'm the outlet for all her frustration, for the impotent entitlement she experiences because the world has been promised to her since the moment she knew the world exists. I'm the one who has suffered because of the so-called affluenza Jerry and Brianne have bred, and the void they can't see—so I'm the only person who can offer Cherish absolution.

Control.

I will forgive Cherish all her faults.

Control.

I will stay here with her. I won't change my mind. I won't hurt her back.

I love Cherish with eyes wide open, the way my mother seems to think I can't. The way Kelly implied I wouldn't, if I understood everything she's done.

Of the two of them—Nichole Turner and Kelly—he's the one I can tell. He's the one in front of whom I can afford to unfurl enough to enjoy the telling. He will be my outlet, one more time.

CHERISH TAKES FOREVER to fall asleep, once her parents leave us. They place pain medicine at my bedside in case I wake again, and they promise her things will look better in the morning, sealing it with a kiss on both our foreheads after tucking her in.

Control.

I'll be too impatient if I focus on Cherish, so I cull myself out of semiconsciousness again. I focus on the fire I can still hear, and smell, and see, and I wait for it to recede. Awake, and attentive to it now, I understand that this blaze—the one that's been overlaying the bedroom like a transparency, like a mask affixed to an image so that it can be altered without changing— is not a collection of smaller flames. An inferno is not a congregation of lesser fires; it is another entity altogether.

Its roar is not a series of crackles and snaps escalated by sheer addition; it is a thunderous bellow all its own. It is threatening because it is singular in purpose. When it reaches, some tendrils scorching one way while some snatch another, it isn't because its mind is divided.

At the foot of the bed, dark flames like shadow flicker and wave, but I know it's fading. In a moment I won't be able to see it at all—but that won't mean that it's really gone. I can always call it back, like Kelly on the lawn outside the gazebo.

I reach for Cherish, while the shadow flames are still just visible. I lay my hand against her back, and a sound escapes her,

like I've released her breath with my touch. Like she was waiting for it, and now she'll rest. She didn't see the fire encircling
the bed. She doesn't know that it filled this room, consumed
the window dressings and the furniture and the walls—so I
tell her.

"Everything can burn but us."

She answers with a soft murmur, and I roll toward her, leaving the fire to fade completely. I lay my head between her shoulder blades and breathe deep before the warm aroma is gone
with the color of the flames.

"I forgive you."

I take her phone from her bedside table and text Kelly, so
that I can tell him, too.

Gazebo. Soon.

I don't expect to surprise him a second time. Cherish really
hasn't been in contact with her ex-boyfriend—I know because
the last message is still the one that was there before I texted
him last. If he's got any sense at all, he'll know it's me.

I know he does when he sees the message but doesn't
respond.

Control.

He'll come.

I put Cherish's phone back and pull on clothes, careful with
the lightweight sweatshirt so that it doesn't rustle too loudly
against my bandaged arm. I don't want to wake Cherish after
the night she's had. It's why I don't touch her face or hair when
I'm back at her bedside, standing over her. I keep a watch, but I
don't reach for her, and I don't speak. I don't remind her what
I've decided—that I forgive her, that I'll take better care of

her—I just stare at the way the moon from the large windows across from our bed bathes her in light.

I want to count out tallies on her skin, or tear a wound into her forearm the way I buried an upturned nail in my foot—only so we'll be the same.

Control.

I don't let myself trace where it would be. I don't let myself count aloud the numbers we won't need anymore. I only pass the time it'll take for Kelly to get to the Whitmans' property by keeping a silent vigil over my Cherish, and not hurting her the way she's hurt me.

Eventually I creep out of the bedroom, down the staircase, make my way to and through the kitchen, then out the door.

The air is still outside, and it's thicker than it was inside the house. It's closer than it was when I was swimming, which seems like it was forever ago. Everything feels different, not just the stagnant atmosphere that will only be broken by thunder and lightning—a violent release of tension so that things can go back to the way they were. The pool looks different, and the garden as I pass it. All the grounds are familiar and completely changed, as though yesterday the world split from the cellophane layer I did not know it wore.

It's the Nichole Turner effect. I feel her as I walk the rolling lawn, see outlines of her through the corner of my eye as I make my way to the gazebo.

Control.

I can't unsee her here, despite the things I've discovered and decided. I can't deny the way this place has changed since she and my dad left yesterday afternoon, or the way she would no doubt suggest that it's my fault. That I am to blame for the way it feels as though a veneer has been snatched away. That I tore it away like a volcano of shiny red crystals erupting from a wound.

Nichole Turner has seized my attention, and it almost costs me an advantage.

He's doing a good job shielding his body with the gazebo post. He's clearly done this before. But when he flicks his chin to the side to move his dreads from his eyes, even the shadow can't conceal that it's Tariq waiting up ahead and not Kelly.

I sent for Kelly, and Tariq Campbell came instead.

I only have a few moments to figure out what that means, so I slow my steps. I tuck my chin close to my chest, pull myself toward center, so that I can think. I banish Nichole Turner from my mind and shuffle through scenarios and probabilities.

Tariq with Jerry Whitman, showing off his bruised hand.

With me, in the kitchen, showing genuine concern. Leaning close a moment later and asking if we could steal a moment away.

Tariq smiling and exposing his best friend's grill.

Kelly on the grass outside the gazebo when I pulled his shirt up to find a gruesome bull's-eye.

Why is Tariq here?

"Hey, babe," he says when I am close enough to hear. He's still behind the post, casually leaning against it with one shoulder, one leg tossed in front of the other. He isn't even facing the lawn; he's looking out toward the golf course. There's something about his voice, even though he called me babe. The same smugness that oozed out of him while he and Cherish's dad talked in front of the grill. There's something chastising in it, whether he means to lace the pet name with it or not. This will be a playful confrontation—I just don't know why.

"I'm surprised at you," he continues, reaching up to absently fiddle with his dreaded fringe before shoving off the pillar with his shoulder. For a moment, the movement puts him deeper in the gazebo's shadow. "Trying to see our boy again when you know that's against the rules. What'll Mother think? How am *I* supposed to feel?"

And then his breath hitches. The laugh lines around his mouth ripple and then evaporate.

It's all I need.

I didn't expect it to be Tariq, and Tariq did not expect it to be me.

"I'm kidding, Fair," he says, tries to recover by forcing a chuckle and sliding both hands into his pockets like I can't see them balling up there. "I know you and Kelly don't rock like that. Did Cherish lose her nerve?"

He's come out of the gazebo and sauntered toward me, touching his hair again like he doesn't mean to, and twice clenching his jaw while it's strategically angled so that I see the way it hardens.

He thinks he's seducing me. He thinks that I am an ordinary teenage girl, or any lovestruck teenager period. That I haven't heard the words he's said—or else that he can keep me from processing them by invoking a crush he has no way of knowing I have revoked.

"Are we not cool anymore?" he asks, and when he's standing

right in front of me, his dark eyes glistening with the light of the moon, he touches my hair.

I told Cherish she was bad at this—but Tariq is remarkably worse. He's reckless while he tries to reclaim the mask he clearly wore with me. He's forgotten the tension he cultivated between us with protracted nervous hesitation. The way that even an embrace seemed forward. He's aggressive now, by comparison, touching me to force a swoon that won't come.

"We must not be," I say, letting my gaze untether from his to wander his face, his eyes trying to follow. "You came here in the middle of the night to find Cherish."

"Come on, Farrah," he says, lacing his voice with a masculine timbre before invoking a pleading tone that's meant to buckle my knees. He wants me to think he can't help it—that need to be believed by me. That it's seeped into his words rather than being attached to them intentionally.

Kelly laughs—I hear him as though he's still there, between our feet. When I glance down, I see him, faintly. I take a step back from Tariq to make room for his best friend, contorted on the grass, some of him swallowed in our shadows, and some of him alight. He's glowing, his face upturned—but not toward me. He isn't laughing at me now.

"You thought I'd be Cherish, and Kelly knew you had access to his phone." I look back up at Tariq. He hasn't recovered, and he won't. He wasn't ready for this, and Kelly knew he wouldn't be. "Like you had access to his grill. What else have you taken out of your best friend's mouth? Don't." I throw my hand up against his lips when he starts to speak. "Don't bother.

You don't have to say that you and Cherish were an accident, because I'm the one you care about. Or inevitable, because you've known each other so long. I don't care enough about you to warrant being lied to."

I can see when he gives up. The mask slides all the way off, and his brow straightens. He swipes his lips across my palm to get from behind my barrier, but his eyes never leave mine.

"I already know," I tell him. "And I choose Cherish. Like Kelly did."

Tariq barks, but it doesn't sound the way his friend's did. He isn't wounded. He isn't felled. He doesn't know he can be.

"Kelly had a choice," he says through a smirk, his lips curling the way Kelly's do. At first glance, it's a snarl, except that the warning isn't that he is preparing to devour. It's that he pities me. "That's the difference between my dad and the Whitmans. Kelly knew what he was choosing."

And then he pulls back. His neck winds in, and I can see by the way his eyes dart momentarily that he thinks he went too far.

I uncoil. Slow.

"What are the rules, Tariq? The ones Cherish was supposed to know."

His jaw is clenched again. It is handsome—now. It *is* revealing this time, because he didn't mean to do it.

There's a war behind his eyes. He's deciding where to go from here. He's weighing whatever options he thinks he has—a process made futile by the fact that he doesn't know how to account for me. He has no idea what I'll do. Kelly hasn't warned him, not about the likelihood of my being here in Cherish's place and not about what I did the last time.

He's going to choose poorly. He would've even if he knew better. Adopted by the judge, and given free rein in the Campbell court, Tariq is just like Cherish—except that he's worse. He thinks he's stronger. Whether because his father metes out judgment and there is an understanding therefore that it will never preside over him and his house, or by sheer possession of the appendage between Tariq's legs, when unmasked, it isn't naïveté beneath. It's something more malignant. Something that is both unaccustomed and resistant to being questioned. It looks out from behind Tariq's handsome eyes at my audacity, and when he flicks his hair from his eyes, he doesn't care whether or not the gesture still affects me.

"What happened to your arm?" he asks, and the words are so leaden that they tumble out of his mouth and thud against Kelly's bull's-eye.

I uncoil more, breathe in deep, though he can barely see the way my chest rises. Soon I will be entirely free.

"The same thing that happened to Kelly's side," I say with the same appearance of calm. Mine is genuine—until Tariq speaks again.

"So you do know," he says, and I shrug with one shoulder to confirm. He relaxes, and there's a sound like a lock successfully picked, a heavy thud and release that only I hear.

I will tremble with adrenaline if I stand too still, so I reach up and touch Tariq's hair the way he touched mine. I roll my head to one side while I look up at him. He knows it isn't him I'm inviting, but this forbidden thing we are finally speaking of candidly. The excitement it elicits deserves an outlet, though, and I part my lips and run my gaze across his until he smirks.

"Won't you be in trouble again?" he asks. "When they find out what you've done? What they'll think Cherish has done?" He takes my chin in his hand and tilts my head one way and then the other, as though testing that I'll allow it. "You'd barely recovered from being poisoned for Cherish inciting that little fight before you went and got whatever that is." He gestures at my arm with his chin. "And now texting Kelly from her phone? You're as bad as Kelly. A real glutton for punishment."

I bite my lip because he expects me to, my mind chewing over everything he says even though I can't seem impacted by it. I don an intentionally unconvincing innocent expression and Tariq grunts amusedly, his hand releasing my chin and sliding to my neck.

"Maybe it's all right, though," he considers, his own head tipping in the process, his eyes roaming from the skin beneath his hand to all the rest he can't see beneath my clothing. "If you tell them it was you. There isn't any harm in the whipping boy and whipping girl hooking up. Mm, I *like* you like this."

He thinks the final phrase is the confession. He barely stifles a groan before planting his lips on my neck, his free hand sliding around the back of me.

I am not here.

I am in the bedroom, and Brianne Whitman is beside me. She's taken the Mylar sleeve so that she can smell the book inside.

She's shivering with excitement while I study the gift.

The Whipping Boy.

It's not for reading . . .

Everyone should have something just to cherish.

Tariq's hands are moving around my waist, his lips parting and allowing his tongue to taste my flesh, but I feel none of it.

Brianne gave me the book. Not Cherish.

I am staring at the sky above the gazebo while I rock with the motion of Tariq caressing me. My hands are on his shoulders, splayed the way they would be if I were racked with satisfaction or arousal, too. Instead I am peering through a hole in the sky that only I can see.

"Cherish never wants to talk about it," I say, forcing myself to whine. "Kelly's so lucky you and your dad have been so open about it."

Tariq is at once smug about compliments and greedy. He devours my words and then can't help but bask.

"I get it, though. I mean, it's taken her this long to catch on, and I wasn't supposed to talk to her about it until she understood." His hands are tightening and releasing around my waist. "Respect her parents' decision," he says like he's repeating an instruction, his eyes rolling as he shakes his head. "But a whipping boy's punishment is only useful if the prince knows it's on his behalf. Or princess, in her case." And then he snorts.

I force myself to speak. I respond without releasing the rage igniting inside me.

"She always acts so confused," I say.

"My dad's right; they've made a complete mess of it. They're just lucky they chose you. You want what's best for Cherish." He looks into my eyes like this is romantic. Like I should be pleased at his acknowledgment, that it means I am worthy in his sight.

"Not like Kelly."

"Man," Tariq scoffs. "He just wanted to stay out of juvie.

He doesn't care about me." He wears a disgusted grimace, and the hand that massages my hip grows rougher. "He doesn't care how generous I am, how willing I've been to share what's mine. All I asked is that he handle my things respectfully, and he couldn't do it. He couldn't help pawing her right in front of me."

It's quiet except for the sound of Tariq roughly kneading my body. He's reliving the night of the fight, and I wait for him to speak again.

"And he had the nerve to hit me back. After everything I've given him. He knew the rules."

My side will look like Kelly's soon, the way Tariq is handling me.

"So he *was* the other guy," I say, leaving my tongue between my teeth teasingly. I could tell Tariq I've seen what he's done, that the bull's-eye he made on Kelly's body allowed me to do damage of my own, but I won't.

"Well," he says, smiling through a shrug. "Dad said it was time for boxing lessons, since Kelly wants to hit back."

"Who needs a punching bag when you've got a whipping boy," I say, and then I attach a smile to it.

"That's right, whipping girl," he whispers as he leans close enough for his hair to brush my forehead.

Now I know. I am the whipping girl. That's what someone thinks. That's what they have made of me.

What's the point if she never sees what she's done?

A whipping girl's abuse must be witnessed by the chosen child.

That's why. Why Cherish had to dress my wound. Why Cherish had to wash my hair. Why Cherish had to clean up my vomit.

We didn't do the kinds of things she and Kelly did . . .

I told Jerry that. That's why my wound at all.

Not because I offended his daughter. Because of what I told him his daughter had done.

I am Cherish's whipping girl. That's why they want me here. That's why they lied to my parents, why their help to my parents came too late.

I was willing to stay. When my parents left the state, when my dad began his new job—that better opportunity that happened to come from far away—I was going to bury my heels in the ground and stay with the Whitmans. I was going to choose the world that Jerry and Brianne made.

They only want one.

My fingers tighten, sink into Tariq's shoulders and back, because Kelly isn't on the ground between us anymore. He's standing behind Tariq.

He wasn't right because he understands Cherish and me. Kelly isn't smart or clever—or he wasn't before he set the trap for Tariq tonight. He has been privy to privileged information. He knows there is such a thing as a whipping boy.

Nichole Turner was right, too.

She knew I wasn't in control and she left me with them.

She left me with the Whitmans because she knows her daughter. She has warred with me long enough to know how this will end. She left me here so that I would end it.

She tried to warn Brianne, and then she warned me.

Brianne and Jerry Whitman were in control, all this time, not me.

The sky continues to tear above the gazebo, and from inside the dark, I hear the fire approach.

She should have told them that it would've been wiser to play this whipping-girl game with an opponent who is weakened by defeat. She could have told them that I wouldn't be.

She could've told them that I would be unleashed.

"It isn't fair," I say, eyes anchored on the inferno that will soon spill out over the sky, onto the version of the Whitmans' property that awaited me after yesterday's events.

"What?" Tariq asks against my neck, where his lips are still caressing, his tongue still sometimes gliding over me before his mouth closes around my skin. "What isn't fair, Fair?"

He's amused himself, but I don't have to play along. He's too distracted by his own pursuit.

"You and I." I draw my fingernails across his shoulder blades, elongate my neck so that there's more to taste. "We didn't even properly kiss. You were so chaste with me—even when Kelly and Cherish were doing whatever."

There's an unmistakable pause in his fondling, and then he starts to draw back.

If he looks suspicious of me, I'll press into sulking, lose interest in his touch because of my personal displeasure with what happened between our friends.

If he's anything else, I'll proceed.

His eyes reflect all the light they've trapped inside, and his hair interrupts his mischievous gaze.

"That *isn't* fair," he says. "I wish I'd known you better; I would've done everything to you."

"I don't need everything, now that you belong to Cherish," I tell him. "Just the kiss I'm owed."

He's doing me a favor. I can tell by the way his lids sink to the middle of his beautiful eyes before he lets his head droop toward me. He's leading with his forehead again, making me wait. Expecting that I am impatient for his lips to return to me. He's taking pleasure in teasing me, so I raise my chin, search his lips with my eyes. He turns his face slightly, so that his mouth is just out of reach, and I let my brow buckle.

Tariq Campbell is a monster. Whatever he was playing at during our stilted, tedious courtship, the game has changed. The fact that I'm a whipping girl has restored the power to which he is accustomed. This clandestine order his father partakes in is not a casual worldview. Tariq's metamorphosis is too startling for that. His previous performance is too impressive. He is a boy taught from a young age the necessity of it—of maintaining the mask. Of perfecting so mild and ordinary a character that no one would think it robust enough to hide anything beneath.

He is the one uncoiled before me. When his tongue glides across my lips before parting them for entry, it is because this is a safe place to reveal himself.

I am not a threat.

I am the Farrah who's lost my place. The Farrah sick with dysphoria, whose reality and world no longer look the same.

I am the Farrah who finally knows; I am Cherish Whitman's whipping girl.

This is my first kiss. The soft but sensual probing Tariq's tongue is performing in my mouth is the first of its kind, so I close my eyes.

It feels pink. Sickly sweet. Tame, given the way his hands were roaming and kneading before. As though he knows he is my first and part of the favor he is showing me is delicate restraint.

But this Tariq is a threat.

This Tariq wore a thick scab across his knuckles, and his best friend's grill inside his mouth. This Tariq convinced me in a way no one else did. I did not suspect him before the barbecue. Not once.

I did not expect that he wanted to come between Cherish and me.

When Tariq's kiss becomes more soft lips and electricity in the hollow of our cheeks, I let my tongue slip forward—and then retract it as though stung. As though I'm unaccustomed to being the aggressor, unfamiliar with how to show him that I want more.

My tongue is a baited hook, and he returns his to me, his hands slipping around my neck and down into the small of my back—and then lower. He's been invited, and he will unfurl his greed completely.

I test Tariq's tip with my teeth, just enough to take hold, my lips spreading into a grin as though to show him what I've done. He responds with an aroused grunt, amused.

I release him, and he barges back in. He swims past my row of teeth of his own volition, because I am not a threat.

I hold him with my lips this time, and Tariq leans in, one hand tightening with the back of my shirt inside. I slowly pull back, so that his tongue is incrementally exposed, and he presses back into my mouth.

His eyes are closed when I open mine.

I bite.

Hard, because this is not a test. I clamp my teeth and force the two rows toward each other as though what's between them is food.

Tariq's eyes are wild, bypassing shock and confusion to hurtle toward pain. He wants to get free, but trying will inevitably worsen this.

When he jerks, as though to tear a layer of cellophane away, I do not release. What he succeeds in freeing from my hold is forced to escape between my teeth. It is the bit that I exposed a moment ago, and nothing more. I know by the sounds he makes—the sounds that do not resemble any I have heard before, even from a monk seal or a fallen boy in this very spot—that it is an unpleasant experience. I taste that even what gets released is not entirely intact. Whatever the top layer of his tongue looked like before this kiss, it is painted on the back of my teeth. The glossy underside has nothing to shed and—if he can distinguish between the two sensations, if he has the presence of mind to contrast them—it must be the more sensitive of the two.

I still hold a good portion of Tariq's tongue between my teeth.

He's trying to say my name. He's pleading.

The saliva that runs from both sides of his mouth spills into mine, some cascading down his face. The light makes it easy to see, a thick fluid glazing us both.

The texture is unique. The deeper I bite, the tougher the

meat becomes—if it can be considered meat. Whatever it is, the tongue of many beasts is deemed appropriate for eating, though I've never had it. I don't know how it should taste, when properly prepared, but with it wriggling in my mouth, I imagine Tariq's tongue is something like a stale gumdrop. Inside, it will be smooth and sticky. I only have to slice through it.

Tariq is hurting himself. He is writhing and wagging his head in desperation, his hands on my shoulders because he doesn't know whether to hold me close or try to shove me away.

It's too late when he understands that I will not let all of him go. He has exhausted the range of agonized, openmouthed whimpers, wails, and cries. He has pleaded in garbled words, spit drowning out what my teeth don't render incoherent.

He can't see the fire in the sky behind him. He doesn't know when it explodes through and what were flames flow like lava down the night sky to remind me what I said to Cherish.

Everything can burn but us.

I cull everything I've uncoiled in my belly, all the power I've unleashed, and I sink it into Tariq.

The wetness isn't all saliva anymore, but it feels the same. Metal has swarmed the inside of my mouth before I reopen my eyes. Tariq is locked in my gaze when I complete my bite. My teeth rest together, my face and chest soaked—and there is something resting quietly inside my closed mouth.

Tariq collapses to the grass below me as soon as it's done. His hands are trembling over the lower half of his face, and he turns to look up at me, his dreaded fringe in his beautiful eyes. He's shaking his head as though he's incredulous—as though there's any use in it.

I want him to show me. I want to see the smooth cross section I have made of his tongue, though what bubbles out between his fingers is thick and red so that I know his whole mouth must be full.

He isn't thinking straight. He seems more confused by the second, so I open wide. I present my trophy on the tip of my tongue so that he understands. The sight of his dissected tissue is like an anchor. He abandons the hysterical sounds he's been making and meets my eyes. His sanity is short-lived. Even though I have remained calm—though I was willing to give him as much time as he needs to reconcile himself with what just transpired—he scuttles backward as though there's a ghost or a boogeyman standing in my place. He manages to fall back against his shoulders before tumbling backward like a barrel being rolled.

I watch him escape, one hand always at his mouth so that there's only one free to push himself up when he loses balance for some reason and the toes of his shoes make drags and divots in the lawn and on the golf course when he gets that far.

When he's a wounded silhouette stumbling along because he can't remember the way he came, I don't know why he calls back over his shoulder, or what—until I turn back toward the Whitmans' house.

"RahRah," is all Cherish can manage, and she watches me take Tariq's tongue out of my mouth.

XV

S he didn't know.

She doesn't believe.

She has only ever seen the monster in me.

"Where did you get this?" she asks when I show her the book.

The Whipping Boy.

"Cherish, it's an antique." It's all I say before her face collapses into tears.

"What does it mean?"

"It means you are too precious to harm, so you let them hurt me instead."

"I don't know what Tariq means, I don't know what Judge Campbell's done, but you know them. You know who my parents are—"

"And I know you keep a log of all the times you've ever hurt me, Cherish. One two three four five."

We're standing on my side of the bed. Tariq's blood is still painted across the lower half of my face, and the book is in Cherish's hands. She drops to the mattress, and her head and shoulders fall as though she is a star collapsing into itself.

"RahRah," she says, and my name sounds like despair. "The tallies are all the times *you* hurt *me*."

Nichole Turner is here. I feel her eyes burrow into the back of me and know that if I turn right now, I'll find her there. She is flickering in and out of the bedroom, as though she is the flame, returned.

I can protect you from one . . .

Whatever I ask Cherish, my mother will hear.

I don't speak. I don't ask my best friend when I have hurt her. I don't ask her whether she has erased a tally for every time I could have hurt her but didn't. I don't ask whether this is all a lie, whether she is as proficient at deception as Tariq was trained to be.

You can't see anything but the story you're telling.

Nichole Turner's voice is always in my head—and then my mother speaks audibly. From behind me, she says what she has always meant. I hear her in stereo, and I know that Cherish can't help but hear her, too.

"Farrah, you are not in control."

I don't reply. I've already admitted it. That I've been too close to the Whitmans; that believing I was in control kept me from suspecting them no matter how many times they hurt me. But Nichole Turner won't let it go.

You can't see—

I slam my hands over my ears, except that they are in fists, and I am stunned. In front of me, Cherish vibrates and I close my eyes to give my vision a chance to restore. In the dark, I search for the fire that became lava that spilled out across the sky so that Nichole Turner can see what I control now that I am completely uncoiled.

This is not my failing; I could not have known the extent.

I didn't understand what they were doing to me—and it wasn't because it was a secret. I was not bested because I cannot see what isn't on the surface. It took my whole life overturning. They required me dysphoric, destabilized. They waited years.

"They're ahead of you," Nichole Turner tells me in front of Cherish, whose eyes I find watching me in bewilderment when I open mine. She doesn't see the lava pouring down the wall behind the headboard, she is so surprised to find my mother here.

"They aren't ahead. They don't even know what they've done," I tell Nichole Turner, my breath coming more quickly at the sight.

Their success at this is accidental.

Cherish had to love me the way only someone missing something crucial could.

They had to love Cherish enough to do all the right things, all without ever considering divesting from the world that endangered her. They didn't want to change the world, so they changed Cherish.

Jerry and Brianne Whitman had to build the void I've filled.

Cherish didn't know. She couldn't have. If Cherish isn't white girl spoiled, if she isn't naïve, if she doesn't have a hollow place carved into the entitlement and selfishness that are her birthright, then *I* am the imposter. Nothing I have ever said or known can be believed.

"I was trying to make it small," Cherish interrupts. "If it was just tally marks in a book, then maybe it wasn't as awful as it felt. I didn't want to think any more about it than that."

"He's going to make it home eventually," Nichole Turner tells me, speaking over my best friend.

"Do you think I'm a monster, Cherish?" I ask, ready with an ultimatum—except that no one is following a script anymore.

"Yes."

The lava scaling the wall behind the bed pauses—but only for a moment. I only have to alter my plan slightly.

"Then so are they."

A new wave of silent tears swells from her eyes and down her face, the way the lava resurges, thick and hot.

"But I can't be the one to convince you. I'm not the villain, Che. I won't let them make me into one. You have to prove it to yourself."

She won't know how. I am counting on it.

I kneel down in front of Cherish, take her hands, and then lay my head over them as though our knuckles don't jut into my cheek.

"Your mom will tell you," I say, and nod against our clasped hands. "She'll tell you the truth, if she thinks you're the one getting hurt by all this. They never wanted that."

"I am getting hurt," she tells me, and I lift my head from her lap to look Cherish in the eye.

"I know, Che."

I'VE RUN AWAY in the middle of the night. That's what Cherish tells Brianne Whitman when she goes into her parents' bedroom and only wakes her mother.

I am in the back of the car when Brianne and Cherish take off to find me at the only place my best friend can imagine I'd go.

"Did anything happen?" Brianne is asking her daughter. She's been woken up abruptly and hustled into the night before she could gather her thoughts or alert her husband, but now, as she buckles her seat belt and simultaneously backs out of the garage, her blond hair in a messy bun at the nape of her neck, Brianne only looks like an actress portraying frenzy.

"She left!" Cherish whines, and when she lurches away from her mother's consoling hand, it doesn't give us away. She's white girl spoiled, allowed to return annoyance and mild violence for doting affection. "I told you something was wrong!"

"Calm down, sweetheart." Brianne Whitman cannot accept her daughter's rejection for more than a moment, and she lays her hand on Cherish's leg to rub and then pat her brown skin. "She just went back to the house, I'm sure."

"What if she doesn't want to come back? What if she runs away for good, like Kelly did?"

It's a gambit, assuming information from very limited intel and then testing it. It wouldn't work for me, but Cherish is the one asking where Kelly has gone and why Tariq had access to his phone—despite the fact that I'm the one with something to give him. There's a trophy in the white box nestled inside the circle of Eloise Whitman's heirloom bracelet, and I have decided to gift it to Kelly. For exposing Tariq to me, or for at least placing Tariq like a sacrifice before me at the gazebo if he couldn't have known how well I'd excavate the truth. Kelly wouldn't have known what I can do if I hadn't sealed his judgment in the Campbell house the night I went to find Cherish. He couldn't have known if I hadn't brought him to his side on the lawn outside the gazebo. But he knew Tariq, and I didn't. I have more than repaid any debt I might have to Kelly, but I will give him the tip of something more when Brianne tells Cherish where he went.

I know Brianne will answer by the way she glances away from the road at her daughter and then can't help but glance again.

"What?" Cherish presses, a hint of concern in her voice. "What is it?"

"Kelly didn't run away, baby," Brianne tells her, and when the car slows to a quiet and creeping stop at the next sign, I know she is going to idle here. It is the wee hours, and there will be no cars pulling up behind us, forcing us to move. "Cherish. Kelly didn't run away, but—he isn't going to come back."

I am lying on the short carpet behind the back seat, compressing it further still and feeling the solid frame beneath it. The carpet is a thin veil meant to make the harsh metal structure look like something soft and welcoming, rather than the monstrosity it would be in its natural state. It takes so little to trick the eyes, but I am lying on the thin deception, and the cold, unmalleable frame is bleeding into me until I start to shiver.

"Kelly is going to prison," Brianne says, and I can hear the tears welling up in her blue eyes.

"Prison?"

Control.

I can't sit up; I can't tell my best friend to keep calm. That it's possible to resist hysterics no matter what you hear and no matter how unexpected. There's no way for me to communicate that we must keep control.

"Kelly isn't going to prison. Judge Campbell wouldn't allow it." Cherish says Leslie Campbell's title and name with ease, like there are many things she has refused or doesn't have the capacity to simultaneously process. She wants to know whether her parents are monsters, but without a personal incentive, she has left Tariq and his father as they were. As they are and have always been in her mind. She bucked away from her mother but speaks of him without malice, and I understand how so many of them escape repercussions. "Kelly's just a kid."

"I know that's how you see him, Cherish, but he's not like Tariq. Kelly's gone through so much, and it's hardened him. Leslie tried to save him, but he didn't want to be saved."

"What happened?"

"Kelly got arrested a few nights ago, with one of his younger brothers. It doesn't surprise me that the boys were smoking or using, but Leslie said they had enough on them to be charged with possession with intent to distribute."

I shiver almost to the point of vibration in the back of the car. I will make the whole vehicle rattle in a moment.

Control.

It isn't working. Justice is a blindfolded woman who looks

too much like Brianne Whitman for her lack of vision to matter, and when her scales are equal, they still tip.

I look up at the car's ceiling and am relieved to hear the fire on the other side. I can breathe more steadily when the roof begins melting, the metal buckling at the heat of the lava as it creates a gaping mouth and the red-orange liquid begins dripping around the edges. The night sky is above me now, and I fix my gaze on it while Brianne Whitman relays a lie.

"But he made a stupid mistake," she says, and she doesn't mean the possession that would never have landed Tariq Campbell in handcuffs. "He took a plea deal to send his brother home, when the boy would've ended up in juvenile court anyway. Leslie could've helped him, the way he helped Kelly. Now he's the sole defendant, and he's going to be sentenced as an adult."

Cherish isn't like me. She was there tonight, somewhere hidden behind Tariq and me, but she doesn't put it all together. She won't understand what Kelly has done until I tell her, and I don't know whether I'll try. There are things I couldn't know.

What did Tariq do to warrant the punishment that Kelly has defiantly worsened for himself?

How pure is this game the families play? How often is a punishment displaced correction for their beloved children, and how often is it meant to keep the whipping child in line?

I'm willing to bet that like the bull's-eye on Kelly's side, the Campbells' abuse isn't always Tariq's punishment. Kelly's ingratitude is reason enough to involve his younger brother in the fraudulent charges and replace him.

The sky shining above the hole I've melted in Brianne's car is a bruise, black and blue, with stars like the blood of burst capillaries stippling the surface, and distant gases clouding the edges with a molding green.

Control.

It's Cherish who needs me. It's Cherish I said I'd forgive and protect.

I'll bury Tariq's tongue, and Kelly with it. After tonight the thing that connects us, the likeness, will be destroyed. There will be no whipping girl the way Kelly ensured there is no more Campbell whipping boy—not from his bloodline.

When Cherish sobs in the front seat, her mother leaning over the center console to embrace her and moan sympathetically, there is nothing Brianne or Jerry Whitman would do to interject. Her tears are required.

They're the ones who did this right. Between Tariq and Cherish, only she suffers when the whipping children do. Only she loves me the way a beloved child must for the pain of the surrogate to matter. Whatever the Whitmans have done, they believe in it. They believe in Cherish's need of it—and at the baptism, we will make Brianne tell us why.

When we arrive at the home where my family used to live, Brianne doesn't pull into the drive even though the house is still unoccupied. While she parks alongside the island on which Cherish and I buried the last one's remains, I see that another white post has been staked into the lawn. Another transparent box holds pamphlets extolling the desirable qualities of what once was the Turner home.

Like the Whitman property after last night, after Nichole Turner came and together our conversation began the unveiling that Tariq completed, this place looks different. The sky above it has split, and it isn't the fact that the sun will soon rise. The color that is bleeding into the sky is the fire that began in my dream. The fire that will burn everything but Cherish and me.

I wait while she walks to the back of the car and opens the door for me.

"Farrah," Brianne says, but she isn't calling my name; she's identifying me. She is questioning my presence because while she expected to find me here, she did not know she'd brought me. "Cherish . . ."

The woman stays beside the car as though the effort it is taking her brain to make sense of this impedes her motor skills. Her brows cinch and spread and then repeat, her mouth slightly opening and then failing to close completely.

"Come on, Mom," Cherish tells her, as she and I cross the street and begin up my driveway. The command itself is enough to compound Brianne's confusion—that the confusion is hers alone, and the daughter who was so recently frightened and unaware in the car is not out of sorts.

We've gotten to the fence and I've reached over to unlatch it before Cherish and I turn again and find Brianne exactly where we left her.

"Come on," I say, and then I disappear into the backyard, leading Cherish by the hand behind me.

We have time to undress before we see Brianne again. She's moving elegantly, though she doesn't mean to. Her hands float around her body as though searching for some guide rope that will make this descent safer—which means that some part of her knows it isn't. If Cherish were at all intuitive, it would be as good as a confession, the way Brianne's chin tilts one way and then the other. She is as worried as if these surroundings are foreign and she can't know what she'll find, despite all the times she's laughed and lunched here.

"Cherish," she begins, still resembling a brilliantly trained stage actress, her movements and her voice filled with a perfect trepidation and concern. "You said Farrah ran away. What's going on?"

Cherish won't reply. The gate was the threshold. Now that we are by the pool, where the lights still shine, rippling through the water as though the light itself is enough to interrupt it, Brianne must supply the answers.

I extend my hand to Cherish and lead her into the pool. The water breaks to accept us, the way it always has, even though we ease in instead of jumping. The entry must be slow and silent. Brianne Whitman must have time to watch her daughter and me walk into the water, so that she recalls what the security guard said.

"Cherish, what's going on?" she asks again, and there is a storm approaching. I can feel it in the water that sways away before returning to slap my naked torso, and I can hear it in her voice.

Her cell phone rings.

"Cherish," she says again. She's trying to steady this scene, whatever it is about to become, by steadying her voice. She says her daughter's name like a gentle command.

"Don't answer that," I tell Brianne, standing shoulder to shoulder with Cherish in the water.

As though my words alert her to the sound at all, Brianne fishes out her phone and looks at it.

It's Leslie Campbell. Or Jerry Whitman, who's only woken up because he received the call from Leslie Campbell and is calling to find out where his family is—where I am.

"Don't answer it," I repeat, and when her eyes raise to find me over her screen: "You'll miss the ceremony. Be present with us; Cherish wants to share this with you."

Cherish has been watching her mother, too, but now she sinks into the water. She lowers herself in until her chest is submerged, and then lies back, her legs lifting back to the surface. When she is floating beside me, I easily pull her around so that Cherish's body is between her mother and me.

Brianne's eyes dance. From her daughter to me, to her daughter, to her phone.

"None of this should worry you," I tell her, and then I press her daughter underwater.

Brianne's mouth falls open as though to match the action.

"What's the matter?" I ask, and Brianne's head turns involuntarily from side to side.

"Farrah . . ."

"Watch what happens if I try to remove my hands." I lift them and Cherish grabs my wrists, forces me to stay attached, to continue the baptism.

A tear slips free and runs down the length of Brianne's face. She is so thin I think I can see her heart slamming against her breastbone; this will not take long.

"We've done this so many times before. You were warned," I say of the night Cherish and I came here last. "What could be different about tonight, that you have cause to worry what I might do to her, Brianne?"

"I don't know, Farrah." She sounds breathless. "I don't understand any of this. Why did you girls bring me here? What are you doing?"

"We're proving something to each other. That we trust. That we can be trusted. That we won't fight back. I can hold Cherish underwater as long as I like and she won't ever try to escape me."

Brianne sputters out a sob, her face collapsing at last, her hands rising to cover her mouth.

"But why should that worry you? It's the same for me. I don't resist Cherish. Even when I think she's hurting me. Even when I thought she made me the whipping girl."

"Please, Farrah."

Brianne Whitman is on her knees. I haven't felt Cherish tense once beneath my hands, the way she does when holding her breath first becomes an effort, and her mother is already at wit's end.

"I'm so sorry that we hurt you, Farrah, please."

There is no defense. No argument, no denial. It is over before I've begun—but I am already uncoiled. The sky is already severed. It bleeds red-orange; it spills lava across the treetops and the gables of homes nearby. It lights up the world so that everything outside the backyard fences glows. Brianne and Cherish and I are the only things left untouched, and this pool.

"She's my baby girl. Please don't hurt Cherish."

That is why this will work. It's why it has. The reason the Whitmans imparted Cherish with a gaping flaw is the reason she needs me, is the reason they chose me, is the reason Brianne would rush out of bed without her husband, is the reason she did not answer her phone, is the reason she is on her knees. Because she loves her child, wholeheartedly and without defense. There is nothing self-preserving in it, and it will be the death of her.

I pull Cherish out of the water.

She doesn't gasp or buckle forward dramatically to try to catch her breath. Her hands stay around my wrists, and we rest our foreheads together while she quietly recovers—though I open my eyes in time to see the way she watches her mother out of the corner of hers.

Cherish is mine. We are here, baptizing each other again, because it is true. We belong together, and she agrees.

"She has to tell you why." I speak softly to Cherish because she is so near.

"Cherish." Brianne is still crying softly. "Come here, sweetheart. Please."

"She won't come in after us unless you ask her to," I tell my best friend when I see the worry try to move from her mother to Cherish like an airborne contagion. "You have to make her watch, or you'll never know the truth. I am not the only monster, Che."

She nods against my forehead, her eyes returned to me.

Brianne Whitman's phone is ringing again.

"Cherish, it's Daddy. Come tell him everything's okay."

She's holding out the unanswered phone, dangling it in a desperate attempt to reclaim her daughter from me.

"Farrah hurt Tariq," Cherish tells her, and I am as stunned as her mother. We didn't agree to this. This is not part of the ceremony—telling her mother what happened outside the gazebo. But she keeps going, her hands still around my wrists. "That's what Dad's calling to say. He wants to know where you are, because he thinks she's going to hurt us, too."

"Cherish," her mother says pitifully, prostrated on the stone outside the pool as though demonstrating a misleadingly simple stretch that will become increasingly difficult and painful the longer it's held.

"But why would she?" Cherish asks as though there was no interruption. As though she is unmoved by her mother's emotion— except that she is clamping my wrists more tightly and I can feel the way she shivers. "Why would Farrah hurt us, Mommy?"

"Because she's your whipping girl," Brianne says, and then her forehead falls as though it might connect with the ground. It doesn't, and she nods instead. "Daddy and I hurt her so that nothing would ever hurt you."

The woman sits back against her heels now, her fair hair flying and falling in wisps, some catching against her wet eyelashes, some attracted to the corner of her mouth. She is every cinematic representation of beautiful despair. She is built to be lovely even as she falls apart.

"Let's call Daddy, Cherish," she suggests, her eyes wide as though she's stumbled upon an escape. "He'll tell you anything you want to know," she promises, like she hasn't put together that I already do.

"Did Jerry poison my toothbrush, or did you?" I ask, and her eyes leap to me and then between Cherish and me. "You know as much as he does. You've done as much as he's done."

Brianne licks her lips, her eyes returned to mine, and lifts her chin. When she breathes deep before opening her mouth to release it, I don't know what she'll say next.

"You love her, Farrah," she begins. "I know you do. It wouldn't have worked if you didn't."

Her shoulders sink and this time when her phone rings, none of us react. It is decided. The world outside these fences is aflame, and everything can burn but us.

"I hate that the world is this way," she tells us. "I hate what this country's done to you—but there's no taking it back and there's no denying how beautiful it's made you."

Cherish's grip slackens, and when I cut my eyes to see her, there is a look I've seen many times before. It's the way she looks at me when she is weak or confused and thinks that my strength means I'm the villain, that I made her so. At last it's directed appropriately.

"The more we learned, the more aware Daddy and I became of just how many roadblocks this country has intentionally put in place to disenfranchise people like you . . . the more beautiful you became. All of you. The more we realized that you don't see it."

Nichole Turner walks into the yard, and Brianne Whitman continues as though she doesn't sense my mother behind her.

"Black Americans, you don't realize how much you've benefited from all the pain and suffering. Being forced to be resilient and authentic in ways white Americans can never be. You don't wonder what you'd lose if these systems were dismantled completely." Brianne lets her chin fall into her chest and when her full weight presses into her legs trapped beneath her, her ankles twist and so do her hips until she is sitting flat on the ground, her legs bent beside her.

"We need the pain, but you couldn't stand to see your own child experience it firsthand," I say when she seems to have exhausted the energy to tell it. "Something about her being yours altered that conviction."

"But then she met you," Brianne exclaims, enlivened again and reaching out to me while my mother approaches her from behind. "And you showed us what to do. When she was hurt, you hurt yourself, and we knew. You could hurt for her."

I wrap my arm around Cherish when her shivers become full-body tremors that rattle her neck and teeth. She is hearing the truth from her mother, the way she had to, and it is threatening to overwhelm her. Her body itself is trying to reject it, to stop her mind from processing what Brianne Whitman is confessing, so that Cherish can remain naïve and coddled and WGS. She can't unknow this now, but the void her parents built in her has left her frame unbuttressed. Weaker under pressure, and easy to debilitate.

Cherish is a work of art, and I have the Whitmans to thank.

"We decided it that day, after the nails," Brianne tells us. "And we wanted to do it right. We wanted to be safe. So we discussed it with Leslie."

"You don't mean safe," I interject. "You mean you wanted legal protection."

"We wanted his advice—that's all. And then he put a name to it, he said it was called a whipping boy, and he was so much more ostentatious than we would ever be. He could afford to be, but it was only ever out of love, for us." Brianne looks at Cherish with eyes as wide as saucers, as though she needs her daughter to believe. "Daddy and I only wanted what's best for you. It's the only reason."

Cherish is holding on to me. Our foreheads are pressed together and one of her hands is still around my wrist because she's too overwhelmed to remember to let go.

"There's a way that this could sound plausible," I tell her mother. "It could sound well-meaning and tragic, ignorant but not malicious. There's always a way when the victim looks like us and the perpetrator looks like you."

Nichole Turner stands above Brianne Whitman, looking down on the woman, who has a strange expression of hope in her eyes, as though she doesn't know where I might be going from here. I know the words, but when my mother looks up at me and curves her lips upward just so—just enough that her infantilizing dimple winks at me—I know how it ends. Nichole Turner does what I always knew she could. Without speaking she conveys everything. She tells me how Brianne will be enticed into the water and how Cherish will come out of it with me.

"This could all have been out of love, Brianne—except that you enjoyed it."

"I didn't—"

"You told me what I was. You gifted the book to me, and you sat so close I could feel you trembling with delight."

She falls quiet, and it speaks volumes.

"Having and loving a Black daughter doesn't change that you wanted to toy with me. You wanted me to know."

"I gave you the book because we could finally begin. We'd

waited so many years, for you to be positioned just so, and all that time, we knew Cherish needed this—"

"You made dating Kelly a punishable offense so you'd have an excuse to hurt me. You wanted to do this."

"Yes," she interrupts me this time. "But only for Cherish's benefit."

"Then once more," I say. "For Cherish's benefit."

I roll my head to look into my best friend's eyes.

"Baptize me," I tell her, knowing that both our mothers can hear. "The way you did the last time."

Cherish's chin snaps to the side, and despite everything she is looking to her mother for shelter.

"RahRah, I can't. I'm too upset. I don't want to do this anymore."

"Che. I baptized you."

"I know, I just don't want to mess up again—"

"You were perfect. Whatever happens, you always are."

"What if you drown again?"

Brianne shoots back up onto her knees.

"Cherish," she says, her voice raised.

We have to do this now, before the fire goes out or the neighbors alert security again.

"Then there'll be no more whipping girl," I tell Cherish, lacing my fingers behind her neck to keep her close despite her mother. "If I drown, only you'll be left to face the consequences. You'll be a whole person, the way they didn't want you to be. The way they can't help you be."

"I love you, RahRah," she tells me.

"Even if I'm a monster?" I ask, and I know what she'll say.

"You aren't the only one."

She disconnects our foreheads long enough to lay her head on my shoulder just as my mother lays her hands on Brianne Whitman's shoulders.

Cherish is still wet when we wrap ourselves around each other, and her baptismal water soaks through my underwear and my skin.

She can't know what's going to happen next, but this step is crucial, the way she knows that she could lose me, that I would sacrifice myself for her to be a better Cherish. A complete Cherish.

I bury my face in her neck, too, and then I pull back before she's ready.

"Baptize me," I tell her, and then I go down.

"Cherish," I hear Brianne Whitman cry out before my ears are underwater. "Don't!"

My best friend's hands find my chest, and one atop the other, as though to do compressions, as though to bring me back to life, Cherish pushes down and I go all the way under.

There are warbled sounds, as though Brianne has lost all decorum and gone into a frenzy immediately.

Through the water, I keep my eyes on Cherish, and for a moment she is looking back at me. Despite the noise and the way the light creeps up the sky from all sides, eating up the darkness and promising to rain down thick, burning red-orange when the destruction of the darkness is complete.

When Brianne finally gets in the pool, it's like an explosion disrupts the water and I turn my head to find her legs shooting out as though she doesn't know there's no use trying to run.

She is crying out for Cherish to stop, to pull me out, and I hold Cherish's wrists so that she doesn't give in before her mother arrives.

Brianne is too frantic; the faster she tries to move, the slower she seems to go. She is exhausted by the time her hands land on her daughter, but taking hold of Cherish does nothing to bring me up.

"Cherish, let her go!" Brianne shouts as she wrestles her daughter and finds for the first time that she is no match in strength. I can hear her now that she is directly above me, though the water sloshes around me, and even though I hold my breath, I feel the burn as some invades my sinuses.

"Why? So you can punish her instead of me?" Cherish demands. "Isn't that the way a whipping girl works, Mommy? Won't one of us have to pay? Why can't it be me? Am I not strong like they are? Don't you want me to be?"

"No," Brianne cries. "Cherish, please!"

"Baptize her," Nichole Turner tells me from outside the pool, and I plant my feet on the bottom.

I erupt from the water, taking hold of Cherish so that she doesn't fall back—only Brianne does.

The water moves in the space between us as though it has traded places with the air, as though it has all risen with me. As though it is mine, like the fire and the lava.

Brianne is off-balance, her whole body contorted, half in and half out of the water, her thin hair already plastered to her pale skin. When I take hold of her, she doesn't know to resist.

She is underwater with little effort, and for a moment neither she nor Cherish fights back.

The water that's been airborne crashes back into the pool, and the world inside the fence is quiet.

I am holding Brianne Whitman underwater, when my mother speaks.

"Control."

I must not do this alone. Cherish is bewildered somewhere behind me, but I have to bring her back.

"Cherish, baptize her with me," I say, tension entering my voice when my best friend's mother collects her bearings and understands what is happening. She's thrashing now, and though she is slight, I cannot hold her down without Cherish helping me. I won't.

"Cherish," I say again—but she's already beside me.

Cherish is looking down into the churning water, but her hands are at her sides.

"Che."

"They're monsters. But they love me, RahRah."

"They love you, Che, but it doesn't matter. They didn't think you could be strong without struggle, and they kept you weak so you wouldn't see that the world they made for you only exists here."

Brianne almost breaches the surface, and I focus for a moment, gritting my teeth to force her back under.

The calm insistence returns to my voice as quickly as it escaped, and the whimpering shriek Cherish made settles below the surface again when her mother does.

"You can't be them, Che. You can't. And you can't keep us both. They made sure of that."

I don't give her the ultimatum. I don't tell her that it's Jerry and Brianne Whitman or me—just remind her that it is the dynamic they forged.

"Help me, Che, so they can't hurt me again."

It takes her longer than it should, after everything her mother said. After all the things she told us that apply to everyone who looks like us. After saying words that people who love and learn and sound the way the Whitmans do shouldn't be capable of saying, it shouldn't take Cherish long to come down on my side.

But I'll forgive her. Cherish is the one I'll protect, the one I'll always love even when I hate her. And she belongs to me now, the way I told Kelly she did. The way Tariq knew she did when he saw that she had witnessed and never tried to stop me.

Cherish is baptizing her mother with me and I am swallowed up in rapt intoxication. I am rocked by waves of Brianne's resistance quelled by her daughter's forceful response. I case off her mother to test Cherish's pressure, and Brianne Whitman cannot break free.

I let go completely, stumble back in the water, and witness. The sky is red-orange, and the fire is raging outside the fence, but now the water is changed, too. The light that cuts through has transformed the pale and slight blue-green to the color of the flame, and as Brianne struggles against her daughter's baptism, everything burns but Cherish and me.

Lights turn on in the house next door, but it's too late.

Soon it will all be quiet.

Cherish only stops pushing down when her arms sink below the surface to her shoulders because there is no more resistance.

When she finally lets go, her mother bobs up toward her and Cherish screams as though unprepared for the consequence of what she's done.

"RahRah." And I'm at her side, pulling her away and toward the edge of the pool. I lower us both to the stairs and hold my Cherish close.

Brianne Whitman's body tilts underwater, slowly turning so that her back can crest, and I shield her daughter's eyes with one hand, shushing her.

"We're safe now," I whisper, and close my eyes to feel the way her arms tighten around me, this Cherish who is capable of so much more than her parents or I thought. "You saved me."

"What happens now?" she asks, and I know what she means. I know that she is asking whether there will be another baptism when Jerry Whitman arrives, so I reassure her.

"Your dad will be here soon."

"I'm scared. He's gonna see what I've done."

"He has to," I tell her, rocking gently on the step, the way we did the night she drowned me. "But it's okay, Che. He loves you more than anything. I wouldn't have let you do it if he didn't. He'll do whatever it takes to protect you. He'll rewrite the world again, for your sake."

"What about you, RahRah?"

I'm still swaying with intoxication, at being in the water with Brianne's body, at having watched Cherish hold her down. I'm too overwhelmed with it to tell her why I'm safe. Why it had to be her, why she had to hold her mother underwater, and how Jerry Whitman will know that the void they created in their daughter has been entirely filled. I inhabit her, and without me, she'll fall apart. It's their fault that Cherish needs me to survive this.

No more whipping girl; now I am her guide.

"He wants you safe, Cherish," I manage. "So he'll protect me, too."

"Then you'll still come home? You won't leave me, after everything they've done?" she asks, and I kiss Cherish on the top of her head. Squeeze her back while her mother's phone starts to ring again. In the distance, around the front of the house, I hear it faintly echo, as the phone the call's originating from is close by.

The fire outside the fence darkens like it will soon recede, and the light in the sky dims so that it's only daybreak. Nichole Turner is gone, and Brianne Whitman bobs in the water.

Control.

"*You're* my home," I tell Cherish. "That's what we'll tell him."

The fence creaks, and before he speaks, I know Jerry Whitman is here with us.

"He has to know that we belong together."

CHERISH FARRAH

BETHANY C. MORROW

Discussion Questions

BOOK
ENDS

DUTTON

DISCUSSION QUESTIONS

1. From the first chapter, we learn from Farrah's perspective that she felt "angry. Defensive. Like an ordinary teenage girl, when all I'm ever doing is pretending to be one." What did you think she meant by that at the time? How did your understanding of her assertion that she was only pretending to be "an ordinary teenage girl" change over the course of the book?

2. When she introduces us to Cherish and the Whitmans, Farrah says, "Color blindness requires the kind of delusional naïveté that I have only ever believed in Cherish." How is it believable in Cherish? Discuss the fallacy of color blindness, both how it's portrayed in the novel and how it appears in real life.

3. While musing on Cherish, Farrah narrates that, "I only studied her because I had to know whether there was someone else who could construct a mask that convincing." What is Farrah referring to when she mentions a "mask"? How does it relate to the larger themes of the book?

4. Farrah knows that her mother, Nichole, sees beneath the façade she puts up in a way other people do not. She believes that her mother thinks just like her because of it. Do you think Nichole is similar to Farrah? Why or why not?

5. Cherish claims that "Being a spoiled white girl when you're Black is literally my favorite thing ever." What does being "white girl spoiled" mean to Cherish? How does it differ from the way Farrah relates to the idea?

6. The book is told from Farrah's perspective, which means we only see Cherish through Farrah's lens. Taking a step back, how do you think Cherish feels about Farrah based on how she acts toward her? Are there times when you think her feelings toward Farrah shift throughout the story?

7. In the novel, Farrah is desperate to hold on to control even as the life she knew is being pulled out from under her. How much of this attachment to her old life (her childhood home, possibly her school, etc.) is an expected reaction for anyone losing these things, and how much feels out of the ordinary?

8. Farrah says that when she was younger, she was able to see things that other people weren't able to, such as Mrs. Whitman's "golden halo." What do you make of Farrah's ability to visualize certain sounds and see things that other people aren't able to?

9. According to Farrah, she and Cherish "cared too much about proving ourselves to each other in the secret way we somehow devised without ever putting it into words." What are they each proving to the other person? How does this play out in the novel?

10. *Cherish Farrah* is one of the books that is helping to establish the genre of social-horror novels, along with other media like *Get Out*, *Us*, and *Watchmen*. How would you characterize the social-horror genre after reading the book? Visit https://youtu.be/XXeaKsD4Tik to hear more about the genre from the author herself.